Legitimation League , Oswald Dawson

The Bar Sinister and Licit Love

the first biennial proceedings of the Legitimation League

Legitimation League , Oswald Dawson

The Bar Sinister and Licit Love
the first biennial proceedings of the Legitimation League

ISBN/EAN: 9783337406172

Printed in Europe, USA, Canada, Australia, Japan

Cover: Foto ©Andreas Hilbeck / pixelio.de

More available books at **www.hansebooks.com**

EDITH LANCHESTER.

THE BAR SINISTER

AND LICIT LOVE.

THE FIRST BIENNIAL PROCEEDINGS

OF THE

LEGITIMATION LEAGUE,

WITH FOUR PORTRAITS.

EDITED BY

OSWALD DAWSON.

PRICE ONE SHILLING.

LONDON: WM. REEVES, 185, FLEET STREET.

LEEDS: GEO. CORNWELL, 4, UPPER MILL HILL.

—

1895.

CONTENTS.

FRONTISPIECE : EDITH LANCHESTER.

PORTRAITS OF THE VICE-PRESIDENTS } BETWEEN PAGES 152 AND 153.

PAGE.

OBJECTS, ETC. 6

ANNOUNCEMENT 9

WILLIAM F. DUNTON.
EMMA M. A. DUNTON.
MILLICENT DUNTON.

CHAPTER I. THE DIALECTICAL MEETING 11

„ II. FIRST ANNUAL MEETING 21

„ III. A REPORT OF THE REPORTS 56

„ IV. A SOLICITOR ON MARRIAGE 69

„ V. THE LEAGUE'S SOLICITOR'S VIEWS ... 80

„ VI. A VICE-PRESIDENT'S VIEWS 87

„ VII. THE CORRESPONDING SECRETARIES' VIEWS 99

„ VIII. LEGITIMATION AND LICIT LOVE ... 107

„ IX. THE " NATIONAL REFORMER " CORRES-
PONDENCE 114

„ X. UNIVERSAL LEGITIMATION 122

„ XI. THE PRESIDENT ON THE BAR SINISTER 128

CHAPTER XII. MARRIAGE AS SLAVERY... 141

„ XIII. LABOUR AND LEGITIMATION 143

„ XIV. WHAT IS LICIT LOVE? 145

., XV. THE NEW LEGITIMATION ACT 148

,. XVI. HONOUR TO WHOM HONOUR IS DUE ... 150

.. XVII. A WIFE'S SISTER DEBATE 153

., XVIII. THE WOMAN AND THE LAW 159

„ XIX. NATURAL CHILDREN IN FRANCE ... 168

., XX. THE BAR SINISTER AND LICIT LOVE ... 174

., XXI. MR. MILLAR ON MARRIAGE 205

.. XXII. STATISTICS OF ILLEGITIMACY 211

.. XXIII. NATURAL CHILDREN AND PERSONAL
RIGHTS 218

,. XXIV. AT THE BEDFORD AGAIN 225

.. XXV. THE SECOND ANNUAL MEETING ... 236

„ XXVI. THE ADVERTISING AGENT'S VIEWS ... 252

„ XXVII. THE GREAT LANCHESTER CASE ... 258

XXVIII. THE FIRST LEAGUE MEETING 264

.. XXIX. DR. BLANDFORD'S BACKERS—AND THE
LEAGUE'S 278

., XXX. THE SECOND LEAGUE MEETING ... 289

„ XXXI. ASYLUM OR GAOL? 305

FINISPIECE : LILLIAN HARMAN.

THE LEGITIMATION LEAGUE.

President:
WORDSWORTH DONISTHORPE, Inner Temple.

Vice-Presidents:
J GREEVZ FISHER, Chapel-Allerton, Leeds.
J. C. SPENCE, 2, Darnley Road, Royal Crescent.
London, W.

Corresponding Secretaries for London:
JOHN BADCOCK, St. Brelades, Vicarage Road, Leyton, E.
TOLEMAN GARNER, 4, Westbury Place, Green Lanes, N.

Honorary Secretary:
OSWALD DAWSON, Harman Villa, Seacroft, near Leeds.

Treasurer:
GLADYS DAWSON, Harman Villa, Seacroft, near Leeds.

Bankers:
THE LONDON AND MIDLAND BANK, LIMITED,
Kirkgate, Leeds.

Solicitor:
BENJ. C. PULLEYNE, Albion Walk Chambers, Leeds.

Notifying Clerk:
ARTHUR CORNWELL, Albion Walk Chambers. Leeds.

Advertising Agent for London:
EVAN STREACHAN, 295, Strand.

OBJECTS, RULES, &c.

To create a machinery for acknowledging off-spring born out of wedlock, and to secure for them equal rights with legitimate children.

Membership of the League is open to anyone who signifies in writing agreement with its objects. and who subscribes to its proceedings.

Members who are disposed to render material support to the cause are invited to subscribe to the funds of the League.

Membership, whether or not accompanied by a donation (or subscription beyond the amount of the published price of its proceedings), does not carry with it any control of the funds of the League, or power to alter its constitution.

THE LEGITIMATION LEAGUE.

NEITHER law nor custom gives its sanction to the duel, and neither may be said to countenance pugilism even in its milder forms.

The day when married people will no longer be left to fight it out is dawning with a momentum unparalleled in any previous period since the mooting of the first divorce bill.

Much of prejudice, and that by no means founded solely on what has been termed the Indeterminate Co-efficient of Supernaturalism, has allied itself with what is either the show or the substance of reason, in counteracting the forces which seek to dispel the gloom.

The day of emancipation is doubtless distant, and little hope of accelerating the dawn lies down the devious path of legislative endeavour.

Whilst each for himself or herself must weigh the personal damage—the ostracism of society, the detriment in business, and any other considerations of like character – all must realise that the line to be pursued is that which has led all other pioneers in history to attain their ends, the line of active or passive rebellion against the effete laws and customs of the time.

No active defiance of law is involved in dispensing with the seal of State sanction which is withheld from all who rebel against the slavery of marriage. Though their alliances are illicit they are not illegal, and their children, though illegitimate, suffer injuries remediable by legislation which few would rate as momentous save where the entail of property is concerned.

The really grave difficulties are encountered in the conflict with custom, and here, as ever, the multiplication of offenders will soften the austerity of the condemnation.

Those wishful to forward the cause, and willing to live together without the bond of State wedlock, are invited to register their alliances before the Notifying Clerk of the Legitimation League, and to acknowledge their children born out of wedlock.

It is not essential that consent be given for the public advertising of these alliances, but as the registers will be open for inspection by any member of the League, or by any persons on payment of a fee (whether or not such persons may be presumed to have a direct interest in ascertaining the information therein contained), the League covenants with every registering party that the latter will not seek to make it responsible for any injury arising from unauthorised and indiscriminate publication.

Those who wish to advertise their alliances and to publicly acknowledge their children through the medium of the Legitimation League, must give consent in writing to the Honorary Secretary:—

Oswald Dawson,
Harman Villa, Seacroft,
nr. Leeds.

The Legitimation League.

—

We, William F. Dunton and Emma M. A. Dunton. formerly Emma M. A. Briggs, of [*21, Newington Crescent, London, S.E.*] having since the 12th of November, 1892, lived together as Mr. and Mrs. Dunton, and being now so styled and commonly known, hereby give formal notice of our alliance.

We hereby also acknowledge the parentage of Millicent Louisa Dunton, born the 4th of February, 1894, and announce our determination to similarly regard as acknowledged children any future issue of our union.

We consent to the publication of this notice in such manner as the Honorary Secretary of the Legitimation League shall see fit.

Read by us this 19th day of July, 1895, and signed before Arthur Cornwell, Notifying Clerk to the Legitimation League.

W. F. DUNTON.

EMMA M. A. DUNTON.

Witnessed by

OSWALD DAWSON,
Harman Villa. Seacroft, nr. Leeds.

ARTHUR CORNWELL,
Albion Walk Chambers, Leeds.

NOTICE.

———

Any alterations in the registrations made before the Notifying Clerk of the Legitimation League must be made in writing, signed and dated.

Verbal intimations can be taken no cognisance of under any circumstances.

CHAPTER I.

THE DIALECTICAL MEETING.

HAVING been invited by the Dialectical Society of London to address its members on the subject of Legitimation, the date of the eleventh of October, 1893. was fixed, and an address was given by me in the rooms of the Pioneer Club. Dr. C. R. Drysdale occupied the chair. The following is the text of the paper :—

MR. CHAIRMAN, LADIES AND GENTLEMEN.

I daresay it is highly probable that there are assembled here to-night apostles of the most diverse schools of political thought. For anything I know there may be present those who in their own persons maintain the old-fashioned traditions of Liberals and Conservatives. It is more likely, I imagine, there are those who are to be classified as Socialists and Individualists; whilst at the tip of the wings the inevitable Communist and Anarchist is sure to turn up. You will have inferred from the character of these introductory observations, that the discourse you have so graciously invited me to deliver to your society this evening, is to be a political one. In a measure this is the case; yet it is only so in a qualified fashion. The movement for legitimation is, as apprehended by me, a movement for Freedom—for the abolition of one State function : the poking in of the nose of State at nuptial proceedings, and the pinioning of the hands of the parties, in a general way, to all time, when those proceedings are over—or rather as soon as the parties have signed their names, even if true marriage should never subsequently ensue. The movement is accordingly much more of a social than a political one,—so far as any question of practical politics is concerned, it is as far out of the field as Snowdon is out of the sea. And it will be well for it to preserve this relation for many a day to come. When you make a question practical, it frequently happens you have to adopt many vicious practices. You have to chop it, to adjust it, to postpone it, to ally it with some other practical question, and do divers other deeds quite familiar to practical politicians. In the matter that we have in hand there is nothing of this sort. *Punch* long ago dealt with this question of marriage, and his advice is the most succinct summary of our crusade that you could possibly have. *Punch's* advice to those about to marry was " Don't." We say the same, for if you intend waiting till you can repeal the marriage laws, the worms that have consumed the marrow of your bones will have sunk a thousand times beneath the mould of your graves. We will, therefore, take it for granted that the feeling against marriage should express itself in personal action rather than in legislative endeavours, and then ask, Does it follow that there should be no subordinate feature of that action which may have a practical or even a legislative side ?

Procreation is intimately connected with marriage, and as involving other persons than those who make the contract, may surely be said to lend itself with more fitness to the concern of outsiders. Any register—were such established or even proposed—of the unions of two persons, Edwin and Angelina, or other parties —would interest people far less than the nature of the relations of these to any possible children, their several duties, powers, and so forth. It is even conceivable to me that some obtuse legislator might recognise that he had nothing to do with the dealings of adults, and yet that he had some official word to say when it came to a question of children. When a child is born it becomes a citizen ; it has not to wait for registration or any kind of inoculation even, and the first problem of State which presents itself in the person of the helpless infant is, who is to be responsible for its keep? Many answers to this question have been attempted, and the most elaborate one in the direction of an improvement of the present laws is that framed by the Committee of the Personal Rights Association, and published in a leaflet entitled "The Maintenance of the Children of Unmarried Parents." Extended responsibilities of a legal order are sought to be imposed upon the father of natural children—a sum to be paid down for medical and other expenses attending the birth of the child; the periodical payments are to be made to some duly credited officials and not to the mother direct, and various stringent procedures are to be adopted to secure that the father duly discharges his legal obligations. The proposed legislation is of a sort that may most reasonably commend itself to reformers, and if I ask to be excused from giving any opinion upon it myself, I do so simply because the subject handled is one with which the Legitimation League has nothing whatever to do. The projected Bill does not, so far as I am aware, propose that all affiliated children shall be legitimated. If it did, I should then endeavour to resist it to the utmost of my power. The failings, of weakness or of wantonness, which have as their result the birth of unwelcome babes, are surely sufficiently punished by the weight of the saddle of pecuniary responsibilities arising therefrom, and with the disgrace which will mark the period of life when these failings are to be found, without the addition of a stigma, which shall last with the lifetime of the child, by reason of the latter being the legitimate offspring. It is, I presume, unquestionable that many of the brightest stars of our political, our social,—I suppose I might also add, our philosophical, if not even our clerical firmaments—have in the exuberance of youth, committed themselves in such a way that there is room for a doubt as to whether their first-born are really entitled to a primary place from a chronological standpoint. Many, indeed, of our exalted ones have probably at some period of their prime, learnt the meaning of the word "bail"; yet no one proposes that because a man has once incurred the displeasure of a proctor at his university, or of a policeman on his midnight patrol in Piccadilly. that he shall be saddled till his dying day with some sort of an incubus. On the other hand, our laws happen to be such that an action for libel would lie if these misdeeds were irrelevently brought in during the quondam culprit's electioneering campaign, or on his appointment to directorates, or. and here to use a

vulgarism, here's the rub, at his wedding-day When
a man enters the state which the Church call holy
matrimony, which the law endorses as holy, which
public opinion endorses as holy or any synonymous
term, he is supposed to leave his past behind, and the
just sentiment of our laws and of most of our people,
see the horror, the cruelty, the absurdity, of stamping
upon the earliest issue of his righteous alliance any
other seal than that of first-born ; and upon the next
issue of his righteous alliance that of next heir, the
brother or sister of the first-born, and so on. And
here it is, ladies and gentlemen, that we encounter
the most remarkable aspects of the little crusade
which you have so kindly asked me to expound to
you this evening. This almost universal sentiment,
which, as I have pointed out, has received the seal of
the law ; this doctrine that the children of holy
alliances and the authors of those children, the
parties to such alliances, are entitled to freedom from
the perpetual resucitation of libellous charges against
their priority of status from previous children of
origin less holy—this idea has met with strenuous,
conscientious opposition from most of those who
have given this movement for legitimation the weight
of their support and the valued time of their consideration. I cannot, even if I would, dismiss in any
flippant way the force of the hostile feeling—feeling
which has found expression—against the views which
a minority of us hold. It is considered that an
injustice is inflicted upon the children of these earlier,
these unholy, unions, these unions of vice and shame,
of ignorance or carelessness, if they are to be classed
as illegitimate. There are two answers to this
objection —of course I do not say there are no more

than two. The first is this, the State must have some method of dealing with the property of intestate persons, and considerable awkwardness would arise if the children of putative fathers could put in a claim of next of kin in event of intestacy. The children of putative fathers would be those who had been affiliated, and as a great many children born out of wedlock never are affiliated—sometimes for very obvious reasons—it follows that an illegitimate or unaffiliated class would still be retained; either this or at any time upon the death of an intestate, any and every illegitimate child who had not been affiliated could claim to be the "legitimate" heir of the intestate. Those who disagree with the minority of us contend that there would be no grievance or absurdity about such a state of things. And so, as the song might say it, that is just where we differ.

The second answer to the objection to this, the removal of the bar sinister legally—the establishment of universal legitimation—would *not* remove the stigma of being born in what is now an illegitimate manner. If, by legislative process, illegitimacy ceased to be a legal disqualification to inherit anything from someone, or a legal disqualification of any kind, it would not then follow that illegitimacy would be abolished; and, indeed, by no political manœuvring can you remove that stigma which attaches to those whose birth has been improperly, unrighteously brought about. A bastard is a bastard, and to make him a legitimate one, by abolishing all illegitimacy, leaves him a bastard still. If legitimation would in reality confer upon bastards any benefits of other than an artificial kind, I should be most delighted to set these advantages in one scale and the evils in the other—the evils to the child itself, which, as I have elsewhere endeavoured to show, are of an appreciable character, and the evils to its relations—and rejoice in an open mind awaiting the result of the process of weighing the two. Supposing, for instance, that it were the law that an illegitimate child were ineligible for election to any learned profession, or not allowed to deposit its money in any Government Savings Bank—not that I approve of these institutions—I should be very anxious either to abolish the law which ordained this, or, if this were not feasible, possibly to abolish illegitimacy. A bastard should suffer no legal disabilities whatsoever. The sufferings which it may fall to his lot to receive at the hands of Society are eternal, or, at any rate, they are quite independent of the manœuvres of those who set themselves to promote bills or abolish laws. The constructing of the politician or the destroying of the Anarchist will leave the bastard where he stands to-day.

A very natural question which will now arise in the minds of many is this : What do you propose to do ? I have devoted by far the larger part of my time to explaining what we are not going to do, and why we are not going to do it ; now comes the question, What do we want to do, and why do we want to do it ? We aim at extending legitimation to a limited class, the acknowledged children. It may at the first sight be considered that this proposed step is a mere piece of political dodgery, of attempted utilisation of the Parliamentary machine for the propagandism of one's own particular views. Well, I think there are very good grounds for the proposal, based upon abstract considerations, and superior to many of the pretensions to necessity for legislation set down in the preamble of the politician. The acknowledgment of a child is an acceptance of responsibility, and gives a claim to ownership. Surely these titles should be rightfully held by the parents of the children, and, we consider, wrongful would it be to hold that the right of ownership should be invalidated if the two parents of a child decline to make another and totally different contract, namely, that of living together for life. A question which arises, which we must allow to arise now, notwithstanding the difficulty of it, is whether any contract between the parents is a necessity of the case,—with the subsidiary question whether, if not a necessity of the case, it should nevertheless be open to the State to take any cognisance of contracts made between two adults of opposite sexes who wish to form an alliance the result of which is or may be parentage. It is, indeed, quite within the pale of theoretical politics that a system of provision for the mother of a man's child should be arranged, such provision to comprise the support needful for her for a period prior to the birth of the child, and during its early years; and to be of no fixed amount, but according to the arrangement—which might be quite indefinite as to amount—of the parties concerned. Any legislation on these principles need be nothing more than an amendment of the Bastardy Laws, but there is one reason why it should be differentiated, and that is that the offspring would not be bastards. We do not send a bailiff to collect taxes unless they are considerably in arrears. The upshot would therefore appear to be the retention of " marriage " in so far as State cognisance of a contract between two adults who are possible parents is concerned, and the substitution for marriage of a contract which has time limits determined by the incapacity of a woman taking part in procreation to maintain an economic independence. It is not likely that women will be able to provide out of savings, or dowries, or by any plan of insurance, against the contingent expenses of motherhood ; and these expenses being of an order which men are by our present laws called upon to pay —or to part pay—even when unwilling, there is no reason why they should not contract to pay them when willing.

As the law now stands, a man is not called upon to pay for a stillborn child ; a wise woman would contract with a man—if her confidence in him had any limit—for provision in event of her maternity, even if maternity with her shall be motherhood of the stillborn. When should the wise woman make that provision ? Obviously before she incurs the risk of becoming a mother of children, stillborn or otherwise.

It is well known that it is not necessary to have any contract at all in order to entitle an aggrieved person in a love transaction to actual redress. In other words, an action for breach of promise may lie before anything has been signed. I know it to be quite open to question whether this state of affairs is right and proper. Assume that it is so, however, and it will not be a very great development of the principle involved to ask the State to recognise the arrangements of persons who privately register themselves as parents of possible children. There can hardly be a doubt that many registrations at private offices would be frivolous and farcical, and to ask the State to differentiate between such and serious alliances without laying down the lines upon which such differentiation is to be made would be attempting too much. To ask the State to register, and to differentiate before undertaking registration, would be a far more dangerous procedure. As a piece of practical politics, the recommendation we should offer in the matter of action is that the State should accept the registration of persons who agree to take a name in common, and to give to the issue of their union their own name, to be liable for such issue in the same way, to the same extent, and for the same length of time, that married people of the present day are now liable, and that the power to terminate the contract should not be brought into force until one year after the registration.

Mr. John Badcock opened the discussion, and was followed by Dr. Alice Vickery, Miss Law (Honorary Secretary of the Society), Mr. F. W. Read, Mr. W. S. Crawshay (Editor of the *Liberty Annual*), and others, including the Chairman.

CHAPTER II

FIRST ANNUAL MEETING.

THIS Meeting, held on 31st March, 1894, at the Bedford Hotel, Covent Garden. was advertised as a " Meeting of Members and Friends. Admission Free. Questions invited." An attendance of about five-and-twenty persons, many of whom were ladies, filled the room. Mr. David Oliver took a shorthand note. Mr. WORDSWORTH DONISTHORPE, Barrister-at-Law, President, took the chair, speaking as follows :

Ladies and Gentlemen,—This is the first annual meeting of the Legitimation League. The inaugural meeting was held about a year ago in Yorkshire—at Leeds. I think I will first call upon our honorary secretary, Mr. Dawson, to give us a report—not a formal and written, but an oral report—of the progress of this League during the past year, and to read any letters of interest which he may have in his possession. After that I will call upon the Treasurer to present the balance-sheet.

Mr. DAWSON : Mr. Chairman, Ladies and Gentlemen,—I have apologies from the Vice-Presidents, who write stating that they are unable to be here to-day. Mr. Fisher writes :

"CHAPEL ALLERTON,
Friday, 30th March, 1894.

" It is a great disappointment to me to find myself unable to enjoy the pleasure and privilege of assisting at your meeting to-morrow.

" To-morrow's conference will mark an important epoch in the movement, and will, I trust, be marked by the adoption of resolutions conducive to the progress of your efforts for the removal of obstacles which prevent people from establishing any one of their known natural children in exactly the same position which such child would have occupied if born within the bands and bonds of hallowed and legalised wedlock. Possibly the best first steps to be taken in the early future, if the income of the League suffice for the necessary expenditure, will be to formulate modes of declaration of parental acknowledgment suitable for pre-natal and post-natal registration, and to arrange, if possible, for the acceptance and enrolment of these declarations at a scale of fees designed to be or to become self-supporting.

" The internal and external criticism which the motives of the League have undergone ought to help to clear the ground and point the way for further action.

" Whatever be the extent to which, mainly owing, as is pretty well-known, to your liberality, the campaign may be pushed, it seems now to be growing upon public conscience that liberty demands that parentage in the fullest sense of the term ought not to be for ever made dependent upon the adoption of conformity to modes of sexual partnership blessed by theology, admired by fashion, and upheld by the present law of this or other lands.

        "Very faithfully yours,

                "J. GREEVZ FISHER."

From Mr. Fisher's co-Vice-President I have also a letter, a somewhat remarkable—well, an admonitory letter, from which I will now read portions :—

"When you cease to hold the reins of conduct, and calling others to your aid, embark on a public voyage ; when you begin to discuss the step forward of public action, in which you will only be one of the crew . . . . it becomes me to vacate my ornamental position as one of the Vice-Presidents. . . . . . . Let your life recommend your at present *outre* views. Do everything quietly, pose as decent and severely respectable, and in two years your private example and demonstration would do more to advance your cause than a dozen rowdy meetings or a hundred pounds spent in advertising. Get over the feverish desire to demonstrate, and I feel sure that, domestically and socially, many happy and innocent hours of enjoyment are before you and Mrs. Dawson.

        "I am, believe me,

           "Always yours sincerely,

              "F. ARNOLD LEES."

The Solicitor to the League, who unfortunately cannot be with us at the commencement of this meeting, but who will join us later on, sends a paper of practical suggestions, of which the following paragraphs form the conclusion :—

"Constitute of the governing body of the League certain of them who assent thereto, Trustees. Let parents desiring to make a settlement vest in such

Trustees the real or personal estate with which they wish to endow their offspring, and let such Trustees hold the same upon the trusts and directions they, the parents, shall give relative thereto, and let such trusts and directions be recorded in a register signed by the parties, the details to be worked out by subsidiary rules framed by the Governing Body of the League.

"It may, however, be necessary to remark that under this head the Trusts might, according to the existing law of England, be held to be bad as void for immorality, and could not, it is thought, in any event be applied in favour of a *futuro in esse*.

"In conclusion, if the Archbishop of Canterbury and a few other distinguished divines could be induced to become members of the governing body of the League, it would greatly increase the number of its admirers, and lead many wandering sheep into the beneficent fold of the Legitimation League."— (Laughter.)

Mr. AUBERON HERBERT writes as follows :—

"I am much obliged to you for your kind invitation. I cannot accept it, both because I shall not be in London, and because I have put off mastering up to the present the principle of the Legitimation League, so that I don't know how far I am or am not in accord with you.—Very truly,

"AUBERON HERBERT.

"FALMOUTH, *March* 25th."

Mr. W. STEWART ROSS, expressing his inability to be present to-day, wrote also as follows :—

"I have considerable, but not unqualified, sympathy with your evangel. . . . . . If any subject be sacred it is the inherent affinity of the sexes, but no subject that affects human happiness and well-being is too sacred to be decently and rationally envisaged and discussed.—I am, dear sir, yours faithfully,

" 30*th March*, 1894."   " W. STEWART ROSS.

Mr. WHEELER wrote me thus :—

" HOLLOWAY. N., 23*rd March*, 1894.

" I am sorry that a prior engagement at Hastings will prevent me from attending the meeting of the Legitimation League. This I the more regret as I should much like to make the personal acquaintance of Mrs. Dawson and yourself, who have shewn such courage in this matter. Trusting I shall have that pleasure some day, I am, yours truly,

" JOSEPH MAZZINI WHEELER."

Mr. R. L. PHILLIPS writes from Arts Club, Manchester, to be enrolled as a member, and furnishes an account of his own experience for reading at this meeting, at which he regrets he cannot be present.

" DEAR SIR,   " 28*th March*, 1893.

" I went, in 1871, to the Coast of Africa, Congo district, and have resided there almost continuously until the year 1887. It was considered the correct and respectable thing to engage a native mistress, and I did like others, but holding that such unions should not be a matter of mere animal convenience, I formed the intention, and gave it expression, to consider myself as the husband of the woman who lived with me. She was the daughter of a powerful chief, and we were considered by all her family as man and wife, though no ceremony of any kind was performed.

"I have had five children, three of whom are now alive. I may say that these temporary unions are the rule in the country of which I speak, and contrary to the general presumption, they are usually as lasting as circumstances permit. Middle aged men do not send away their faithful partners through a desire for novelty, as is generally supposed would be the case in England, were the marriage laws relaxed. But if a couple are really ill-suited, they generally find it out in the course of a short time, and they go their ways in order to find more suitable partners. This seldom happens, and I should seriously assert that as a rule African girls make more domesticated and useful wives than do their educated and accomplished sisters at home.

"As to the question which has been raised as to status and rights of children if temporary unions were allowed, I should like to say a few words. Are we worse than savages not to love our children? When do men withhold affection from their offspring, and deny them the reasonable chance of success in life? When do they disown them, turn them adrift as outcasts? Not when the youths are wild, not when they are dishonest, unprincipled, expensive to keep. Not necessarily then. No, the only case of a father's affections becoming estranged is when he is ashamed of his son, at least, this cause is, in ninety-nine cases out of a hundred, the true cause of estrangement.

"If a man is ashamed of his boy, or shamed in his boy, for they are one and the same feeling from birth. he will shirk his responsibilities, not otherwise.

"It is the unfortunate children of clandestine intrigues that suffer from birth, and I am very sure that I, that you, that anybody else who is bold enough to do as we have done, will be able to give object lessons on the subject to those around us, as to the probability of our disregarding our duties in these matters.

"I have perhaps written at tedious length on a subject which has probably been more peculiarly your study than mine, but I hope that a re-statement, by an independent hand, of opinions which I believe you share, may not be uninteresting nor uninstructive.

"I am, dear sir, yours truly,
"Oswald Dawson, Esq."   "R. L. PHILLIPS.

I regret I have not a communication from Mrs. Victoria Woodhall Martin to read to you to-day. However, I may say that at Mrs. Martin's request Mrs. Dawson and I visited her, and derived much encouragement from the "God-speed" she wished for the progress of the crusade.

Another veteran reformer, Mr. Thomas Squire Barrett, who formerly edited a journal, *The Present Day*, largely devoted to sex reform, is not with us; so from my letter collection I read you two received from this pioneer.

"WISTERIA HOUSE, BERKHAMSTED,
"DEAR SIR,   17*th October*, 1893.
"I have just bought the 'Verbatim Report' of the Legitimation League, and am deeply interested in it. I am thoroughly with your views. The subject has had my warmest sympathy nearly all my life, but especially during the last thirteen years.

"I will gladly join your League.

"I am, dear sir, yours sincerely,
"THOMAS SQUIRE BARRETT.
"Oswald Dawson, Esq."

Under date " 24*th October*, 1893.

' DEAR SIR,

" . . . . . I send you herewith a small cheque, one guinea, for the funds of the Legitimation League.—(Cheers.) . . .

" In *practice* it seems to me that the only real benefit Legitimation would carry would be the inheritance from intestate parents. Possibly it appears to you, as it seems to me, that if children unacknowledged by parents had power to claim a portion or all of intestate estates, it would open the door to much fraud. Whenever a rich man died without a will there would surely be claimants saying they were children of the deceased, and this would cause much trouble and expense even when the claimants did not succeed in their suits ; and there is also the possibility that by means of perjury many claimants might succeed who were *not* the children of deceased.

"I am, etc.,   T. S. BARRETT."

I may say that during the course of the past year we have had several letters from people who have been interested in our League, or I may say, involved, and who have required legal advice upon matters relating to illegitimate children, and this advice has always been sent at full length by Mr. Pulleyne, Solicitor to the League, free of all charge. As to the work which has been done in the course of the year, personally I am quite satisfied with it, although we have not yet got many members. A great many people have written to us (as you see from the letters I have just read, as well as from the letters read at the inaugural meeting), to express sympathy with the object of the League, but unless persons have actually stated that they desired to become members, we have not so considered them. We have not asked anyone to join the League. It has rested entirely with every individual to say whether he cared to become a member or not. I was told the other day that we ought to have a form of application for membership. Well, that may be good policy or not, but I am quite satisfied that this League should be small in numbers and, perhaps I may say. almost prefer it.

Most excellent work has been done by the Corresponding Secretaries of the League, Mr. Badcock and Mr. Dupont. It is quite impossible now to give you an adequate conception of the value of their services.

As to the work done in the Society beyond correspondence (we have had nearly 300 letters to deal with during the year of one kind and another), the work includes an address delivered by myself by the invitation of the Dialectical Society and before that Society on the 11th of October last. That address will be reprinted in the Proceedings of the League, the second volume of its proceedings. We have, moreover, had a number of "drawing-room meetings," at which the Vice-Presidents, Mrs. Dawson and myself, and at times other friends, have been present. We have not held any public meetings between the first or inaugural meeting and this present one. An account of what has taken place at most of these drawing-room meetings has appeared in *The Yorkshire Evening Post*, and sometimes in other newspapers. The gist of the papers and addresses has always been reported in *The Yorkshire Evening Post*, and a great many copies of that journal have been sent to sympathizers with the League.

It is undoubtedly a fact that the League has not been carried on for a year without there having been something partaking a little of the nature of acrimony in the management of it. There has been a correspondence in the *National Reformer.* Well, some rather unkind things were said in the course of that correspondence. The controversy arose through a letter of my own, and the vice-presidents set to work to argue the matter out amongst themselves. Well, we have only two vice-presidents now instead of three, but the *Reformer* correspondence is not responsible for this fact, and I have great pleasure in saying that that is the only change which has occurred in the year in the *personnel* of the League. We have the same president to-day as we had a year ago, and we have the same treasurer and the same corresponding secretaries, and the same vice-presidents, save that circumstances—circumstances of a private character, and not divergences on matters of principle or policy— have led to one gentleman withdrawing. Although there has been this storm in the *National Reformer,* the two remaining vice-presidents are on perfectly good terms, and the difficulties then raised have now been settled. Another article (one, in fact, of extreme importance, as bearing first of all on the subject of the *National Reformer* correspondence, and one that should be read by everybody at all interested in the work of this League), is the article on " Bastardy," in the January number of the *Free Review,* from the pen of our President. I would just take this opportunity of reminding you that in *The Modern Review* of this month I have been privileged to state the case for this League in an article on " Legitimation and Licit Love." A number of copies of this magazine are on the table at the other end of the room, and I hope everybody present interested in the subject will take one away.

With regard to the press generally, I am glad to say, we are triumphing. At first *The Leeds Mercury* one of the most respectable papers in the country—declined to insert our advertisement, but now there is a full announcement in that journal of our meeting to-day and there is an advertisement of my article in *The Modern Review*, " Legitimation and Licit Love." Then again, those of you who have read the report of our inaugural proceedings will perhaps remember how *The Leeds Times* violently attacked us in a leader headed " Wife or Paramour." Well, when I was going up to London to the Dialectical Society's meeting, the gentleman at the head of *The Leeds Times* came and asked me if I would send him a report of the meeting in London, and I did so, and the same gentleman comes to the office of the Legitimation League for all our publications. Hence, you see, we are making progress, though slowly, for I think you will agree that if those who exercise their power as editors to prevent us obtaining a hearing at the very inception of a new crusade, also those who are fiercest in their denunciation, will give us space not merely for advertisements containing terms like " Licit Love," but for reports of our doings in cities other than Leeds, we have some reason for encouragement and pride. (Cheers.)

Mrs. DAWSON, Honorary Treasurer, read the Balance Sheet for the past year, which was as follows :—

Balance Sheet for the Year ending 31st March, 1894.

Read at the First Annual Meeting of Members and Friends held on that day at the Bedford Hotel, Covent Garden, London.

𝔇r.   ℭr.

RECEIPTS.	£	s.	d.		EXPENSES.	£	s.	d.
Subscriptions	317	8	6		Advertisements	220	14	6
The receipts by sale of Publi-					Printing and Stationery ...	61	3	8
cations may be taken as					Salaries	3	13	6
balancing the expenses					Rent of Halls	4	3	4
of postage and papers.					Fares	1	4	2
					Bank Charges	0	7	6
					Balance in Bank	26	1	10
Total	£317	8	6		Total	£317	8	6

Bankers—
The London and Midland Bank, Kirkgate, Leeds.

GLADYS DAWSON, *Treasurer.*

The CHAIRMAN : Has anyone any question to ask with respect to the report and balance sheet ?

No question was put, and the balance sheet was consequently adopted.

THE CHAIRMAN : Ladies and gentlemen, the presidential address at the inaugural meeting was chiefly occupied with the legal aspect of the question, but to-day you will not expect from me anything more than a few words of business. I propose to inquire mainly into the reason for the very small membership of an association which must, in the nature of things, elicit a very considerable amount of sympathy from all classes in the country. (Hear, hear.) There must be some reason for this. As a matter of fact, the number here to-day is considerably larger than the number of persons who assembled in an upper attic two thousand years ago, at the inaugural meeting of an association which now numbers. I believe, 300 millions or thereabouts. As to the reason of the smallness of the number, I think it is due to the fact that we unintentionally leave ourselves open to misrepresentation. To a certain extent we misrepresent ourselves. I was asked by our honorary secretary to bring some ladies here. I am glad to see that there are some present, but I confess in my own circle they are alarmed— they are afraid. They say " We sympathise with the main object. the alleged object of the associa- tion. but we think it means something more, and we do not care to mix our names up with an association which *may be* of a somewhat different complexion." The objects of this association are misunderstood by the great bulk of the people, who will not take the trouble to find out what our purpose is.   Now what is the object of our League? It is a simple one, it is definite, it is clear.   We aim at reforming the law as to legitimation.   That is our whole object : nothing more, nothing less.   The law of legitimation, as everybody knows, is merely a branch of the law of evidence.   The State says, "We are compelled, whether we wish it or no, to distribute the personal estate of an intestate.   There is no way out of this difficulty.   We *must* do it, otherwise there would be a scramble."   The law observes what men do as a rule when they make a will, and follows this custom.   What they do *as a rule*, the State does in cases of intestacy.   We observe if a man leaves a widow and children, he leaves a certain amount of property to his widow, and a certain amount of property to his children.   As a rule a man who has no children leaves rather more to his wife : half, as a rule, will go to the wife, and the rest to his father, if his father survives, or, if not, the rest will be divided between brothers and sisters, and so forth.   We have noticed these things, and based the law of intestacy upon these observations.   What can we do that is fairer and better?   So far there is no quarrel.   It is what any sane person would do.   A certain part of the estate is to be distributed amongst the children of the deceased.   The term used is "children," and that term has to be defined.   Disputes arise.   Three or four individuals rise up and say "we are children of the deceased."   Then, from some obscure quarter emerges some one else who say, "I also claim to be be one of the children of the deceased."   Then it is absolutely necessary for the State, or whoever undertakes this function, to make a rule whereby it can be ascertained who are really the children of the deceased, and who are not. In order to do this you must make rules quite as clear, as precise, and as comprehensible as those relating to agreements for the transfer of land. We all know that, according to the Statute of Frauds, an agreement for the transfer of land has no effect, is not binding, is not even considered worth attention, unless it is in writing. It is a simple matter to put it in writing, and thus avoid endless litigation, confusion, and dispute. Similarly in the case of children, there is no conceivable difficulty in registering the fact that two certain persons are the father and mother of a particular child. There is no difficulty whatever in doing that, but when it comes to the particular form which is required by the State, here our quarrel begins. Up to this point we have no quarrel. There is no Government on the face of the earth, no State in existence, where individualism had advanced so fast and so far as it has in this country ; — till to-day, in the matter of property and testamentary powers, we have absolute liberty without any qualification whatever. The last few limitatious have been swept away in the present reign, at the commencement of which a man could not absolutely cut off his wife and children. In France he cannot do it now. All these limitations of freedom of bequest have been swept away, and now we in England have absolute liberty on the lines of individualism in this matter. Only when we come to the formality itself do we find ourselves in opposition to the law. The State says : " In order to claim sonship with any given person, you must furnish evidence that the said person and your mother were married at the time of your birth." Very well, that would be a very salutary provision if the word marriage meant what it ought to mean, and not a form with which certain incidents are bound up, which can only be described as very serious, and to some extent calculated to defeat the ends of the State itself. The responsibilities attached to the formal ceremony of marriage are so great, that many people prefer to dispense with it altogether, rather than incur such immense liabilities. To begin with, the contract is a life long contract, and can only be dissolved in the way we know. I need not go into that at all. Our quarrel with the State begins when we come to this question, – What should be the liabilities attaching to marriage, what should be the duties of married people, and what should be their liabilities? If marriage were, as it originally was, and as it will eventually be,—merely a contract to provide for any offspring of the union within a given time, say twelve months,—a contract renewable from year to year,—it is doubtful whether any illegitimate children would be born in this country at all. So long as this is not the case, and so long as we cannot hope for the present by legislation to abolish the extraordinary system of permanent marriage, which is utterly out of harmony with the development of the legal system in every other department of human affairs ; so long as it is impossible for us to abolish this system of compulsory permanent marriages, it is for this society to devise some other means by which children born into the world without this safeguard, without this formal recognition of legitimacy, may become in some way legitimated. I have not come here to propose any particular system, but let it be distinctly understood that this association has been formed with this object, and no other object whatever ; and when we are mixed up in published statements, as we have been in some northern papers, with all kinds of schemes, and of systems of social and moral philosophy, let it be clearly understood that we have nothing whatever to do with any of them. It is no more honest to charge the members of this association with the advocacy of free love, or promiscuous sexual intercourse, than it is to charge the anti-teetotallers, or the Liberty and Property Defence League, with sympathy with drunkenness and debauchery, vice and excess. I think the best course for us to pursue would be to issue some form of manifesto or circular making it fully, and clearly, and explicitly known that we have nothing whatever to do with free love, or with the rights of unacknowledged children, or with affiliation orders, or anything of the kind ; and and that our sole concern is reform of the law as to the legitimation of offspring. (Applause.)

Has any lady or gentleman any question to ask either of myself or of the secretary as to the objects and principles of the movement ?

Dr. DRYSDALE : Am I right in saying that one of the chief grievances of those who have so-called illegitimate children, but who are really married, is that in the event of the death of the father the death duty to be paid on the property left is higher by 10 per cent. than is the case when the children are legitimated ?

The CHAIRMAN : They have to pay a higher duty than legitimate children.

Dr. DRYSDALE : Would it not be well to embody that as one of the points considered to be unfair in the present law.

The CHAIRMAN : I am distinctly in favour of equalising the death duties, and more particularly of equalising them in a very simple manner, namely, by abolishing them altogether.

Mr. M. D. O'BRIEN: Are the questions asked now the only questions you will allow to be asked?

The CHAIRMAN: Now is the time to ask any question.

Mr. O'BRIEN: I want to know if the League acknowledges the legitimacy of the wedlock to which its circular refers? I have a number of questions, and I will give you them either separately and you can answer as I put each one, or you can put them down and answer them all at once.

The CHAIRMAN: Will you ask your first question?

Mr. O'BRIEN: Does the League acknowledge the legitimacy of the wedlock to which its circular refers? I have the circular here. The word "wedlock" is mentioned in your circular where you state the aims of your League. You state your object to be—" To create a machinery for acknowledging offspring born out of wedlock, and to secure for them equal rights with legitimate children." I am referring to that word "wedlock," and therefore, I say, does the League acknowledge the legitimacy of the wedlock to which its circular refers?

The CHAIRMAN: Most unquestionably—yes.

Mr. O'BRIEN: If the League does acknowledge this wedlock to be legitimate, then how can anything be legitimate that is not born in it, and of the persons who are implied by the League to be locked in it? How can things which are not equal to the same thing be equal to one another?

The CHAIRMAN: I confess I find some difficulty in understanding the question propounded. As far as I can gather, it means this : if wedlock is recognised as legitimate by the League, nothing else can possibly be recognised as legitimate by the League. That is not at all my view. We regard the regular marriages of the Church, or of Quaker meetings, or by the State official at a Registration office, as perfectly legitimate ; and we also regard Scotch marriages and marriage by advertisement as perfectly legitimate.

Mr. O'Brien : If this "wedlock" itself be not legitimate, then how can the legislative putting of those who happen to be born out of it upon the same level as those who happen to be born in it be warrantably called "legitimation"?

The Hon. Secretary : Perhaps I may interpose and answer you by quoting a passage from my article in *The Modern Review* :—"The Legitimation League has nothing to do with the facilitation of divorce, or with any other amendment of the Marriage Laws. It seeks as few modifications of the English law as possible ; and it is not pledged to sweep away any existing institution. Persons who marry and approve of marriage as a concern of State may join the League, which is as elastic as the phraseology of the 'objects' will possibly permit. All we require of members is the modicum of toleration needed for the avowal of willingness to concede to such as prefer that in their own individual case State marriage shall be superseded by the 'living with' system. the rights which lawful wedlock confers upon offspring."

Mr. O'Brien: I have one or two more questions. Is not the standard of legitimation the fact of being born of parents who have agreed to and carried out monogamy ?

The Chairman : I fear not. I very much regret to say there is very little monogamy in this country.

I believe under our system there will be a great deal more. There will be a great deal more monogamy and less pretence.

Mr. O'Brien : What is there at present to hinder people from acknowledging offspring born out of wedlock by making special provision for such in wills, or by giving to such whatever they are able to give out of their own private property?

The Chairman : There is nothing whatever to prevent that being done.

Mr. O'Brien : Does the League want a legislative machinery for providing that if a man seduce a woman while she is living in what the League itself calls "wedlock," the offspring of such seduction shall be entitled to inherit the whole or some proportionate share of the seducer's property, in case the seducer should die intestate?

The Chairman : That all depends on whether the seducer acknowledges the child or not. If a man has been such a blackguardly fellow as to seduce a girl——

Mr. O'Brien : "Another man's wife," I said.

The Chairman : That all depends upon whether the child has been legitimated according to the form proposed by the League. If the child were legitimated by the father and mother—and nothing can be done without that consent—the child would naturally inherit as any other legitimate child would.

Mr. O'Brien : Suppose a wealthy man has 100 children by women whom he has seduced while living in what the League calls "wedlock," would the League propose that, in case the man dies intestate, every one of these 100 children of dishonour shall inherit some share of his property?

The CHAIRMAN: If they were legitimated they would succeed. Whether all children born out of wedlock are properly called " children of dishonour " is a matter of opinion, and to a great extent perhaps merely a matter of religious fanaticism.

Mr. O'BRIEN: No, a matter of truth, sir. However, you will only allow me to put questions and not make remarks. Is not the League an organisation for putting the offspring of vice upon the same level, in regard to inheritance, as the offspring of virtue? In other words, is it not a League which is conspiring to hinder the continuous carrying on of truth as it is in nature?

The CHAIRMAN: It is a League the object of which is to put the children of what you call " vice " on the same footing with the children of " virtue." I believe that is the expression you used.

Mr. O'BRIEN: Is not the League an organisation for trying to achieve the hopeless task of circumventing that unalterable law of nature in accordance with which all attempts on the part of parents to run more than one family are necessarily followed by suffering in the children of such attempts?

The CHAIRMAN: No.

Mr. O'BRIEN: Is it reasonable to expect that a supreme administrator of law will authorise the distribution of unwilled property amongst children whose vicious parents have not carried out that clear and natural duty of which monogamy is the only complete expression?

The CHAIRMAN: I think the probability is that the children to which you refer, the real bastards of the people, will not be legitimated, and hence will not participate in the advantages which legitimated children will enjoy. I cannot quite follow your question as to the great administrator.

Mr. O'BRIEN: Don't you admit a supreme administrator of the law?

The CHAIRMAN: I admit that at present there is a State, and that there will probably continue to be a State for some time.

Mr. O'BRIEN: Don't you admit a supreme individual—a supreme administrator of the law?

The CHAIRMAN: No.

Mr. O'BRIEN: All right. Then I will put my other question—Have either parents or children a right to what is not reasonable?

The CHAIRMAN: Clearly they have not a reasonable right to what is not reasonable.

Mr. O'BRIEN: Are any of the forms of polygamy or polyandry reasonable?

The CHAIRMAN: Perfectly reasonable, but not now expedient, I think. We have found by studying the history of peoples that both polygamy and polyandry are failures. Monogamy has proved to be a better system of sexual relation than any other, and those nations which have adopted that system have prospered better than other nations where it has not been in vogue. Therefore we think that the monogamous system is quite capable of standing by itself without any artificial bolstering up by law and police.

Mr. O'BRIEN: If you believe that the system can stand entirely by itself, what do you mean by using these words in your pamphlet on " Love and Law ": " The husband's liability for the children of the marriage would continue for the space of say one year, contingent on the wife's fidelity. And the wife would be unable to marry again during that period without forfeiting the settlement on the child's behalf"? If you mean that the monogamous arrangement is to stand by itself, why do you not say "We will have no law"? Then I could understand your position. But you say you want law, and now you say you want no bolstering-up by law.

The CHAIRMAN; No; I want fulfilment of contract. I want the State to see that when a contract is voluntarily entered into, it shall be fulfilled. I want the State to enforce the fulfilment of contract—not to control the relation of monogamy.

Mr. O'BRIEN : Are not men and women so constituted that they can only efficiently do their natural duties in relation to one family, composed of persons who are all the children of the same father and mother; and is it not a fact demonstrated by all history that in proportion as men and women depart from this individualistic oneness, they undertake a task which is as impossible as the efficient and harmonious service of two masters?

The CHAIRMAN : I quite agree with every word of that.

Mr. O'BRIEN : If you agree with every word of that, and if—as you said a few minutes ago—"wherever polygamy and polyandry have been tried they have proved failures," what do you mean by saying that polygamy and polyandry are reasonable?

The CHAIRMAN : Certainly reasonable.

Mr. O'BRIEN : How reasonable, if they have been proved by experience to be failures?

The CHAIRMAN : Everything is reasonable or not, according to the circumstances of time and place. Polygamy and polyandry were both perfectly reasonable, perfectly expedient and desirable, in certain phases of human development. What was reasonable then is probably not wise now. It is reasonable, but it seems to be unwise. Most people agree with me upon that point : but it is a matter of opinion.

Mr. O'BRIEN: Does the President of the League think it would be rank tyranny and bad policy for him to forbid his own children, if he has any, from sexual indulgence amongst themselves because they cannot appreciate monogamy, just as he thinks it would be tyranny to prohibit them from singing "Little Bo-Peep" and "Sing a Song of Sixpence," because they cannot enjoy the superior music of *Il Trovatore* and *Faust*?

The CHAIRMAN : I think it would be an act of tyranny on the part of the parent, and I approve of it ; I think benevolent despotism very desirable in the nursery.

Mr. O'BRIEN : My next point is about the agreement : Does the person who calls herself Gladys Dawson mean, when she gives "notice," she will "not be known by any other name or signification whatever," that she will not change her name directly she sees a more charming man than the person who calls himself Oswald Dawson only ? (Order, order.)

The CHAIRMAN : Order, order.

Mr. ASHDOWN JONES : I move that no further questions from Mr. O'Brien be allowed. (Hear, hear.)

Mr. TOLEMAN GARNER : I beg to second that.

The motion was carried.

Dr. DRYSDALE : If I may now be permitted to make a few remarks, I wish to congratulate the society that is now making its way in this country upon the admirable address we have had to-day from the chairman. I am sure it must have been a great privilege to any of us who take an interest in human affairs to have heard such a logical address. It is seldom that one has an opportunity of hearing anything of the kind. What between conventionality and stupidity one scarcely hears anything worth mentioning at the present time. I consider that this Legitimation League is certain to succeed if only the members have the courage to go on. Why do I think so? I think it is evident that this League must ultimately succeed. for have not France on the one hand, and that most enlightened part of Great Britain —Scotland—on the other hand, always allowed persons to legitimate their children at any time they like? Any one of us living in this large city can at any moment cross the borders into Scotland and legitimate his children in the course of half-an-hour at a magistrate's. When that is the case it is perfectly clear that it is absurd for us in this country to go on adhering to obsolete and ill considered views which we have inherited from our ancestors,— ancestors who, as Mr. Bentham always reminds us, were simply barbarians. It has been too much the custom to regard whatever our ancestors thought or did as being clever. How could they be guily of anything clever when most of their time was occupied in murdering each other, and when they had little or no time for reflection upon civilized affairs at all? (Hear, hear, and laughter.) We have now come to a time when we have grown up a little, and we ought to adapt our laws so as to make human beings happy so far as law will conduce to that end.

And I am convinced that a nation like Great England will never consciously make unfortunate children suffer for any purpose whatever. Unless the lawyers can tell me, I cannot see what object the law serves in treating unfortunate children as it now does. Personally, I have an immense respect for the law, because I really know nothing about it, and people are apt to admire what they do not understand. (Laughter.) I do not understand how a great country like England, with so many eminent lawyers, should allow this blot to remain on the Statute Book of the realm—namely, that even when parents bequeath to their illegitimate offspring their property by will, the State has the meanness to take from those children 10 per cent. more duty than it exacts from children born in wedlock. This is as much as to say to the children, " we (the State) will teach you the disadvantage of being born illegitimate." How can you teach a child in that way? I think all of us, whether we are members of this League or not, must condemn such mean conduct on the part of the State. Many of us would, no doubt, be very glad to join this League if we dare. Unfortunately, we are not all in a position to afford to care not one straw what the public thinks about this league. Many people would join the League if it were not for the fear of something more dreadful than anything I can express, that is, of being forced to live in indigence.

Mr. TOLEMAN GARNER : Mr. Chairman, ladies, and gentlemen,—Perhaps I may be allowed in a humble way to support the observations of Dr. Drysdale, or rather to supplement what he has said with regard to the existence of this league. I suppose, to the vast majority of those present, I am little short of being an absolute stranger, and personally I am only too painfully aware that I am placed at considerable disadvantage in speaking upon the subject in which you are so deeply interested. I must say that the principal object of the League is one which should have the decided support and heartfelt sympathy of everybody capable of thinking and arriving at a practical conclusion for themselves. Womanhood or manhood once attained, it seems to me that this legitimation question becomes of almost paramount importance. We owe it as a duty to thousands of little ones, as a duty in our own interests for self-protection, and in order to afford justice to mothers, as well as to bring innumerable callous parents to their senses, to leave no stone unturned to bring about an alteration of the present state of the law, and to educate public opinion to this end. I take it that, in expressing these views, I am simply echoing the sentiment of every lady and gentleman present with, I am afraid, one exception. (Mr. O'Brien : " Hear, hear.") As a member of the Malthusian League, the president of which, Dr. Drysdale, is present here to-day, my wife and I have done what we could to train numerous friends in the way in which we think they should go. Without the least desire to be egotistical, I think if hundreds of young couples who get married would only join hands with us in this matter, the cause which has brought us here to-day would stand on a vastly different footing from what it does at the present time. In conclusion, may I say that I shall be delighted if I am allowed in my humble and inadequate way to assist the cause forward on every possible occasion with voice and pen. (Applause.)

Mr. Badcock : I am not much of a public speaker, but I feel called upon to justify my existence as the London corresponding secretary of this League. I have corresponded during the past year rather considerably on questions relating to the sexes and filial relations, but most of my time has had to be spent upon my own education in the matters with which the League is concerned. My principal quarrel with this League is that it has not gone any further than a simple statement of its objects. We all belong to it because we hold that the matter of wedlock should have nothing to do with the status of the child. Having got so far, what other steps should be taken becomes a matter for discussion. The questions in which we are interested are coming up now. As we all know, present-day novelists are treating of the relations between the sexes. As to my own opinions, they are mobile at present, and I am always glad to hear the expression of the views of others. I do not feel inclined now to enter into the question as to what should be the proper status of a child. The great difficulty in this matter is with regard to intestate property. That is the difficulty. What I object to is the statute law itself.

Dr. Alice Vickery : With the permission of the Chairman, I should like to mention that I have received a copy of the weekly bulletin statistics published in the city of Paris. The number of births for the week is arranged in three columns. The first column is, "The Legitimate," the second column, "The Illegitimate, but Recognised," and the third column is, "The Illegitimate." Now, my belief is — I am not quite certain—my belief is with regard to inheritance that the "illegitimate children but recognised" rank equally with legitimate children in France. If that be so, I think it would meet the position which the League wishes to take up at this moment. If this were conceded, it would lead on further, no doubt, in course of time. I am perfectly in sympathy with the League as it stands. I sympathise very much with its objects. It has scarcely gone far enough to please me, but this is a question in which, perhaps, you cannot go too slowly. It is necessary to begin with something that will be fairly, readily recognised, and as the question is debated and discussed, no doubt the programme of the League will be widened in order to allow others to enter in who take a much wider view.

Mr. J. C. SPENCE : The object of the League is said to be—"To create a machinery for acknowledging offspring born out of wedlock, and to secure for them equal rights with legitimate children." As an engineer I have had considerable experience in designing machinery, and one of the principal conclusions I have always come to is to trust to working machines rather than machines that have not been working. The statement of your object that you desire to put children born out of wedlock on the same basis as those born in wedlock, implies that wedlock does secure the proper acknowledgment of children. We want the acknowledgment of children in some form. We do not want to confine it to Roman Catholic marriages, or marriage in an English church or a Registry Office. What we want is to have marriage contracts which the parties themselves make up to suit themselves. I believe the principal fault of wedlock is the "lock," and you cannot get out of it without doing something very often humiliating. Marriage is now supported by the great weight of sentiment, and, personally speaking, it seems to me to be the right institution. We should maintain it as far as we possibly can, and I would suggest that this League should become a supreme Marriage Reform Association, which will register marriages that cannot be enforced by law at the present time,—marriages, however, that will be accepted by Mrs. Grundy, whose recognition is a very important item in the matter. These irregular marriages—like the marriages contracted by people of the infidel religions—will be acknowledged socially. They will have the social sanction, and that is a great point gained. I think a good practical way of getting much truer ideas into general use would be the adoption of a system of registering irregular marriages, that is, contracts deliberately drawn up between man and wife or man and woman arranging for the children or offspring of such unions, and for inheritance, but with no perpetual clause in them.

Miss EDITH VANCE : If it is not presumptuous for a young member of the League, I should like to say a word or two on the future working and welfare of it. It seems to me you have worked in the best possible way in the circumstances hitherto, because, as every-one knows in connection with movements of this kind, it is first necessary to convert individuals, then groups, and then classes. I should like to suggest that in future your form of membership should be more widely circulated, and that the conditions of membership, including your minimum subscription, should be made known. Many persons would join the League, and are entirely in sympathy with it, but they are deterred from doing so because they think it is a much more " swell " affair than it really is, and they are afraid they would not be able to pay the subscription. That has been one of the things mentioned to me by friends. They want to know what is the subscription, and what they are to do in order to become members. Then I think we might easily get friends to deliver addresses at most of the progressive societies. The National Secular Society, I think, would only be too pleased to give you a platform and a hearing.

The HONORARY SECRETARY : The subscription to the League is the price of its publications. Everybody who joins as a member is supposed to buy the publications for himself. If he sends anything over that, all right. The treasurer is glad to receive anything that comes to her net. I am exceedingly obliged to Miss Vance for her suggestions.

Mr. DAVEY : The last speaker, Miss Vance, has cleared the path for me. When I first saw an announcement of the formation of this League I was really under the impression that it was a high-class sort of institution, with a large fee to be paid. From what I have now heard, however, you may put me down as a member, providing its literature is not sent out in five guineas' worth at a time. (Laughter.) With the objects of the League I am fully in accord ; and our friend in the corner, Mr. O'Brien, has certainly raised my opinion of the society. (Hear, hear.)

Mr. CRAWSHAY : I should be very anxious to support the League if it gave a little more prominence to the equalisation of the duties in regard to inheritance—if it went in for putting them on an equal footing. I think it is a barbarous state of the law that a person who happens to have been born out of wedlock

should have to pay this extra duty of 10 per cent..
and sign his name to a form which says "he is a
stranger in blood to the deceased." That is a dis-
graceful state of things, to which, I think, more
prominence should be given. I do not think any
prominence is given to it in the statement of the
objects of this League. Mr. Donisthorpe is for doing
away with the duties altogether. That hardly meets
the difficulty. It would be easier to equalise the
duties than do away with them. The former would
be a step in the right direction towards their ultimate
abolition. Then several of the speakers said they
were not prepared to support the League because it
does not go far enough. Dr. Alice Vickery said,
however, that it was a good thing to go slowly at
a time. The League draws the line at unacknowledged children, and that appears to many of us not
to be consistent and going the whole way as the
League should. I for one may say that I should be
very anxious to support this League on account of
that barbarous distinction made between legitimate
and illegitimate children, if it would be a little more
explicit and satisfactory with regard to the question
of non-acknowledged children.

Mr. BADCOCK : There is a movement on foot
among the advanced Socialists for raising the duties
on legitimate children's inheritance.

Mr. ASHDOWN JONES : With regard to non-
acknowledged children, there is a certain amount of
difficulty in legitimating all of them, because it is
sometimes difficult to know from which father they
inherit. It is often a question of very great doubt.
I do not see how we are to legitimate them all in the
sense of inheritance, because many of the fathers

don't know their children, nor do the children know their fathers. (Mr. O'Brien : " Hear, hear.") With regard to acknowledged children, I think it is a barbarous state of things that because two individuals want to acknowledge children, the law should step in and say " No." I want to see first this wrong righted.

Mr. J. C. SPENCE : I understand you are trying to get up a system of registration ?

The HON. SECRETARY : I have offered a sum for the purpose to be placed in the hands of trustees. It is very essential indeed that the records of registration should be permanently accessible, and accessible in the usual business hours or during specially advertised hours. Mr. Pulleyne, Solicitor to the League, agrees to let us have one of his offices, subject to a two years' notice to quit. He himself or his clerk would undertake the registrations. We should have the use of the office and a safe in which to keep the books. This would be in consideration of Mr. Pulleyne receiving the fees, or a share of them—a substantial fraction of each fee for trouble, and the interest on the sum of money deposited with trustees for rent during such period as the responsible officers of the League had use of the room and access to the records in the safe.

A MEMBER of the LEAGUE : Why should Mr. Pulleyne have all the fees ?

The CHAIRMAN : I am afraid that scheme will hardly work. I question whether Mr. Pulleyne or anyone else would be allowed to take fees under the circumstances. There would have to be some consideration for the money, and the consideration would not be lawful. I very much doubt whether there could be anything more than a voluntary registration without any payment whatever. It is a very interesting point, and I should like to see it decided.

Mr. YATES : Under the law as it stands at the present time, whether a child be legitimate or not, its father can have his name inserted on the certificate.

The CHAIRMAN : There is no difficulty if a father likes to put his name on a register, he can do so now. And it is commonly done with the consent of the mother.

Mr. CRAWSHAY : I beg to propose a vote of thanks to the Chairman.

Mr. JONES : I heartily second that.

The motion having been passed *nem. con.*—

The CHAIRMAN : I thank you. It is more pleasant to be received in this way than to be hustled out of the hall as I nearly was at the meeting in Leeds a year ago. There were twenty times the number then present, but the Leeds meeting was not so unanimously favourable as this. I think we have only one dissentient, my friend Mr. O'Brien, with whose writings we are all familiar and so much admire. I am sorry we cannot agree upon this marriage reform question. He holds peculiar views on this question which do not seem to me to accord with the general principles he has adopted.

Mr. DAVEY : I move that the best thanks of this meeting be given to Mr. and Mrs. Dawson for the extraordinary efforts they have made to advance the interests of this League,—a self-imposed task they have worthily fulfilled. I am sure our hearty thanks are due to them.

Miss VANCE : I have great pleasure in seconding that, and before the next annual meeting of the League, I hope to have the pleasure of hearing an address on the objects of the League somewhere in London. I will do my best to secure a platform and a welcome for any representative of the League who may desire to deliver such address.

The motion having been adopted unanimously,

Mr. DAWSON said : I am sure I thank you very much for your kindness in passing this vote, but it was really not needed.

The proceedings then terminated.

A REPORT OF THE REPORTS.

A HALF-COLUMN report of the meeting occupied an excellent position in the pages of the *Weekly Times and Echo* on the following morning. Copies of the issue were posted to all members and friends.

The fullest account was given by the *Bedford Mercury*, which I partially reprint here.

"THE LEGITIMATION LEAGUE.

"The first annual meeting of the members of this new League was held at the Bedford Hotel, Covent Garden, on Saturday last, Mr. Wordsworth Donisthorpe, the well-known barrister, president, in [the chair ; a representative of this journal accepted an invitation to be present, and went to town for the purpose,—not that he was in full accord with the meeting, but is always interested in any crusade carried on in the name of progress and liberty. The society is young and is on somewhat new lines, its objects being to 'create a machinery for acknowledging offspring born out of wedlock, and to secure for them equal rights with legitimate children.' Though it is new, it is likely to be heard much of before long, for it aims to confer a status of respectability upon the acknowledged children of unmarried parents, by giving them legal recognition with titles to succession. . . .

"The President, a man of broad views as well as of great courage, briefly opened the proceedings, and asked the Secretary, Mr. Oswald Dawson, of Leeds, to make an abstract of the letters received, and to give the annual report. Mr. Dawson, who has been the moving spirit of the League from the outset, was cordially welcomed. Letters had been received from Mr. Greevz Fisher and Dr. Arnold Lees, the vice-presidents, the former sending several suggestions for a 'Declaration,' which he thought might be used as a manifesto of the object of the League. Their solicitor, Mr. Pulleyne, of Albion Walk, Leeds, sent several sheets of similar suggestions, believing that if the public knew more of the League they would support it. What was required was a simple Code providing for the registration of non-State-tied marriages, and for the filing of declarations of fatherhood and motherhood. Mr. Beaumont, solicitor, of Hull, and others, also wrote, including some who were not yet convinced of the advisability of supporting the League. Mr. Phillips, writing from Manchester, gave striking testimony gained by his residence in the Congo district of Africa, and bore witness to the faithfulness of the women in that land. Mr. Dawson then sketched the work of the year, instead of presenting a written report. . . . The Treasurer (Mrs. Gladys Dawson) read the financial statement, showing receipts £317 8s. 6d., and expenses amounting to about £290, leaving a balance in hand of £26 1s. 10d.

" The President then gave an address, in the course of which he enquired into the reasons for the small membership of the League, the chief one being the fact that they were misunderstood, and were liable to misrepresentation. Ladies fought shy of it, and he was glad to see so many ladies present, ready to take their share in this unpopular attempt to secure justice for the children. . . . Their object was to reform the law as to the legitimation of offspring, not to alter the law of bastardy. They had nothing to do with promiscuous or free love—for liberty had no sympathy with vice—and he thought their best course would be to issue a manifesto, as suggested in several of the letters. Mr. Dawson remarked that he hoped his article in the *Modern Review* would answer the purpose of such. There was a copy at the door for every visitor.

" Questions were invited, and Mr. M. D. O'Brien asked several, and the President answered them promptly and clearly ; but as they were growing more and more intensely hostile to the League, the audience agreed by resolution to refuse permission to Mr. O'Brien to waste any more time of the meeting. Sympathetic remarks with the League were made by Dr. Drysdale, the well-known physician, who regretted that the public were still largely influenced by mere conventionalities and stupid customs. France and

Scotland both made legitimation very easy, so that it was absurd for England to hold out as she now did. The nation should adapt its laws to make human beings happy, and not allow such blots as those which make a man's natural children pay 10 per cent. legacy duty, and gives them only nine-tenths of the property their father intended them to have. An interesting discussion followed, among those who spoke being Mr. Toleman Garner, Mr. Badcock, Dr. Alice Vickery (who spoke on registration of births in France), Mr. J. C. Spence, Miss Edith Vance, Mr. Crawshay, the Secretary, and others.

"In the evening Mr. and Mrs. Dawson entertained a large party at the annual dinner of the League, in the hotel, and a sumptuous affair it was. The menu was excellent, flowers charmingly arranged, and, wonder of wonders at a dinner— the speaking was both pointed and short. Mrs. Dawson gave "The Queen," the company rising ; and then the place of honour was given to "The Press," proposed by Mr. Badcock and responded to by Mr. Legge, of the *Modern Review*. Mr. Spence, author of "The Dawn of Civilization," gave prosperity to the Legitimation League as one of the efforts to get rid of many inherited and slavish notions which came from mediæval times. They dated from the time when women were practically slaves, and to clear them off was the reform most needed to-day. Mr. Dawson replied and spoke of the desirability of the proposed Registration office, where the records should be open to public inspection at all reasonable hours ; and then referred to the social ostracism which he

and others encountered through this advocacy of
their views. Songs were given by Mr. Gordon
Heller and others, and a most pleasant evening
was spent by all present."

The other singer was Mr. John Banks, whilst
Mrs. Harding, in each instance, favoured us with
accompaniments on the piano, and Mr. Toleman
Garner with a recitation.

On the following Monday the *Pall Mall Gazette*
posters announced, in large letters, " Legitimation :
A Strange Feast." Here follows " Some Notes of a
Dinner Party," extracted from that newspaper :

"THE LEGITIMATION LEAGUE.

"SOME NOTES OF A DINNER PARTY.

" The card of invitation said that the organization which was going to celebrate its anniversary
was ' The Legitimation League,' with headquarters
at Albion-walk Chambers, Leeds ; that the annual
meeting would be held on Saturday afternoon, and
would be followed by dinner at the Bedford, in
Covent Garden, at six. ' I have always had much
admiration,' writes a *Pall Mall* contributor, ' for
the folly of those who would try to restore the
fortunes of the exiled Stuarts. It looks so
chivalric and essentially out of date. Therefore
I dressed and went to the Bedford. Of course I
was late, for the Legitimationists had the absurd
idea that six really meant that hour, and not half-
past. The diners were just sitting down. It was
a mixed gathering ; there were ladies present,
and of the men some were in evening dress, some
were not. There were two or three striking
personalities in the room. One was the lady I

afterwards learned was Mrs. Oswald Dawson, who is associated with the founder of the League, Mr. Oswald Dawson, in its work. Another was Mr. Wordsworth Donisthorpe, of the Inner Temple, president of the League. What he did there trying to restore exiled Stuarts puzzled me, and while engaged trying to solve the puzzle dinner was served. I had for neighbour a fair Lorrainer, and judiciously questioning her as to the League, found that she, like myself, was a stranger and a pilgrim within its gates The absence of any emblems of the banished Royal family, the scraps of conversation which came flitting towards me as dinner progressed, suddenly brought with the baked meats a realization that I had fallen into a happy error, and with the sweets I felt as Carthew did in the Currency Lass Public-house, 'a strange sense of wading deeper in the tide of life.' I was in the most sentimental of companies—marvellous, too, that it should come from hard-headed Yorkshire —for I began to learn that these were folks for whom the marriage tie had no attractions, and who were ready where the joint fancy struck them to agree to be husbands and wives for times and seasons only. I am a most respectable man, but some of the ladies were pretty, the gentlemen were quite unconventional, and there was a sense of the sweetness of stolen waters over it all which constrained me. Mrs. Dawson proposed 'The Queen.' It was after that the ladies produced their cigarettes. Mr. Gordon Heller, a singer of worth, who like myself was a mere guest, entertained us, and at last Mr. Oswald Dawson rose

to reply for the League, to my further enlighten-
ment. Mr. Dawson was, I may explain, the
founder of the feast, as well as the League. He
is a man of medium height, heavily bearded, with
kindly eyes gazing at, I mistrust me, an unsympa-
thetic world through gold-rimmed spectacles. He
was down on our present marriage customs,
those relics of days when the Catholic Church, as
the proposer of the toast had said, laid down its
stupid laws about the relations of the sexes.
What they aimed at in the League was to create
an organization which will agitate for reforms in
this particular, which will enable people who have
agreed to live together without accepting the civil
contract, to register their determination, with its
period of duration, and also secure the legitimiza-
tion of children born out of wedlock. Mr.
Dawson spoke of the social ostracism which he
had suffered. ' As it happens,' he said, ' my wife
and I—though you know I am not a husband in
the ordinary sense—do not care much for company.
and it does not affect us,' but one judged that in
Leeds the new movement for the perfect equality
of the sexes has its opponents. What they were
eager to have was a machinery which would serve
to further their aims. It might be called the
Legitimation League, or the Licit Alliance Association—any name they liked. He supposed he
could not use the words Free Love Alliance,
because it was liable to be misunderstood. At
any rate, he was glad to see them all, and hoped
to meet again when progress was more marked,
for some legal difficulty would compel them to
find a solution, a werk he commended to the

president—Mr. Donisthorpe—and would the waiter
bring in some whisky, which the waiter did not
do, but continued the champagne, and I recol-
lected I had toasted the League and Mr. and Mrs.
Oswald Dawson, and was not over sorry. Though,
as I said, I am a most respectable man, but it is
an age of new views, and life is worthless unless
it is lived. Besides, the champagne was very
good."

Extracts from the above sketch appeared in the
Yorkshire Evening Post, whilst other Leeds papers
also took note of the event. Amongst these was the
Skyrack Courier, which, in addition to a report of the
meeting, gave a half-column also of comment. I
subjoin the following extract :

"THE LEGITIMATION LEAGUE.—The recent
annual meeting in London of the Legitimation
League, which has its head quarters at Leeds,
again directs attention to this institution. Mr.
Oswald Dawson, of Seacroft, as is well known, is
Secretary to the League, and is certainly doing his
utmost by tongue and pen to make it and its
objects known throughout the country. . . .

" . . . Such ecclesiastical ideas about
illegitimate children as prevail in other countries
abroad, and have more largely prevailed in this
than now, founded upon a barbarous Mosaic code,
as they are, ought not to be allowed to continue
in existence in Great Britain. . . . .

" . . . The State is guilty of extraordinary and most illogical inconsistency in this
matter. It permits of marriage being reduced to
a mere civil compact by being celebrated at the
Register Office, and yet perpetuates by its legisla-

tion the old spirit of proscription and prejudice towards the hapless child born out of wedlock, which originated out of the belief that civil marriage, or marriage without a priest, was immoral. The State itself sanctioned what, in the eyes of the church, was illegitimacy ; and yet— playing fast and loose with the ecclesiastical sentiment—while striking at the foundation of that sentiment by establishing the Register Office, pretended to conciliate it by maintaining the old disabilities of illegitimate children. . . .

" I might say that since there can be no true marriage without love, the children resulting from the many loveless mercenary matrimonial unions of the day are, morally, quite as illegitimate as those legally known as such, though, of course, equally as innocent."

Waddington's " Guide to Leeds" devotes a page of information to the League, from which I take the following sympathetic note.

" Our marriage laws are an uncivilised, barbarous congeries of mistakes which lead to endless litigation and untold misery. Considering that the sum of human happiness is increased or diminished by the interest taken, it is rather strange that people should be afraid almost to think on matters which the profoundest jurists and the most learned prelates of all the churches of Christendom have always manifested interest in."

Waddington's " Guide to Scarborough " put the case for the League lucidly.

" THE LEGITIMATION LEAGUE OF LEEDS.

" According to the view of the President and of the founder of the League, Mr. Oswald

Dawson, of Leeds, the legitimacy of a child
should depend simply upon the fact that it has
been duly acknowledged, and should not be determined solely by the circumstance that its parents
were legally wedded at the time of its birth.   The
most natural retort to this contention seems to us
to be the question why should people who so far
defy the laws of society as to dispense with the
marriage ceremony which the law prescribes,
wish to place themselves or their offspring under
shelter of the law by securing for the latter the
status of illegitimacy, especially as the principal
benefit attaching to legitimacy, the title to inherit
in event of the intestacy of parents, can be secured
by the simple process of making a will.   To this
the reply of the League is that the illegitimate
child, even though entitled to money under a will,
has to pay a higher rate of duty than the legitimate child, and that, were this not the case, it
would none the less remain an injustice that the
illegitimate child should suffer from the negligence
of the parents to make wills, whilst his brethren
born in wedlock do not so suffer.   The League,
however, whilst duly recognising the legal disabilities involved, is not slow to perceive and to
proclaim that the chief gain to be sought is 'the
investment with a respectability of those who
object to the prevalent custom of modern matrimony, and for their offspring—for duly acknowledged children.'   Those, indeed, are the closing
words of Mr. Oswald Dawson's address at the
end of the first volume of the League's proceedings.
How he may develop the idea in the second
volume, *The Bar Sinister and Licit Love*, will,

we presume, sufficiently show. The expression, 'Licit Love,' makes us think he intends to show the way, in theory, of obtaining some sort of legal recognition for the sort of alliance which, before the founding of the League, he had entered into with a lady who by public advertisement in York-shire and other papers declared that she had 'for some time past used and adopted the surname of the above-named Oswald Dawson,'—the above-named having at the same time made a slight change in his name (merely dropping one of the Christian names), seemingly for the purpose of enabling the lady whose advertisement of change of name followed his to refer to the 'above-named.' Whether this is to be the system which it is seriously proposed shall replace, among such as prefer it, the practice of marriage, or whether it is simply a part of such system, remains to be seen. Those who, with ourselves, confess to a curiosity to see how this startling project of legitimation is to be developed, will await with interest the advertised publications."

The *Yorkshire Owl*, in a full page review of our inaugural publications, reproduced the frontispiece of the "Proceedings," and described the President's pamphlet, "Love and Law," as a very remarkable production. Continuing, the *Owl* said—

"His essay, as we have indicated, is a most remarkable one, not only on account of its candour and outspoken nature, but also by reason of the amazing subtlety with which its barrister-author deals with all the argumentative hosts of the enemy. To those who look upon marriage as a purely · human adjustment of the sexual

relations, Mr. Donisthorpe's logic will be conclusive. It was said of Shelley's union with Mary
Wollstonecraft, that the poet acted upon a social
theory —with sincere conscientiousness—which, if
generally adopted, would bring shipwreck upon
thousands of English homes. The learned author
of this essay goes a long way towards demon-
strating that Shelley's theory might become a
national practice without any such dire result.
The essay ought to be widely read : it opens up
more avenues of thought than perhaps even the
author intended."

Mr. J. Morrison Davidson, barrister-at-law, who
is a well-known journalist, devotes over a column to
the Legitimation League in *The Weekly Times and
Echo* of June 3, 1894. Mr. Davidson is compli-
mentary, and partially sympathetic. He looks to the
time when our " well-intentioned efforts " will be but
" the mere memory of a barbarous past." The
barbarity, I fear, has not so much relation to the
compulsion involved in legal marriage as to the
possession of private property implied in the label-
ling of people as legitimate heirs. Whether or no
there would be legitimacy and illegitimacy under
Socialism I cannot tell. There would, I presume, be
no baronetcies or other titles to follow the family
line, and no acres or stocks to inherit. But it is
conceivable that certain privileges might be possessed
by parents, as of naming the vocations they wish
their children to be put to by the State, or by the
children themselves in view of special services
rendered by their parents to the State, as, *e.g.*,
exemption from military service ; and if this be so it
will be needful to know who are the parents, and of

what children they are parents.   Indeed, I opine that Socialism will have left its own advent far distant in the barbarous past ere, say. the eldest or only son of a great benefactor will be asked to regard himself as other than a gentleman of leisure.   Similarly with respect to property.   Is it proposed to nationalise the trinkets, the family Bible, and the old arm chair ? If not, there will probably be some one *more legiti-mately* entitled to take possession of them than others.   Then what about the property in what we may call the moral goodwill of the old home?   To nationalise the site when you cannot nationalise the associations of it would indeed be hard.   Then who is to have the choice of dwelling there?   Will not the wife, or the paramour who was recognised, or the children who were acknowledged, have a prior claim over the stranger, other things equal?   If so, then the State must know who were these with prior claim, and in this, as in all these instances. there will be need for a Legitimation League if the acknow-ledged children who are born out of wedlock—if any wedlock remains—are not to be left out in the cold.

———

CHAPTER IV

A SOLICITOR ON MARRIAGE.

THE paper contributed by Mr. Charles M. Beaumont, of Hull, a paper too long to read at the meeting, is printed below *in extenso*. Mr. Beaumont wrote an accompanying letter which is also here printed.

" DEAR SIR,

" I am obliged for the notice of the Legitimation League meeting, but regret that I shall not be able to leave Hull for that day.

" As promised, I enclose an article on the marriage question, which please publish in any way that will assist the objects of the League.

" With compliments to yourself and Mrs. Dawson, and with best wishes for a successful and useful meeting.

" Yours sincerely,

" CHAS. M. BEAUMONT."

" Hull, 29*th* *March*, 1894."

THE MARRIAGE LAWS—WHAT THEY REALLY ARE.

By the majority of English people the marriage laws are accepted as an all-sufficient standard of morality : conformity with them is held to be moral, non-conformity immoral, and the suggestion of any important alteration in them is usually hailed as scandalous.

Whether we are concerned in upholding or up-setting this view, it is essential to useful discussion that we should know just what these marriage laws are. They affect the most important and most sacred relation of life, and no one has the slightest right to lift a voice in favour of their enforcement or other-wise who is not acquainted with, at any rate, the main outlines of them.

In the first place, our marriage laws are not, as they are generally supposed to be, a code for the pre-vention of immorality. Let it be clearly understood that in England we have no law against ordinary sexual immorality. The man or woman who wishes to be immoral need not hide his depravity from the police, they may boast of it openly if they choose, they are committing no offence against their country's laws.

It is usual for staunch supporters of they know not what, to hurl against advocates of marriage reform the dreaded expression " Free Love." Let me inform these that " Free Love," in its most oppro-brious meaning of unrestrained license of sexual intercourse, is permitted by our laws; if " Free Love " is to be made illegal our laws must be, not upheld, but altered.

Our marriage laws do not effect any but those who voluntarily submit to their jurisdiction by undergoing the formality of a legal marriage ceremony. This ceremony is not compulsory. A man may have one wife or a dozen; a woman one husband or a dozen, without going through this ceremony, and to such the law has nothing to say, either for or against. But to those who perform the ceremony, what is the effect of their so doing? Most people seem to think that the law undertakes to see to the performance of the solemn marriage vows set forth in the Church service, to sanction their fulfilment, and to punish infidelity.

No so, however. " With all my worldly goods I thee endow " is a promise of which the law takes no notice whatever, but leaves the performance to the conscience of the promissor. Vows to love and cherish, honour and obey, English law is not so foolish as to attempt to enforce, having no means of controlling people's sentiments or affections. It used to go so far as to compel, or try to compel, an unwilling mate to reside with husband or wife under pain of imprisonment, but has given up that task as impossible.

As for punishing infidelity; in the first place the law knows but one narrow meaning for that word, and that is adultery. Indifference, hatred, and contempt may exist between husband and wife without breach of the marriage contract as interpreted by law. Only in case of adultery can the law perceive infidelity. And then, what is the punishment? None. Adultery, like other immorality, is no crime at law and entails no legal punishment. The utmost that the law will do in case of adultery is, to admit its powerlessness by formally professing to loose the bond which has already been broken. Some people seem to regard an order for alimony as a kind of fine imposed as a punishment for misconduct. It is nothing of the sort. It is merely a continuance of the liability that the husband took upon himself at marriage. If a punishment at all, it is a punishment incurred, not by breaking the marriage contract, but by entering into it.

We see, then, that, except to those who voluntarily accept their jurisdiction, our marriage laws are a nullity. Even to those who submit to them they are a nullity in so far as any control, or attempted control, over affections or conjugal behaviour goes. What, then, is their function? Simply this, to regulate the financial relations of the legally married.

The law cannot control affection, but it can control the purse. To this end, then, our marriage code confines its attention. The moral liabilities undertaken with marriage are beyond its power. The pecuniary liabilities thereby incurred, it can, however, enforce.

Let us see how far it succeeds in fulfilling this humble function.

The liabilities implied in legal marriage are shortly as follows :—The husband becomes liable to maintain the wife so long as they both live and she continues to reside with him and fulfils the legal idea of fidelity; that is, refrains from adultery. At the death of either, this liability ceases, so that if the husband die first, and wealthy, he may leave his wife penniless, no matter how much his wealth may have been contributed to by her assistance. On the other hand, his liability is not put an end to by any other misconduct of hers ; she may prove unkind as a wife, useless as a helpmate, dangerous as a mother, altogether a burden grevious to be borne, and still her right to maintenance remains the same. If her rights are not diminished by bad conduct, they are not increased by good conduct. She may work at keeping his house or educating his children, may assist in his business, or manage it entirely, and, at least in the absence of special agreement to the contrary, no part of the proceeds of her work becomes hers.

As to the children, they belong, generally speaking, solely to the husband, to the neglect of the mother that bore, nursed, and perhaps trained them, though she is liable for their maintenance in case of his failure to maintain them, as she is also liable to maintain him if she should be solvent and he destitute.

In case of separation with the sanction of the law, that is, where the court finds that either of the parties has been guilty of any of the few breaches of conjugal duty which the law takes cognisance of, it enforces the above liabilities. If the parties separate without appeal to the law, it leaves them to fight out their financial matters without its aid ; which means practically this, that if one party to a marriage has money and the other none, the monied one can inflict a vast amount of misery on the other, to which that other must either submit or run the risk of starvation. Even where an offence has been committed which the courts would recognise, the great expense of proof often makes redress inaccessible to the moneyless one.

Now, without going so far as to say that this financial arrangement is contrary to common sense, it is quiet conceivable that a couple might desire, having special tastes or under special circumstances, that their money matters should be regulated on a different basis to the above. The husband and wife may be willing to be answerable to one another for a greater responsibility towards their children than the meagre one which can be enforced through the Guardians of the Poor. The wife may be desirous to have some rights secured to her over her prospective children, and the husband may be willing to agree to this. The wife may desire that if she throws in her lot with her husband, works with him, shares risk and loss with him, she shall have a share in the profits also, and the husband may think this just and be willing to assent to it.

The law says nothing against such arrangements, so long as they steer clear of what it calls "immoral consideration," a thing not difficult to do. The law offers a ready-made marriage contract, the best, I suppose, that it has hitherto been able to devise, but it does not enforce it upon couples. It refuses, and rightly, to assist them to make, barter, and sale of sexual favours under any other contract but its own, but it permits them to arrange their merely pecuniary matters as they please.

But though the law offers no opposition to the application of common sense to a marriage contract, social prejudice does. Society likes to have an easy, hard and fast line drawn between right and wrong, so as to save it all trouble in ascertaining facts when it wants to pass judgment. It seizes the readiest rule to hand, however unsuitable, and decrees that the acceptance of the legal code of financial liabilities shall be taken as the dividing line between morality and immorality. The consequences of making a pecuniary contract the standard of morality are, of course, ridiculous. Penniless beauty sells herself to wealthy lust openly and candidly, but she secures the maintenance by going through the marriage service, and that is moral; though the children of such a union may curse the morality that brought them into the world debarred of physical, mental, or moral health.

On the other hand, Mr. and Mrs. Dovecot may love, honour, and cherish one another, share their means honourably, and fulfil all their vast responsibilities to their children marvellously, but they cannot go through the marriage service, because Mr. D. was tricked into a marriage when a boy with an adventuress, who then left him with all his valuables, and is now nobody knows where. So the lives of Mr. and Mrs. D. are immoral and shocking.

Mrs. Ingenue was married when a young girl, not knowing what marriage meant, to a man whose treatment of her was such that she was obliged to leave him years ago, or suffer degradation and misery herself and perhaps become the mother of children whose lives would be a curse to them and all around them. She meets a man with whom she could be happy, and ventures to go through the marriage service with him. A telegram arrives to say that her first husband is dead. With immense relief she finds that her act is no longer immoral, but moral. The death of her husband in the nick of time, though at the other side of the world, and though they would never have met again, has made all the difference. After a year comes a telegram from the first husband himself, saying that he is alive, and wants money.

Horrible! all that year she has been living in immorality without knowing it, for the social code makes possible the absurdity of unconscious immorality. After a vast amount of expense and trouble it is discovered that the first husband is really dead, the last telegram having been a dodge by a villain to extort money. Society, which had righteously deserted Mrs. I., now comes back again, though still fearful what Mrs. I.'s morals may turn out to be until it has seen Mr. I.'s body held safely down by a good heavy tombstone. If the second husband has been too poor for the expense of inquiry, Mrs. I.'s morals would have remained shocking.

Mrs. Green was married for her money by a villain who fortunately set her free by being smashed in a railway accident. So she marries (profiting by experience) a real good fellow, and has several children and is happy. But Green turns up again; his railway accident was a ruse to get out of the country, having robbed a bank. But he has been caught, served his time, and now comes back to claim his wife. She is a weak creature, prevents her second husband from strangling Green, and goes back with him, leaving her children motherless. But then turns up an old pal of Green's, who confesses that the marriage service with Green was a trick, and invalid. So Mrs. Brown may now go back to her husband if he will have her, he being now entitled to a divorce, for she has offended against Society's law even while seeking to obey it. Brown will be vexed at her having left him for a period of concubinage with Green, and if she pleads that she was only obeying, to the best of her ability, the social law, he may well reply that if that is social law the social law is an ass.

Such absurd instances of wives reduced to concubines and children disinherited by technical flaws in marriages may be multiplied infinitely. Do not our novels abound with them? People regard such accidents as inevitable, but does not their possibility show that there is something, say, just a trifle artificial and arbitrary in our social code of morality?

I suppose Society would ask plaintively, " If we take away its present code of morality, what would we put in its place?" Society must have something to get into a state of holy horror about. Well, there is plenty of that without discussing the question of how Mr. and Mrs. So-and-so will divide their property when they are tired of each other. If a man endeavours to escape his natural responsibility to the children he has begotten, leaving them to seek food, clothing, and education in the gutter; if a man tries to retain possession of a woman by reason of her pecuniary dependence upon him when he has no hold on her affection; when parents encourage a daughter to sell herself to an old *roué* for money or rank, there is plenty of work for Society's censorious faculty, and work highly needed, too. As for my idea of what the marriage laws should be, it involves simply a practical application of the evident principle that man or woman should be held responsible for the natural consequence of their own acts. Every parent should be held responsible for the maintenance and education of his or her child, under whatever form of marriage born, or if under none at all; and those who tried to avoid that natural responsibility should be held despicable. The man who was naturally responsible for a woman's confinement should be held liable to contribute towards her expenses, and the man who tried to shirk that responsibility should be regarded as a cur. If a man and woman lived together as man and wife, they should be at liberty to make their own contract as to pecuniary matters. If they made no contract, and, separating, could not agree upon a division, the implied contract should be interpreted by the courts exactly as if between two people of the same sex, that is, as a partnership, or as an engagement by one of the other on salary, or as a mere extension of hospitality by one to the other, according to circumstances. Disputes as to custody of children could be settled by the courts as now, but with a better recognition of the rights of the mother.

But there should never be the scandal of a public inquiry into the conjugal relations of the parties, their fidelity or infidelity. These things should not be held to affect the financial question one iota. Love pays for love, fidelity for fidelity ; these things cannot be paid for in money. The remedy for infidelity is not a money compensation, but to part. And no agreement should be held enforceable in marriage any more than it now is out of marriage, by which conjugal favours are made the consideration for a money payment or money value.

I fancy I hear Mrs. Grundy cry in horror, "Why, under such a law people could live together and separate whenever they pleased !" Now, my very dear and respected Mrs. Grundy, allow me to say that that is entirely beside the question. If we had any law at present to prevent people from living together and separating when they please, I might discuss the advisability of it, but seeing that the law at present allows perfect liberty in that respect—at any rate, to those who have or can earn a living — and that the only people bound in marriage against their will are bound not by law but by the accident of pecuniary dependence—an unfairness which I am sure such an estimable lady as yourself does not wish to continue—I think we may put aside the question whether we should force all married people to love one another and be faithful and happy until we have invented some workable scheme for doing so.

Till then let us leave them to sort themselves as heretofore, only let us try to settle their financial disputes, with which alone we have to do, a little bit more justly.

Chapter V.

—

THE LEAGUE'S SOLICITOR'S VIEWS.

I ASKED Mr. Pulleyne,—whose paper of suggestions, read at the annual meeting, evoked
considerable merriment, on account of its concluding expression of hope that the Archbishop of
Canterbury would join the governing body of the
League,—to write a further paper dealing with certain
legal aspects of marriage, for publication in these
Proceedings. He supplies me with the following
article, in which the legal aspect is not, however,
predominant.

An Apology for the League.

It is of necessity that the thinkers in any large
community must exhibit much divergence of thought
in any matter where the human intellect exercises the
limited intelligence permitted it. From this class
spring the originators who are the pioneers of man's
development.

If the idea be but original or can claim some
approximation to originality, then at least something
is gained. New thoughts are evolved in others,

perhaps, to induce some action of the brain power by which to accomplish all that is subject to earthly revelation.

One fatal impediment to civilization, to the progress of thought, has been, not the mystic compound of man's nature but the base use of it. Cunning minds have seized upon that weakest of weak points—the inability to comprehend the mysteries of origin and futurity—while it is the commonest of plagiarisms that the power creating the earth, known by all names to all nations, and we call God, has circumscribed the intelligence of man and prevented their comprehension.

This mysterious region has always formed, will always form, the happy hunting ground of the Bogie-man, of those unscrupulous men who seek power, fame, fortune, notoriety, by trading upon the super-stitious elements of their neighbour's composition. To proclaim a simple and absolute faith in the Creator. an illimitable belief that the founder of the wonderful universe, of which man is the apex, is wisely responsible for origin and futurity, would not suit their purpose. They who throughout all time, in all communities, have successfully diverted the human mind and been the bane of man, they have enslaved their credulous followers by rites unholy, some demoniacal, some brutal, some indecent, others hideous, cruel, childish, and inane ; they have confused, by creeds and rituals, creeds and rituals of all kinds except simple, involved combinations of words, paradoxical, illogical, incomprehensible, absurd ; they have captured the eye by gorgeous ceremonials, the chief of which has been the gaudy and fantastic decoration of its officiators. The underlying principle has been, and will be, the preeminence of the priest, with power, fame, and wealth to follow ; this accomplished, what matters the rest ?

It is claimed for the Legitimation League that its groundwork, if not wholly original, possesses an element of originality which may commend itself to some class of thinkers not pervaded by the glamour of the mystery-man.

The League claims to base its attractions on no Utopian principles. It simply applies itself to remedy a social evil, winked at by society, wicked only on discovery, and which is freely indulged in by every class, from the highest in the State to the lowest.

Expediency shows that for State purposes, for good government, there must be laws regulating the intercourse of the sexes, but if these laws avoid the Greek conception, and are drawn upon lines emanating from the particular ideas of the persons then engaged upon framing them, they may be evolved in such a spirit of arrogance, extravagance, and bigotry, as to create a worse state of things, and to conflict with the immutable natural laws, and in this respect the League ventures to have an opinion, rightly or wrongly, that this exists, when critically examined with reference to the objects of the League.

A hard and fast line can never be safely drawn. " Actions and interests involved in action are not uniform nor invariable any more than are the momentary conditions of health. In regard to health, at one time one thing is beneficial, at another time the entire reverse. The case is precisely similar in regard to moral action. A line of conduct, which at one time has been pernicious, at another time has brought great benefit often to the same individual. It is the duty of those who have to meet any difficulty, to decide for themselves on each occasion upon the circumstances before them, and from the consideration thereof to seek for a principle to regulate their conduct at such a crisis. Men will know whether their conduct be right or wrong, if they survey the whole circumstances in this spirit. Such is the course which the physician and helmsman take, judging of the course which is most consistent with their art, from the nature of each crisis as it arises."

Words of infinite wisdom indeed, of true charity. Let this be the flag of the League, let it flutter forth and brave the battle and the breeze for ever, so long as humanity lasts ; of the widest catholicity, it embraces closely the lowly and despised object of the League.

It is impossible to bring clearly to the mind the good the League seeks to effect, without adverting to the Marriage and Divorce Laws of England. They form an argument from which the League draws its deduction. It must be admitted that all laws of the State are not equal, it is impossible they should be ; they press more hardly on some than others. Englishmen are apt to say that their laws are alike for poor and rich. A celebrated judge in delivering sentence upon a prisoner convicted of bigamy, demonstrated so far as the Laws of Divorce were concerned, how utterly idle this maxim was, and though great modifications have taken place since that time, the same observations in a minor degree will still apply.

Take a poor man whose wife offends every law of the marriage tie—he has his remedy to get free, but only if his pockets are well filled. The poor man or woman can no more procure a divorce than he or she can fly, without money. An expensive procedure has to be instituted, nor husband nor wife is allowed to confess his or her delinquencies, and set the victim free. The legal proceedings must proceed to the bitter end, and in London alone must he or she face the final tribunal, and then prove to the hilt that which entitles him or her to freedom.

What a mockery to a man with a family, whose wages average £1 a week, or to a woman who scarce can earn her daily bread. Deserted and outraged, without remedy, he or she is barred by the legal and moral laws of the country from seeking the companionship of the opposite sex.

A man without the companionship of an honest woman becomes demoralized, depraved, a rogue elephant. The influence of a good female on the male is incalculable, but this is denied by our laws to an impecunious husband.

The rich man greases the legal machinery with gold, comes out of court a spotless character, and can always find lovely arms to console him for the past, duly consecrated by some rite of the marriage laws.

Vir bonis est quis? qui consulta patrum qui leges juraque servat. So the poor man must abnegate the natural laws of his Creator and be a good citizen, as he cannot be unless he obeys the laws of the country.

An inherent right dwells in an Englishman to alter the constitution and laws of his country, if he can effect that object by all lawful means. That is the poor man's remedy, and during the process of hatching the remedy, he must retreat like Galatea to her pedestal, frozen to a block of marble, forgetting that he is of living flesh and blood.

Who is the worst citizen? The poor man precluded by unequal laws, who obeys the natural laws, or the bigoted followers of the hunters in the happy hunting ground? But the consequences of marriage imposed by the laws are too unequal in operation. Marriage may be accomplished with the greatest ease and at small expense, but the knot once tied is a double reefer only to be disentangled by gold. What difference is there between marriage and divorce that they should not be placed upon equal terms, if the contract be a civil one? What grave complaint often arises from one side or the other, rendering the marriage tie hateful without remedy! In what consists the justice of compelling married persons to live together who find themselves utterly unsuited to each other, who learn to hate each other bitterly, whose diverse composition cannot stand the strain of familiarity?

The League does not decry marriage. All suitable persons should marry in some form, but it contends that the laws should place the poor man on a level with the rich, that divorce should be obtained as easily as marriage is effected, so that an earthly hell might be often avoided.

It seeks to place on record, by means of registration, those children born of a union as solemn to the persons interested as if fortified by rites of church, — when man and woman conscientiously dissenting from the laws of England regarding marriage and divorce, ally themselves together to live in all rectitude and faithfulness, selecting, as they are compelled to do, their own form of rite. For the issue of such as these, branded with illegitimacy, the League seeks to establish a system by which, should the time ever arise when concensus of opinion recognises the justice of the claim, rights of legitimacy will be accorded to such. Its registers would not be open to the results of profligacy. To those who degrade their bodies in the pursuit of mere soulless lust, who degenerate into animals, the League holds out neither encouragement nor assistance. Animated solely by views of pure morality, from the League's mode of thinking, they give their very best by seeking to originate a scheme which, whatever may militate against it logically, or the converse, possesses, it is believed, at least some trace of originality.

> " Honour, we say, or honest fame,—
> We mean the substance, not the name—
> Not that light heap of tawdry wares,
> Of ermine, coronets, or stars,
> Which often is by merit sought,
> By gold and flat'ry oft'ner bought,
> But the true glory which proceeds
> Reflected bright from honest deeds,
> Which we in our own breasts perceive,
> And kings can neither take nor give."
>
> PRIOR.

CHAPTER VI

A VICE-PRESIDENT'S VIEWS.

"THE LEGITIMATION LEAGUE.

"A DRAWING-ROOM Meeting of the above league was held at The Langholme, Harrogate, the residence of Dr. Arnold Lees, a Vice-President, on Thursday, 23rd November, 1893. The Treasurer (Mrs. Gladys Dawson) reported the receipt of Mr. J. C. Spence's new work, 'The Dawn of Civilization,' accompanied by a letter calling attention to the chapter on marriage as bearing on the objects of the League. . . . . . A letter was also read from Mr. John Badcock, Junr. (Corresponding Secretary for London), dealing with certain points raised by the Hon. Secretary in the course of recent addresses in London. Mr. Dawson then read an epitome of these speeches, which had been made before the members of the Dialectical Society."—*Harrogate Herald*, November 29th, 1893.

I had the pleasure, at the first annual meeting of the League, of bringing to the notice of a large

audience the new work of Mr. J. C. Spence, entitled
"The Dawn of Civilization," and of making especial
note of the author's proposals relative to marriage.
Mr. Spence was not at this period connected with the
League, and it is interesting to remark that as
an entirely free lance he came to practical conclusions,
and printed them, whilst others were meditating and
lecturing. Whence he drew his inspiration, and how
long before publication, I do not know. I wrote to
my friend, of whose whereabouts I had not known for
some two or three years, and drew his attention to
my address to the Dialectical Society, and our work
generally, receiving from him the following letter :—

"*3rd December*, 1893.

"DEAR MR. DAWSON,

"I am greatly obliged for yours of 27th, and
for the criticism thereon. As to question of priority
between you and me, I believe priority of publication
is accepted generally as the only standard, not
priority of origination, and you are undoubtedly first
there. My MS. had been sent to the publishers
by June, and had been written much before that,
so I did not borrow from you, and probably you had
thought of the scheme months before you proposed
it, and could not have seen my proposal till a month
after you proposed it. Whoever was first to think of
the proposal, you were the first to propose it in
public. Yours, however, is the more sweeping
measure. Until I read your letter, I had not thought
of the question of polygamous marriages. I did not
evade the question, I overlooked it. I
believe a large and influential body of men and
women would now give their support to a moderate
reform which was based on the monogamic principle

—the husband to the wife at the time, but was free from the element of perpetual bondage ; and that by uniting together in a league they would support each other and give courage to many weaker brethren and sisters. If such a league is desirable, both for itself and for its indirect influence, I think it would be more likely to succeed under the title of 'Marriage Reform' than under 'Free-Love Alliance.' . . . . I quite agree with you that no jury, voluntary or compulsory, can adjust the little differences between couples, but still I think it wise to provide in advance a method of adjusting serious differences which may arise in the event of a dissolution of partnership or in case of death. Still, I should think it a mistake if the league insisted upon this condition in the marriages they register ; in fact, the fewer conditions that were insisted upon, the better ; and the greater varieties of terms of partnership the better. With regard to time charters, I am inclined to agree with you as to the action being repugnant. I borrowed the notion from Donisthorpe's article on Marriage, and introduced it—not that I think time contracts good, but I imagine the forces which make, and will for a long time tend to make marriages perpetual, are so strong that the tendency will be too great in favour of people putting up with unsuitable partners, just because they are the partners. To prevent this, a short partnership, with option of renewal, seemed a better contrivance than a perpetual marriage with option of dissolution. Still I think, should a second edition ever be required, I would omit the clauses referring to time bargains, and stick to my own rather than to borrowed notions.—Yours,.

" J. C. Spence."

I refrain from giving any abstract here of this author's theories and schemes of marriage, as expounded in "The Dawn of Civilization," for the League, in place of reproducing the "Indenture" or matrimonial contract therein contained, and the other more important parts of the chapter on marriage in this work, is able to offer the reader a cheap edition of the entire work, with portrait of the author.

The thanks of all interested in the propaganda of the Legitimation League are due to Mr. J. C. Spence for writing, and to Mr. Frederick Millar, the editor of the *Liberty Review*, for publishing an article entitled "Law and Marriage," appearing in that journal for December 1st and 8th. Mr. Spence leads off with a criticism of the suggestion made by Mr. J. Henniker Heaton, that "in the British empire at least there should be a uniform code of marriage and divorce laws for Christians." Mr. Spence is against the "establishment" of any system of marriage, on the same principle that he is against church, chapel, or sectarian establishments, and makes out his case with characteristic clearness. He dwells at length on the subject of legitimation, remarking that "for many reasons it is almost a necessity to limit kinship to such children as are openly and publicly acknowledged by their parents. There is, therefore, no violation of liberty in laying down a law that, if parents wish their children to be recognised as their lawful successors, they must comply with certain legal conditions. So long as these conditions are merely such as experience shows to be necessary to supply proof of identity and definite parenthood, there seems no reasonable objection to such a law. But if the prescribed conditions are designed to enforce some disputed theological dogma, then the law becomes an iniquitous and offensive form of religious persecution. If, for instance, no marriages except those celebrated according to the rights of the Established Church were legal, and the children of all persons married in any other way were treated as illegitimate, the consequence would be that all conscientious dissenters from the Church would be subject to a cruel system of persecution."

I have told the reader where he will find Mr. Spence's article—*Liberty Review*, December 1 and 8, 1894—and whilst I should have liked to have sought permission to reproduce it *in extenso*, I doubt not I shall gratify the reader the more by printing here an article specially written by Mr. Spence for these proceedings.

THE INEQUALITY OF THE SEXES.

I do not here propose to enter into the vexed question of the claims of women to political equality with men, nor to discuss whether they are superior, equal, or inferior to men in mental capacity, moral worth, or æsthetic taste ; but to treat only of some of the consequences that follow from the physiological inequalities which constitute the difference between the sexes. The parts performed by men and women in the reproduction of children are manifestly unequal : from the time of conception to that of birth children form an integral part of the bodies of their mothers, and after birth they still depend for their natural food upon their mother's milk. The mother has therefore direct evidence that every child born of her is her very own ; while the father of a child has no such direct evidence, but must accept the fact on trust from the mother, and the only guarantee he can have is that no other man had intercourse with the mother at or about the time when the child was conceived.

Among races of mankind living in a state of primitive savagery, depending from day to day on the chance supplies of nature, the children receive but little more care or protection than the young of wild animals, and what care they do receive is from their mothers : so that the paternal relationship is comparatively unimportant. Under such conditions the relations between the sexes may be, and in many cases are, but little removed from promiscuity ; kinship and inheritance are only traceable through the mothers.

Among more advanced races, depending less on the spontaneous gifts of nature than on the results of skill and foresight, the relations of the sexes are more definite, the fathers and the mothers of children are recognised, and both parents co-operate in supporting their children. Amongst the highest races, depending least on unassisted nature, and most on the products of art and science, where wealth has been accumulated and inherited from generation to generation, the people are so far removed from abject want that the care and education of their children receives much more attention. The work of the father is generally sufficient to support not only his children but, to a great extent, the mother also. Under such conditions the relation of the sexes is very definite, the parental instinct is developed to the highest degree, men and women toiling harder and sacrificing more for their families than they would for themselves. Where men are expected to support their children and wives they require strong assurance that the children whom they support and who inherit their property should be in fact theirs and no others, and that the wives who share their earnings or property should be strictly faithful to them.

The very different degrees of blame which are meted out to men and to women for unchastity is often quoted as an instance of the tyranny of men over women, but it springs from a very different, and perhaps, natural source—the inequality of the sexes. The ethical sentiment attaching blame to unchastity on the part of women is not imposed by men on women, it is not only approved by women, but almost universally women are far less tolerant than men of aberrations from the conventional standard. All the wonderful and incongruous variety of marriage customs that have prevailed throughout the world at different times and places have their origin in the fact that the mother cannot be deceived as to her share in her own children, while the father can only be sure thas he is the father of any child when he knows that he and he alone has had intercourse with the mother for a considerable time.

However irrational, grotesque, or even disgust·ing the customs and laws governing the relation of the sexes may be at any time or place, still it is evident that they are founded on the central truth that definite relations between the sexes is a necessary condition of any high form of civilisation. The iconoclastic spirit that would destroy every ancient institution merely because it is imperfect, is at least as dangerous and irrational as the worship of forms and ceremonies merely because they are ancient, without any reference to the way they now subserve the purpose for which they were designed. There is no doubt that the customs and laws of marriage and divorce now in force in this country, contain distinct traces of ancient prehistoric times when women were practically slaves, and still more distinct traces of the influence of the theological creed that taught that the " lusts of the flesh " were essentially sinful, and tolerated marriage only as a concession to human weakness. There are many other ways in which the relationship of the sexes is unsatisfactory. The opinion that " marriage is a failure " seems to be rapidly gaining ground. And to judge from the present tendency of current literature, there might seem to be some danger of the institution of marriage being abolished. But the institution, as distinguished from the laws of marriage, is founded on instincts and feelings much too deeply rooted in human nature to be easily overthrown. And it seems to me that the only thing that forms a real danger to marriage is the inflexible and arbitrary system of laws which, although designed to support it, are almost the only cause of its weakness. There can be no doubt that custom preceded law in marriage as in everything else. And so long as fathers and mothers retain the parental instincts now inherent among the higher races of manhood, there will be definite relations between the sexes, and the custom of marriage would survive even if all marriage laws were abolished.

From the legal point of view only those relationships which are contracted in accordance with the laws of the land are classed as marriages. Although conformity to some formal ceremony may be necessary for a regular or legal marriage, it is not of the essence of a definite matrimonial relationship, but merely an

accessory. The ceremonial, formal, and legal conditions of marriage are variable and arbitrary to the
widest extent, the essential conditions are practically
uniform and universal, and these are open acknowledgment of children, and the fidelity of the wives.
Where women remain faithful to their husbands, and
fathers and mothers acknowledge and support their
children, there are the essential conditions of marriage, all laws and customs notwithstanding. When
either of these conditions are broken, there may be
the form, but there is not the substance of a true
marriage.

The natural inequality of the sexes has in many
countries led to a great number of artificial and
unnecessary inequalities being added to that which
is natural,—the women are absolutely secluded
from all men except their husbands ; to be seen or
spoken to by any other man is an outrage on their
modesty ; girls and unmarried women are indoc-
trinated, and accept as natural and proper this absurd
and unnecessary code of morals. But in more
enlightened countries, women and men mix together
freely in all relations of life, business, and pleasure,
except that which is connected with the reproductive
function. And the only guarantees men have of the
fidelity of their wives is their own vigilance and the
sense of honour common among women ; and these
guarantees are in a great majority of cases more to
be relied upon than a guard of eunuchs or duennas.
The open acknowledgment of the relationship
between husband, wife, and children, the close
intimacy between men and women living together
and sharing their homes and fortunes, is the best
possible means of securing mutual fidelity. A woman

living with her husband and children is protected from a thousand temptations and evils ; a man happily married is too well off lightly to imperil the happiness of his home by any course of conduct which would tend to wreck that happiness.

But what about the innumerable cases of unhappy marriages? To this question there seems to be but one reply—they ought to be dissolved, and the sooner the better. If law or custom forbid this dissolution, it is a virtuous act to break the law and disregard the custom. Laws and customs are the outcome of the opinion of some people, and to submit to these when we disapprove of the opinion is an act of servility unworthy a free man. A man may submit to the dictation of other men when the force at their disposal and the penalties which they can inflict are greatly out of proportion to the evils of submission, but he can never so submit in the smallest detail without some little loss of self-respect, and every act of resistance to unjust laws is a service to the cause of liberty.

In matters matrimonial the terrors of the law are too feeble to be worth serious consideration. The breach of etiquette or custom is a much more serious matter, at any rate for women. A woman, if she acts discreetly and does not openly disregard the conventionalities, may be known to be an un- chaste woman, or even a treacherous wife, without incurring much social censure ; but if she disregards the conventional standard, however chaste and pure her life may be, she will be ostracised by the rest of her sex. Some of the noblest among women have have had the courage openly to defy law and custom in these matters, and thousands do so secretly. But only those who have the courage to do openly that which they think proper render service to the cause of freedom, or tend to raise the level of sexual morality. Clandestine relations between the sexes are always open to suspicion. People are in general only ashamed of such relations as are, in fact, discreditable. It is self-evident that those who openly acknowledge their relationship must think that relationship right and honourable ; and if men and women never do anything in secret which they would be ashamed to acknowledge publicly, they will do very little wrong. The one unpardonable sin against the natural law of marriage is for a wife to have secret intercourse with other men than her husband. Such acts, if common, would undermine the foundations on which marriage is based. Deceit in such matters is essentially immoral, but where there is no deceit there is not necessarily any immorality. Where the bonds of marriage are found to be intolerable, and the law will give no relief, then those who would be free themselves must strike the blow. Let them deliberately and openly separate themselves from their wives or husbands, and having done so, there will be no deceit, no fraud, no immorality in marrying again. They may be debarred from contracting legal marriage, but they are morally justified·in evading the law by any means at their disposal.

In a free country men and women should be at liberty to contract or dissolve any partnership they please, on such terms as they may deem suitable. At present the law does not permit this, or rather it does not give a legal sanction to any matrimonial partnership except such as are based on unlimited liability of the partners. The principle of limited liability, only comparatively recently allowed in law for commercial partnerships, is still disallowed in marriage.

Recognising the advantage, almost the necessity, of some form of public registration of marriages, and public acknowledgment of paternity, and the deficiences and arbitrary limitations of the law in this respect, the Legitimation League was originated to supply these defects.

Those who wish to contract regular and definite matrimonial alliances, and to acknowledge and support their children, and to do so openly in the face of the world, but who will not submit to any form of perpetual bondage, can, by registering their alliances with the League, prove that there is nothing clandestine, nothing that they are ashamed of, in their alliance, and at the same time safeguard their liberty. Parents who have children not born in lawful wedlock, but whom they wish to be openly acknowledged as theirs, can register the fact. And although this deliberate acknowledgment of paternity is not recognised at law as conferring the status of legitimacy on children, yet it is the best possible grounds on which legitimacy can be based.

When it is recognised that matrimonial partnerships are not all necessarily of one uniform type, and that we have no more right to enforce on each other uniformity in marriage than in religion, the law will very soon be altered so as to give the legal sanction to any marriage contract people choose to agree upon, and to make the status of legitimacy depend on the deliberate acknowledgment of the parents.

CHAPTER VII

THE CORRESPONDING SECRETARIES' VIEWS.

I ADVERTED, in the first annual report, to the excellent work done by Mr. Badcock and Mr. Dupont. I here reproduce a specimen letter of each. That of Mr. Badcock was addressed to us, and follows after an extract from *Liberty*, which Mr. Badcock was at the pains to copy and forward :

TO ANY NATURAL CHILD.

Sweet babe, when the ignoble scorn and blame
Thee for thy birth, and cry : " Thou hast no name ;
Thou art the child of passion and of shame,"

Ignore them, walking on the world's highway
Full of great purpose ; or, if thou shouldst stay
To answer such poor custom's hirelings, say :

" A name is but a sound to mark a thing
Conveniently for thought ; can it make sing
The silent snake, or give the worm a wing ?

" The only name of worth is that I make
By my own kindly deeds for my soul's sake ;
Illustrious men have walked the path I take.

> "Who reads the verses of Boccaccio
> And then reviles him as a babe of woe,
> Or taunts him as a bastard base and low?

> "Who looks on Fillipino Lippi's saint,
> With grateful heart forgets that it is paint
> Wrought by a hand men say had a birth taint.

> "And who are these, children of sires unwed,
> Born of delirious Love the world wished dead,
> About whose foreheads Fame her light has shed?

> "Catherine the First, De Castro, and Cardan,
> James Berwick and John Burgoyne, Athelstan,
> And Archelaus the Macedonian,

> "Almagro, and too many men of fire
> And force for me to name, since I desire
> Neither your foolish favour nor mad ire."

MIRIAM DANIELL.

"LONDON, *19th September*, 1893.

"DEAR MR DAWSON AND MRS. DAWSON,

"I've just finished reading your book or 'Legitimation League Proceedings.' The only point I wish to dwell upon now is the matter of *caste*, which I am sorry to see you uphold so much. I seek to break it down.

"*On page* 37 : the mere recognition of the Queen's position by the proposal of a 'Royal' toast is in itself so *anti*-libertarian that it will excite the ire of all extreme liberty people who see it. Anyway, to me, 'Royalty' is synonymous with tomfoolery and toadyism and tyranny.

"*Turning now to page* 85 (your address) :—You say, 'a child born of a mother in no sense qualified to traverse the same social stratum as the father, should not be legitimated.' And, although you add 'the child should be affiliated,' you have brought in *caste* as a reason for denying what you would otherwise grant.

" I think that in a true love union caste is necessarily *ignored*. Education, dress, title, money, all go for nothing, as they should in this relation. If a man cohabits with a woman whom he is ashamed to acknowledge, and has children whom he is also ashamed to acknowledge, *it is the man* who requires shaming out. And although I don't uphold laws that give wives and children any rigid claims upon husbands and fathers (except in an intermediate stage while women and children are arbitrarily disadvantaged otherwise), yet it seems to me that if *any* women have a just claim upon the men they have mated with, it is the poorest women—say the degraded prostitutes, if you like. Ignoring the marriage laws altogether, it is seen that those women have more just claims upon the men they mate with who are *least* in need of such privileges. Perhaps it is as Queensberry says, that married women *monopolise* property and position, and so, more or less, increase the poverty of the unmarried females. Anyway, if it comes to a choice of two evils, viz., *either* to give property and legitimation rights to only the respectable (*i.e.*, married or publicly acknowledged), *or* to give all equal property and legitimation rights, then I am overwhelmingly in favour of the latter course. I would much rather abolish all rights altogether, merely (by way of expediency, and in cases where no sufficient counter-proposition was thought more desirable) giving all children whose descent could be proved, a first claim on all property left by their parents WHEN THE LATTER DIED, if the children were minors, and giving them

TOTAL ownership of all property left by their parents when no will was made, and this whether the kids had been legitimated or not.

"I see you are afraid some noble Duke or other aristocrat might have a claim put in by a gutter child or its mother. WHAT OF IT? As far as *natural* rights go, such poor people have quite as much right as the Duke's wedded wife and 'acknowledged' children. If there is to be a difference made at all, I think it should be *in favour of* the despised and neglected women and children.

"By a limited legitimation, as you seek, you create and bolster up *artificial rights*. The fact that a man 'yielded to a temptation' in being seduced by the charms of a prostitute, is no reason for legally excusing him from supporting that prostitute and her child, WHILE holding him to such support when the woman and child have been registered by the State as his ALWAYS. When a man cohabits, he yields to a temptation, whether it is in wedlock or out of it. And what of it?

"The Duke of Normandy had a son by a poor washerwoman, and the son became 'The Conqueror.'

"I admire Goethe for the care he took of a poor girl whom he had a son by, and for the fact that only after the said girl had lived with Goethe many years, and had given way to drink, did he legally marry her, thus giving her a claim upon him in the law's eye, which she otherwise would not have.—Yours,

"JOHN BADCOCK, Junr."

Mr. DUPONT's letter—one of a stock of interesting ones from which to select—was written by him in reply to an Edinburgh correspondent, who had remarked that :

" Mr. Dawson, in fact, limits the scope of his sympathies to the issue of Free Love unions. You extend yours to all natural children. To use a popular phrase, I think he puts the cart before the horse. If he could obtain legal recognition of Free Love " marriage," that of the issue would follow in logical sequence. But to use the wrongs of the children as a lever for the legalising of the legally irregular union of the parents is simply to court failure from the outset."

To this Mr. DUPONT replied :

" *3rd August*, 1893.

" I duly received your esteemed favour of the 25th inst., copy of which I have forwarded to our headquarters, so that your various suggestions might receive full consideration.

" From the expressions contained in your letter I gather the impression that you agree with me in extending our sympathies not only to the issue of Free Love marriages but to all natural children, and this, I may say, is the desire of all our active or sympathetic supporters in Scotland. I shall make strong representations in that direction to our headquarters. I shall also strongly recommend your suggestion of launching a journal as the organ of the League, for I agree with you that such would be the best medium for the purpose of awaking the public conscience and voice to the egregious wrongs which make Pariahs of a portion of our fellow-men.

" Now coming to another portion of your letter. I admit that the removal of legal hardships and wrongs will eventually lead to a gradual improvement in the social standing of the class immediately affected, but I venture to assert that the social stigma which is so deeply rooted in the public mind will still remain practically unaffected until educational measures are resorted to by means of an active propaganda in the press or public meetings. We all know how little legal enactments succeed in uprooting the germs of prejudice and superstition implanted by the popular customs and teachings of former ages, the shadows of which will still hang upon us like a threatening monster, until courageous reformers forcibly break the fetters which have hitherto imprisoned their mind, and boldly proclaim the naked truth to the world.

"With regard to Free Love, I am glad to see that you do not fall into the same error as most people, in that you do not attribute motives of lewdness to the advocates of such a *régime*. Personally it is far from my desire to destroy or in the slightest manner disturb the sacredness, or rather purity, of marriage. But the so-called sanctity of marriage to-day appears to my mind very much like the practice which is common in some parts of Asia when the woman marries for the purpose of being freer in lavishing her love indiscriminately—of course, in that case it is done openly, while here it only transpires through the courts of justice. No, I firmly believe that free unions between the sexes, so far from degrading the chastity of women or lowering the standard of sexual purity, would, on the contrary, stimulate individuals to a stronger sense of modesty, for the sexual desires, like any other desires, are never so strong when free from restraint as when subjected to outward, artificial, and forceful bonds, when the satisfaction of the slightest craving becomes imperative.

"I now come to he last part of your letter. and I must confess that I still cannot agree with your ideas that persons of illegitimate origin or having illegitimate offspring should be excluded from our movement. In the first instance I consider that they have a prior right to voice their grievances, and they simply stand (in my opinion) like an oppressed caste of outlaws, fighting for their rights. In the second instance, *i.e.*, in case of persons who have illegitimate children, their desire to secure for such offspring certain rights and privileges, so far from being considered selfish, they should be held to the highest esteem, for their desire is most honourable. Besides, such action on our part would look too much like pandering or truckling to public prejudice. On the contrary, we should make no concession, but pluck the weed from the very root, for compromises are a proof of weakness and impotency, the exhibition of which would eventually lead to failure.

"Yours sincerely,

"J. DUPONT."

I also reproduce the text of Mr. Dupont's letter to me on this subject, dated *8th August*, 1893.

" Enclosed you will find copy of correspondence with Mr. Wallace, of Edinburgh, which I hope will prove of interest to you, as it will show you the feeling which animates our sympathisers in Scotland.

"His suggestion as to methods represents the general desire of our adherents here, and personally I think if it could be at all possible, a journal to advocate our ideas and lay our views before the public would be a most important factor for ventilating the grievances and wrongs of the class we wish to assist.

" On the other hand, limiting the scope of our efforts to legitimise merely the offspring of Free Love's unions will have a most damaging effect on our movement, and will be most detrimental to our success. From conversations I have had with our supporters in Scotland, I can assure you that, like Mr. Wallace, the general feeling is that our sympathy should be extended to all natural children, otherwise our intended supporters would withdraw their help.

" I trust you will lay these views before the office bearers and give them full consideration.

" Yours very truly.

" J. Dupont."

To Mr. Toleman Garner, a joint corresponding secretary of the League for London, credit is due for the effective way in which he has brought the work of the League before the notice of the readers of divers newspapers. Mr. Garner has not yet elaborated his views with any fulness calling for detailed examination here, but has promised a paper for a subsequent issue of the " proceedings " of the League.

——

CHAPTER VIII

LEGITIMATION AND LICIT LOVE.

THE approach of the first anniversary of the Legitimation League will be regarded with calm by the most zealous of conventional puritans. If it has survived a wonderfully prophesied nine days, it has yet little progress to show in relation to its expressed "objects." These are to create a machinery for acknowledging offspring born out of wedlock, and to secure for them equal rights with legitimate children. The latter aim is entirely legislative in scope; and it is but the nineteenth century—besides which it has taken us a year to ascertain whether legitimate children have any rights at all, or whether that in which they do rejoice is not merely a mixture of privileges and wrongs. Then again, it is going to take us more than a year to settle whether the grammatical construction of the "objects" allows of the securing of equal rights with legitimate children by *all* offspring born out of wedlock, or only by such as have been "acknowledged." The question here involved has been almost the only one which we have discussed, out of conclave, since the inaugural meeting. I append a Bibliography.* In conclave we have discussed the first part of the "objects," and have not seen our way to institute any system of acknowledgment of illegitimate children. For one thing, to specify an initial, though I do not think insuperable difficulty, we have conceived no plan which, if taken notice of at all, would not be liable to such grave abuse by the frivolous (or the serious artfully resorting to frivolity in their antagonism) as to render it more than useless. In relation to this branch of our objects, I have therefore simply to repeat what I said at the inaugural meeting : " We want people to go to the office of some solicitor or solicitors to the League, and draw up such deeds in favour of their illegitimate children as they shall be advised by those solicitors will hold good in law. A register of such deeds will be kept at the offices of the League, and will be open to public inspection." Howsoever elaborately created, any machinery would be woefully incomplete unless it provided for the recognition of offspring yet unborn, upon whom our law allows no settlement. A settlement upon the mother of a man's possible children can be made, but a condition that if one of the parties should discontinue cohabitation the

* " The Legitimation of Acknowledged Children," an Address by Oswald Dawson, in " The Rights of Natural Children," Verbatim Report of the Inaugural Proceedings of the Legitimation League," pp. 80—85. " Legitimation Rights," by John Badcock, junr., and others in *National Reformer*, August and September, 1893. " Illegitimate Children : A Plea," etc., by J. Greevz Fisher (London : Reeves ; Leeds : Cornwell ; 1893). " Bastardy," by Wordsworth Donisthorpe, in the *Free Review*, Jan., 1894. The last-named article should be read by all interested.

pecuniary interest should revert to the other, would have no legal value, or would prejudice the settlement altogether in the eye of the law.

Our law requires that marriage shall precede the birth of a child—that is, if it is to be legitimate. Our ethics decree, with very certain sound, that the formal union of the parents shall precede the conception of the child, and no one, that I know of, is prepared to question the righteousness of this tenet. If Legitimation were the subject-matter of a Bill, provision for the process prior to conception should be made, for the people who marry have this right or privilege ; whilst, as a piece of practical politics— though there is no danger of any of us of this century being mixed up in anything of the sort—I should be willing to limit its availability to cases where formal union had preceded birth, recognising that any extension of the period of acknowledgments of parentage after this would involve a further modification of English law ; a laudable, perhaps, but a respectable propaganda, and one, moreover, already having its champion in Mr. Walter McLaren and his co-adjutors, who have brought in a Bill to assimilate the English with the Scotch law, which admits of the legitimation of offspring by subsequent marriage. The concern of the League with legitimation of this sort is of a subordinate character, theoretically ; whilst practically all it can at present undertake is to register settlements upon born children.

With the affiliation of children under the bastardy laws, the League has nothing whatever to do. It has no voice respecting the question whether pauper parents should receive compulsory support from their children ; but if legitimation should become a " practical politics " matter, enforcement of these duties upon the legitimated would follow, for (as in a previous instance) the withdrawal of the obligations as an attribute of legitimacy would involve a further modification of English law, laudable perhaps—respectable even—but distinct in character. Similarly, where under wills a surviving partner has a life-interest, conditional upon not re-marrying, Courts would probably rule, if Parliament did not expressly provide, that that interest should cease if the beneficiary proceeded to legitimate offspring by a person other than the deceased.

These provisions might be made without violating the cardinal principle of legitimation. A prohibition which *would* clash with the vital element of that idea—the element differentiating it from marriage—is the prohibition of legitimation by persons who have already performed that process in conjunction with a previous partner; and, as that is just the very prohibition which modern society *would* insist upon, as with that prohibition the whole proceeding would be a work of superogation—would be practically a re-enactment of the law of marriage— we arrive at the conclusion that the work of the League does not primarily lie in the political arena. It has not taken a year to find this out. " We don't expect to be popular in this generation," I said to the *Yorkshire Evening Post* interviewer in April last; " nor do we expect Parliament to recognise us in this generation. We are not so much attempting to alter the law, at present, as to ripen public opinion in the matter until it is time to move." Public opinion has long been ripening. Our coterie is not isolated in disapproving marriage as a bond enforceable for all time, dissoluble only by cruelty, collusion, sin, shame, or death. Others are also convinced that Divorce Court records are a national scandal, that the releases should be possible without the revelations, and that any supposed amendment in the shape of "facilitation" of divorce would only aggravate the evils by provoking more readily the lesser degrees of badness requisite to secure the release ; and also "facilitate" deceit by extending the area of collusion.

Many, again, know, from experience bitter indeed, that the cruelties of wedded life are too oft of a character insusceptible of revelation, at times from their carnal but legal enormity, at times from their petty, but sempiternal, triviality. You can no more bring a "scold" into the Divorce Court than you can take her to a ducking-chair ; whilst the mere "tippler" could no more be got there than into a retreat under the Inebriates Act. As to the carnal cruelties of connubialism, I refer my readers to the writings of Ezra Heywood and Moses Harman.* Then what shall we say of adultery ?—adultery of the heart ; a full measure of sin, according to Christ ? If scolding, tippling, and the minor, but recurrent vexations of married life ; if excess and the bestial doings of the nuptial couch ; if these are unadapted for dealing with by the Divorce Court, how shall we expect that division to handle the delicate points of a suit where the petitioner complains of the full measure of sin ?

Furthermore, the Legitimation League has nothing to do with the facilitation of divorce, or

* *Lucifer*, one dollar per annum. Topeka. Kansas, U.S.A. Heywood's "Cupid's Yokes," 15 cents. See also Greer's "Horrors of Modern Matrimony," same price; etc., etc.

with any other amendment of the Marriage Laws, for
a certain healthy reason, aforestated. It seeks as
few modifications of English law as possible; and it
is not pledged to sweep away any existing institution.
Persons who marry and approve of marriage as a
concern of State may join the League, which is as
elastic as the phraseology of the "objects" will
possibly permit. All we require of members is the
modicum of toleration needed for the avowal of
willingness to concede, to such as prefer that in their
own individual case State marriage shall be superseded by the "living with" system, the rights which
lawful wedlock confers upon offspring. The main
right is the privilege of inheriting in the event of
intestacy; the minor right is the privilege of inheriting at a lower rate of duty. Some of us do not
consider that an intestate's possessions should go to
his next-of-kin. Others (including myself) disapprove
a varying duty, regulated according to the destiny of
those possessions. But the barest consideration of
policy dictates that the law should be subscribed to
as it stands, adopting its blemishes and its benefits,
and leaving amendments thereof to other bodies.

There is a corollary to the legitimation crusade.
If acknowledged children are to have certain rights
of inheritance, what about the parents? Wedded
people inherit when their partners die intestate, and
pay a lower rate of duty than strangers. Is the
mother of an acknowledged child to be branded as a
stranger? Are those whose mutual confidence does
not transcend the limbs denoted by the iron cuffs of
the law, not simply by the golden ring, alone to
enjoy licit love? As a practical politics question,
assuredly: yes, by all means, and thanks for every

instalment of mercy. But we are further still from that delectable region now, and it becomes ludicrous to mould our reform on the lines of the possibilities of this pursuit. Yet theoretically the answer seems clear enough. Only unacknowledged love will be illicit love ; the unions of those who are responsible for little accidents in mills and the like, to repeat the phrase which started the storms of the past year,* will be illicit still. The unions of those who are responsible for the " little accidents" whose laughter rings in our nurseries ; who are trained, in Scriptural or other tones, to honour their fathers and mothers ; who share the name and inherit the possessions of those whom they honour, will be the unions of licit love, whether their arrangements have been registered before the Moloch of Modern Marriage or the Protho-notary of a Licit Alliance League.

---

* Even Mr. Donisthorpe, who, I am proud to believe, is in complete unity with me on the vital principles of the League, styles it "somewhat flippant !" See his article in the *Free Review* for January, treating of " Bastardy " with a master-hand.

In the same issue the reader will find the question "Is Marriage Immoral?" answered in the affirmative by Mrs. George Corbett. Some extracts from her article are to be found in Chapter XVIII.

CHAPTER IX.

THE "NATIONAL REFORMER" CORRESPONDENCE.

THE position taken by Mr. Greevz Fisher in the *National Reformer* of August 27th and September 10th, 1893, and subsequently elaborated in his pamphlet "Illegitimate Children : a Plea," etc., drew forth from the President of the League articles appearing in the *Free Review* for January, 1894, and in *Liberty*, May 6th, 1894, in criticism thereof. The substance of these articles has been given in handy form in Mr. Donisthorpe's "Law in a Free State," recently published by Macmillan. My own comments have not previously seen the light. They took the shape of a speech at a drawing room meeting of the League. The text of that address is reproduced in this chapter :—

Dr. Lees : When we last met here we listened to a paper by your esteemed co-Vice-President upon illegitimate children—a plea for their unrestricted legitimation, and at the conclusion of the paper I expressed to you my sense of its high value as a critical enquiry into the subject of legitimation from

a broad standpoint, whilst at the same time I drew
attention to one or two of the flaws in the argument
which impressed me most, and at the instant that I
heard his paper read. The manuscript of Mr.
Fisher's paper was handed to me after its delivery
and sent to press immediately, in time for its production in pamphlet form by the time that I had arranged
to address the Dialectical Society of London upon
this subject. I did not feel it would be fair to make
my paper to the Dialectical an answer, in any right
sense of the word, to Mr. Fisher's, as it was not to
be expected that the latter's pamphlet, having been
published that very day, would be a matter about
which my listeners might be presumed to have any
knowledge ; at the same time there can be no doubt
about it that I felt that the point argued for by Mr.
Fisher, the legitimation of all children, was the point
of all others then in the air, and that my remarks at
the Dialectical meeting had better have relation to it.
I did not follow Mr. Fisher's pamphlet closely, but I
propose to do so more or less closely now. The
author starts out to show that children are " measur-
ably injured " by being " stigmatised by opprobrious
designations as bastards, illegitimate, and the like."
I am afraid we cannot help this ; and what is more,
the proposed " abolition of illegitimacy " will not get
over the difficulty. You will have to abolish the term
bastardy as well ; and I am not aware that the
abolition of a term will help us very materially in the
long run. You may abolish illegitimacy and bastardy,
"and the like," as much as you like from our vocab-
ularies, but the condition of orphanage from other
cause than the death of parents will remain just about
where it was before. Mr. Fisher next denounces

" the imposition of degrading titles " upon those born after this fashion. I am sure it is not my wish to call anyone by any artificially degrading title. I care not what you call them, so long as we know what we mean. If they are to be known by any name at all, that name is likely to have a signification which is of a degrading character.

Mr. Fisher next proceeds to attempt to set forth some truism which I cannot at all agree to regard in that light in spite of his confidence respecting it. He writes, " It would naturally be expected that a wealthy person's natural love and affection would extend to his natural kindred, in degrees proportionate to their propinquity in blood, but the defenders of conventionality in relationships, setting utterly at defiance the threadbare adage that blood is thicker than water, assume that inheritance must (in the absence of formal documentary settlement by will) follow only the course of the conventional. or, as they impudently call it, legitimate kinship." I take this to mean that Mr. Fisher believes that an intestate man is likely to desire, or may be presumed as having been likely to desire, that any children he may have had who happen to be of the order which I have called " chance children," the " result of little accidents in mills or the like,"—phrases which have got me into such hot water in connection with the legitimation controversy—that these children should inherit their share of his wealth. I do not think so.

It will be a matter for grave censure upon me if I mispresent Mr. Fisher in the course of this reply. It will similarly be a cause for censure if Mr. Fisher has misrepresented me, and this I do think he has undoubtedly done. He writes : " Mr. Oswald Dawson has put forward the theory, that in allowing the legitimate child to succeed to property at a smaller percentage of duty, the State is 'rendering a service for which it has received tangible coin.' This is a very extraordinary contention."

I am not aware of having done anything of the kind. I say that when the State receives tangible coin it undertakes to regard the children who are legitimate as heirs—to say that they shall rank in the succession of the property. And this, I conceive, is a far more important service than the excusing them of a portion of the duty payable where the children, who have money left to them by will, are illegitimate.

Then, again, it is said that I appear " to believe that—

    " 1.—Every person be provided with admitted parents.

    " 2.—Every such person be placed, as far as inheritance from kindred is concerned, upon an exact level with avowed and acknowledged heirs."

Neither the firstly nor the secondly of these is true. Where a child's parents are unknown, as in the case, elsewhere brought up by Mr. Fisher, of a child washed ashore after a shipwreck in which its parents are presumed to have been drowned, we should give—the law gives—the child the benefit of the doubt, and regards it as legitimate. Then as to the " exact level " legitimated children under a new law and children under marriage are supposed to occupy, this will not hold, for as a simple matter of fact the wife comes in for one-third of the personalty under marriage, and I have not yet seen my way to allow the same privilege for a paramour. So under legitimation the children really get more than they would were the level exact. If it is hinted that they should be allowed less, I must certainly say I know nothing of such proposal; if this is what we are going in for, then we had, perhaps, better form ourselves into a semi-Legitimation League. To such a scheme I might agree, or might not.

I am sorry that in criticism of Mr. Fisher's pamphlet I should have to call attention to what I must say would strike me as a mere burking of the issue, were this production by anyone less conspicuously honest than Mr. Fisher. He writes: "Two of the Vice-Presidents of the Legitimation League have contributed the dictum, ' Parliamentary statute can alone legitimate, as any child knows,' but this is a mere display of ignorance. Courts have held that persons were the legitimate children of their reputed parents, and their lawful heirs, in one or more cases, where there was no statutory marriage, nor statutory enactment applicable to the case."

I know I trespass on delicate ground in dealing with any aspect of the *National Reformer* correspondence, in which the quoted passage occurs ; but I feel I must venture the explanation that when the two Vice-Presidents used the words " Parliamentary statute," they meant to endow them with at least that slight amount of elasticity or comprehensiveness which might be needed to include the ruling of our courts of law. The rule holds good to an almost universal degree that your child is not legitimate unless you are married to its mother, and this is the state of things we have set out to alter.

Mr. Fisher is impressed by the fact that it "might be hardly fair in some conceivable cases" that the legitimation of a child might "involve the establishment of a boy as the nephew of his adopter's brothers and sisters." Quite so; but the modern institution of marriage labours under a similar incubus, and the injustice is not felt to be of sufficient gravity to warrant a vote for its abolition—at least I have not heard that this is the case. I am supposed to "have been frightened," and to be "timid"—a very absurd thing to say, surely, when we consider that I tell the first interviewer who visits me that there is nothing in my scheme to prevent a man from legitimating offspring by more women than one; and a charge which I feel sure you who are present will regard as very unlikely. Besides, it does seem to me to be such a piece of simplicity to say that the advocacy of the legitimation of *all* children is a *bolder* step to take than the proposed legitimation of the acknowledged ones only. The latter proposal is certainly a more transparent attack upon the institution of modern marriage, for it seeks to place the offspring of alliances unsanctified by State upon a special and distinctive footing from the "chance children," who would be legitimated equally with them under Mr. Fisher's system.

It is said that "if Mr. Dawson were consistent he ought to object to the retention of marriage of parents as a condition of the legitimacy of an individual." Well, this is certainly going a long way. It means that I am to propose to declare all the now legitimate children—the offspring of marital unions— *bastards!* Perhaps I am a bit timid! It certainly did not occur to me to come forward with a proposal of this character.

Mr. Fisher, recurring to his contention that chance children should inherit, claims that their so doing " would not be any violation of the abstract rights of justice." Abstract or not, I think there would be gross violation of the sound principle upon which our laws as to inheritance are framed, which principle is to distribute an intestate's wealth in such manner as we may presume an intestate, in the average of cases, would wish it to be distributed.

Much fun is made in the pamphlet about my proposal to "remove the stigma of illegitimacy on the maternal side only,"—Mr. Fisher wondering whether it is to be the right or left side, or the front or back. It is, however, quite evident that the idea has been misunderstood, notwithstanding its simplicity. For, writes Mr. Fisher, " supposing in the case of highly-placed persons, such presumably as the female heiress to a dukedom in her own right, or any other fanciful high-placement, there were to be a youthful seduction or rape by a groom or a tramp, and that a son were to be born, the father might be very willing to own to paternity, and in fact would quite probably be eager to claim to be the father of one who would, in the course of nature, succeed to a dukedom if conventionally and legally legitimate." The simple answer to this supposition is that if the mother preferred not to acknowledge the child, it would not be legitimate, and it would not " succeed to a dukedom."

Whether the Legitimation League " ought to propose a mode of dealing with the inheritance of paramours," as alleged, is a moot point. It is a difficult one to deal with. When this critical paper was read in this room I pointed out that the subject was one which had long occupied my attention. It can hardly be meant that we ought to lie quiet till we have got the solution of this knotty little point, and are fully prepared with a definite scheme of propagandism in connection with it. We must move a little at a time, and the farthest point which we have yet reached is the adoption of the dogma that only acknowledged children should be legitimated.

Chapter X

UNIVERSAL LEGITIMATION.

A LARGE proportion of the correspondence of the year has had relation to this question of Universal Legitimation. Several writers in the press have defended the position taken up by Mr. Fisher. Mr. H. R. G. Gogay wrote as follows in comment of Mrs. Victoria Woodhull Martin's articles on " Marriage and Maternity," in the *Weekly Times and Echo* :—

"Do you not think, sir, the efforts of Mrs. Woodhull Martin towards improving the race mentally, physically, and morally, would be somewhat aided if that glorious sham known and described as the People's House was to destroy, by legal enactment, the arbitrary distinction—it can be nothing more—now drawn between legitimate and illegitimate offspring? Why should there be any difference made by the law of the land? Holy Mother Church makes no difference. It will baptise, marry, and bury (for a fee) illegitimate and legitimate people, and even ask no questions ! . . . . . Those who made this unnatural law could unmake it, but they will not, for the very simple reason that if every child born to a man claimed by law the same privileges with his 'legitimate' offspring, such a man would think twice, nay thrice, before he did that which would probably bring into the world a being for whom he would have neither regard, love, nor responsibility. The descendants of the cowards who passed this precious law are in Parliament now."

By a further letter it would seem that Mr. H. R. G. Gogay is willing to wield legitimation as an instrument of punishment. In answer to a letter addressed to the same paper by Mr. Fisher, he writes:

"Were all men like the men forming the Legitimation League, Mr. Greevz Fisher and his friends might live in hopes of obtaining by voluntary methods that which I contend can only be obtained by Parliamentary enactment, viz., the abolition of the bastardy laws, thus making no distinction between children born without or within wedlock, and making the man and not the woman legally and morally responsible for the child or children. This would not only discourage libertinism, the forced prostitution of thousands of helpless servant girls, shop girls, and factory "hands," by their scoundrelly employers and overlookers, but should encourage marriage, for it is clear beyond a doubt that no man would care to be saddled legally with the responsibility of offspring by more than one woman ; whereas now any scoundrel can bring into the world any number of so-called illegitimate children at five shillings per child per week for sixteen years. It is farcical, sir, when one comes to think of it!"

Mr Evacustes A. Phipson wrote on "Children's and Women's Rights" in these terms :—

"Undoubtedly, so long as illegitimate children are subject to disabilities, it is most important that parents should have the right to legitimatise them by subsequent marriage. But the great thing is to abolish every law distinguishing legitimate from those ill-naturedly termed "bastard" children, and to give all absolutely equal rights, both as towards their parents and the community."

Lucinda B. Chandler, reviewing the "Rights of Natural Children" in *Lucifer*, April 13th, 1894, proclaims that the claim of the objects of the League is "far out of the way in its implied breadth and scope of justice. . . . The child is still the ostracised party. . . . That the State has no right to stamp any child with the odious title of bastard, or to discriminate in favour of the child born in wedlock, as to inheritance when the father acknowledges his paternity, so that it is necessary that he should make a will in order to deal justly with offspring they fail to see. . . . The rights of natural children will be secured by a much more radical rectification of wrong and unjust statutes than Mr. Oswald Dawson proposes."

"Spes," a lady writer with whom I have since been in correspondence, addresses a plea for universal legitimation to the *Weekly Sun*, March 23rd, 1895, beginning thus :—

"I have just read that powerful book of Grant Allen's, 'The Woman who did.' which appears to me to emphasise more than ever the necessity of recognising *all* children as *legal* offspring."

With some thinkers, at any rate, belief in universal legitimation is a consequence of their adhesion to the principles of Anarchy. I give in illustration the following letters received from Mr. H. Davis :—

"August 9th, 1893.

"DEAR SIR,

"I have only just become acquainted with the fact that you have started 'The Legitimation League,' a notice of which appeared in the columns of *Liberty*, a New York Anarchist advocate, edited by Ben R. Tucker, which I have only just now had the opportunity of reading. I am fully in agreement with the object for which the League is formed, and I am therefore anxious to be of service to the cause. I am also anxious to obtain further particulars respecting the work of the League. I think it right to tell you at once that I am an Anarchist of the Tucker type, and it is because your endeavour is in a line with Anarchism, that I am anxious to be of service. I think there is a good field for work here, and believe that there is a large amount of latent feeling in favour of such a movement, which only requires to be brought out and developed. Awaiting further particulars.

"I remain, yours,
"H. DAVIS."

"Oswald Dawson, Esq."

I sent Mr. Davis further particulars and also referred him to my letter in the *National Reformer*. I give here his answer thereto :—

" *August* 14*th*, 1893.

" Sir,

" Your letter to hand this morning. I have noted your letter in the *National Reformer* referred to, and I must express myself disappointed on learning your attitude on the question of illegitimacy. When I first became acquainted with the fact that the League had been formed, I was under the impression that the scope of its aim was much wider than appears from your letter in the *National Reformer*, and I was the easier led to that conclusion from the fact, or supposed fact, of the uncompromising attitude of yourself and your wife on the question of marriage. Nay, more, even in your letter to the *National Reformer* you quote Mr. Greevz Fisher—one of the officers of the Legitimation League—as claiming for the same the endeavour to abolish the evil of illegitimacy by self-reliant methods, without the aid of Parliament. On further perusal of your letter, however, I find there is no warranty for such a statement, much as I could welcome it. When you have gained all for which you are striving, legal disabilities are not at an end, as one might suppose from the statement of Mr. Fisher. The most that could be claimed for the League's programme—when attained—would be that a step had been taken in the direction indicated, the ultimate result of which appears very doubtful, to say the least. Surely it is easily conceivable that there are many ' good ' men and women whose children would fall under legal disabilities, simply through non-compliance with the new act on the part of their parents,

and thus would *they suffer from no fault of their own.*
There are statements in your letter which seem fundamental from your point of view, which might easily
be controverted and, I think, disproved, were it
necessary to do so, such as the importance of a name
for the child, etc. Suffice it to say, that from my
standpoint the total abolition of *all legal disabilities*
in connection with sex relationships is the one thing
that is necessary and the only freedom worth working
for.

"I could better understand the position of the
League if it sought the cloak of respectability, and
desired to coquet with Mother Grundy ; but I do not
believe this of either yourself or your good lady. I
am only surprised, and somewhat pained, by the
inconsistency of your position.

"Wishing you more light and a wider range
of view.

"I remain, yours respectfully,

"H. DAVIS."

"Oswald Dawson, Esq."

Chapter XI

THE PRESIDENT ON THE BAR SINISTER.

MR. FISHER is usually clear and intelligible, but I confess I am utterly at a loss to understand his short treatise, entitled, " Illegitimate Children," or to make out the drift of his " plea for the abolition of illegitimacy." He seems for once to have completely confounded law and custom. In the belief that he is riding a tilt against the law, he is in reality merely condemning the popular use of unbecoming language. He complains that certain persons are " stigmatised by opprobrious designations, such as bastard, illegitimate, and the like." So they are : similarly, other persons are stigmatized as " mashers," " negroes," " lunatics," and even " females." . . . I know many women who wish they had been born men : they regard " woman" as a term of reproach. Will Mr. Fisher get up a crusade for the abolition of femininity ? . . . . Now, Mr. Fisher is no Don Quixote, and there must be some reasonable explanation of his attitude. And I think I have found it. He actually believes that illegitimate persons are saddled with legal and political disabilities. There are several passages in his pamphlet which confirm this conjecture. He proposes (p. 12) "to repeal all laws defining illegitimacy." There are no such laws to repeal. A bastard has all the rights of an ordinary citizen. He exercises the franchise, he can hold land, he can inherit land from his own issue (that is to say, his only possible relations), and he is in all respects on the same political level as his legitimate fellows.* All the State does is to say to him (and to everybody else), "if you wish to rank as the son of any particular man, you must show that your mother and he were already married at the time of your birth." When Mr. Fisher says this is a foolish regulation, and too narrow a condition, I agree with him. If it is based on morals, it is too loose, because it ought to require the claimant to show that his parents were already married when he was begotten. And if it is

---

* There is only one slight exception to this law, and it tells in favour of the bastard. And this is termed the case of *bastard eigné* and *mulier puisné*. Here the bastard, though unable to furnish the required proofs of sonship (for the State will not accept even the testimony of the father as sufficient to justify it in foisting the child upon the family), is brought up in his supposed father's house as one of his own children. A legitimate child, that is, one able to furnish the required evidence of sonship, is born. If then the father dies, and the *bastard eigné* enters upon his land, and enjoys it to his death, and dies seised of it, then the eldest legitimate son and all other heirs are totally barred of their right. Blackstone regards this as a sort of punishment on the *mulier puisné* for his negligence in not entering during the bastard's life, and evicting him. But this does not explain why all other heirs should likewise be barred. It should be added that this rule applies only when the two sons are by the same mother, who was unmarried at the time of the first son's birth but married at the time of the second son's birth.

based on other considerations, it can be shown to be unnecessarily exacting. Here we are all agreed. But when it is proposed to abolish *all* conditions, I stare in blank amazement. What is to prevent the first boy in the street from claiming Mr. Fisher as his father, in making use of his credit, and in succeeding to his property among the next of kin at his death,—supposing him to die intestate? Surely this is not the intention of the writer. Then what can it be? Is it this? That each child is to be allowed to say, " I am the acknowledged son of somebody, but I decline to say of whom." But any child can say that now, and the State will not interfere with him. It is only when he claims to be the son or daughter of A B, that, in the interest of A B, the State says, " Prove it." Surely this is right and necessary. It is a very serious thing, not only for A B, but for all his kith and kin, to have a new relative foisted upon them. For purposes of kinship and succession the proofs must be convincing and conclusive. We may differ as to what they should be, but surely we shall all agree that they should be of a vigorous and thorough character.

" The conventional connection between so-called legitimate kinship and heirship is to some minds indissoluble, and the extraordinary phenomenon is actually witnessed of certain fearless thinkers incapable of performing such a simple analysis as supposing them to exist apart." (p. 9.)

I am then singled out as one of these unfortunates ; and I am charged with having discussed the question of inheritance and succession to the almost total exclusion of all others, in my presidential address to the Legitimation League.

I did so; but I had not then a glimmer of suspicion that any one present actually believed in a *status of illegitimacy* above and beyond the mere denial of a special kinship. I should as soon have thought of condoling with Mr. Fisher on his being stigmatized as the non-brother of the Czar of Russia. So he is; but does that constitute what Mr. Fisher calls "an individual status," as distinguished from "a relative or reciprocal one"?

I fear I must admit having used language in my presidential address which almost justifies the interpretation put upon it by Mr. Fisher, unless carefully construed in the light of the context. I said, "It seems hard that innocent children should be branded with a life-long brand of bastardy, as the result of folly or impatience, or it may be weakness, over which they had no control." What, in order to be more explicit, I ought to have said, is this: "It seems hard that the State should insist on branding as bastards those whose parents are willing and ready to remove the stain." This is what I understand to be the object of the League; and had it been more than this, I for one could not have taken any part in its establishment.

Bastards are as likely to be brave, and have shown themselves as brave, as others. True; but it is probable they will inherit the moral flabbiness, the uncontrollable impulse, the selfishness, and the lack of self-respect which usually characterise one or both of the parents of illegitimate children. This is a stubborn fact, which is not only antecedently probable, but actually observed. A man, for example, who is disowned by his father on account of the inferior social position of his mother, or because of the ephemeral and unholy tie which bound them—such a man is very likely to inherit his mother's incivic weakness and folly. And the children of immoral parents are no less to be shunned and suspected than the children of diseased, deranged, drunken, or low-caste parents.

No name-giving can mend or mar them. Under any system, until human nature rises to a higher plane, these ill equipped citizens will be born to excite our pity, but they must ever remain the bastards of the people. You cannot wring happiness out of vice.

It is not necessary to blame the bastard, any more than the mongrel, in order to admit that he is or was less entitled to respect, on the average, than his legitimate fellow-citizens. One attaches no blame to the ugly woman—in correct Victorian English, the plain woman—from whom one is constrained to withhold admiration, nor to the poor idiot, whose imbecility we pity but despise.

I have a couple of thorough-bred Irish terriers: one of them is, in Victorian English, a lady-dog; the other is not. Now, I can sell the offspring of this union in advance for a long price. But if the gentleman takes a walk, and, inspired by original sin, becomes the father of what Mr. Oswald Dawson styles a "chance pup" by a mother who is a half-bred pug, then that pup would not fetch a shilling in the market. He might grow up to be an affectionate, plucky, and clever little dog, but the chances are against him. And in any case, without attaching any blame to him personally, we should call him a mongrel and a cur, and he would be shunned by all dog-fanciers.

To sum up, the State is not really concerned with the kinship of citizens except for what may be called work-house purposes. That is to say, if a child is found, the State endeavours to find the mother, and having done so, helps her. if necessary, to indicate the father. The decision of the court on this point is based on probability, and very often in face of the denial of the person accused. It is an absurdly unjust and antiquated proceeding, and should be utterly abolished. In the meantime the State does not pretend that such a decision establishes any kinship whatever. It does not even make the child the son of the putative father. The child still remains *nullius filius* in the eye of the law, although the law has just asserted its knowledge of the father. The total effect of the decision is to render the most probable father of the child liable for its maintenance for the first thirteen years of its life, at a cost not exceeding a sum of about £150, and this only in case of the mother's inability to contribute to the child's support. Otherwise the State makes the mother wholly responsible for the child's support for the first sixteen years of its life.

Some persons (including Mr. Fisher among the number) seem to think that affiliation and legitimation have something in common, which they have not. It would, indeed. be a strange " reform " to rest the title to thirty thousand acres and an ancient name upon the bare opinion of a couple of justices in petty session, with no better safeguard against their stupidity or bias than an appeal to quarter sessions. And yet this is what Mr. Fisher must mean by making *all* children legitimate : though even this does not make clear what he would do in the case of children, alas! no inconsiderable number, of whose paternity not even the mother can hazard a guess.

Finally, as to the liability of the child for the maintenance of its parents in old age and infirmity, it is enough to say that the present position would remain unchanged. Let A. B. register a certain child as his own; let him bring him up, maintain and educate him, and then suppose proof to be forthcoming that the child is not his son; in such case, it may be urged, the child would be in a position to repudiate all liability, and the father would come upon the rates. True, such a case might arise; but so it might now. The birth of a child in wedlock is only a *prima facie* presumption of its legitimacy. The law permits the point to be brought into controversy.

The next question we have to answer is this: Does the present-day law of England, relating to parent and child, succeed in excluding from the ranks of legitimacy only or mainly the children of dissolute and inferior persons? Does it not rather exclude many of the worthy, and include many of the unworthy? If we find that this is so, we shall have good ground for altering the law relating to legitimacy. Take a few instances. Is the man who, years after his wife's death, asks the hand of the loving sister, who has ever since watched over his children and presided over his household, rightly dscribed as a victim of sudden and selfish passion? Or is *she* more likely than other women to be actuated by sordid motives? Again, here is a man whose wife has for years been confined in a lunatic asylum. He meets with a woman in his own station of life, who is willing, in spite of society's reproach, to share his lot for better or for worse, and to hand down his name and his blood to posterity. Is there any reason to suspect inferior moral qualities in either of these two? Moreover, there may be many, there are many, who entertain the strongest conscientious objections to perpetual vows. They will not promise what they may be unable to perform. With every reason to hope that they may be suited each to each through life, they dare not swear as to the remote future. Does this self-possession and scrupulousness indicate a low moral tone? Precisely the reverse. Believers in monogamy, they are not believers in the ability of youth to forecast the tastes and yearnings of maturity. Yet they have sufficient mutual faith to trust one another, and to await with hope the unseen developments of time. Surely none will be found to pretend that the offspring of such unions are likely to inherit unsocial and immoral qualities. Perhaps I should be venturing upon thin ice were I to plead for the youth and maiden who, in the summer madness of love, so far forget themselves as to yield to impatience. It is unnecessary for me to do so. Here, as it happens, they have the support and sympathy of the law of England—of the very State itself. "For if a child be begotten while the parents are single, and they will endeavour to make an early reparation for the offence by marrying within a few months after, our law is so indulgent as not to bastardize the child, if it be born though not begotten in lawful wedlock." Such are the mild words in which the severe Blackstone essays to whitewash the somewhat lax morality of this Christian State. And the English law permits of divorce and remarriage, which is a distinct violation of the monogamic principle. And Scotch law is even more unprincipled than either. Then why beat about the bush, and make believe? Let us face the truth boldly. The State has given up all hope of upholding the monogamic principle by force. It recognises the folly of trying to make men moral by law. Then away with all this cant and coercion. The monogamic principle will take care of itself. It is a natural tendency, and not an artificial creation of the State. And what, after all, are these vaunted virtues which the State professes itself so anxious to uphold? And these vices it is so anxious to suppress? What virtues do our present marriage-laws preserve? Patience, self-control, prudence, constancy. Yes; and what compensating vices do they encourage and engender? Sordidness, life-long prostitution, deception, and secret faithlessness. To what else is due that cesspool of abominations, the marriage-market? Then let the law leave morality to take care of itself, and restrict its energies to the redress of injuries, and to the doing of justice. In the particular matter of legitimation, let it fall back on the father's acknowledgment of paternity supported by sufficient evidence, as the one test of legitimacy; and leave the rest to the advancing good sense of sane men and women.

Mr. Fisher's fear lest a couple of tramps should call at the register office and register themselves the parents of the Duke of Bayswater's first-born, is not a well-grounded fear: for, as I have pointed out, registration constitutes a *presumption* only, which would be very easily disproved.

Says Mr. Fisher: "A claimant father not only appoints the claimed son his heir, but appoints himself the son's heir." And this brings me to the State's fourth reason for busying itself with the kinship of citizens. I postponed the discussion of this fourth reason, because it belongs to another class of legal questions. It is an outgrowth of the old law of status, and is quite out of harmony with our extended system of free contract. Time was when a man could devise no part of his property as he thought fit. Certain definite persons had claims upon it which he could not resist. Such persons were related to him by blood, and their rights formed a most intricate and complex web. How carefully these tables of consanguinity were chronicled and preserved among the titled and propertied classes, is evidenced by the fact that Henry IV. of France succeeded to the throne through the sixth son of a predecessor who died about three centuries earlier, during the whole of which time his blood-rights had, so to speak, smouldered in the form of parchment. Now this system, though scotched, is not yet killed. Mr. Fisher is right, therefore, when he points out that a man, by registering himself the father of a child, by that very act " appoints brothers, uncles, and their female counterparts, as well as cousins and other relatives." In short, a man could by this simple process create and manufacture an heir out of a stranger in blood to the detriment of the lawful heir. But here again this is frequently done under cover of marriage, and in both cases it merely creates a presumption, which can be rebutted by the production of sufficient evidence.

It is an old maxim of English law that God, not man, makes the heir. In other words, the tenant for life cannot supplant the heir *apparent*, except by the dangerous process of killing him. He cannot adopt an older child, and so put a stranger over his head.

But he can and does supplant the heir *presumptive* by the simple process of marrying his washerwoman, whereby the plans of the Deity may be somewhat modified, and the purity of the family blood considerably tarnished.

Any man can disinherit his children, or any of them, by will. He is not even compelled to leave them a reasonable subsistence. The child's ancient right to the *pars rationabilis* has been taken away in every case. By an Act passed in the reign of William III., if a Roman Catholic refused to allow his Protestant child a fitting maintenance, with a view to compel him to change his religion, the Court of Chancery might compel him to do what was "just and reasonable." And in the reign of Anne, a similar remedy was provided to force Jews to provide a suitable maintenance for their Christian children. But both these Acts were very properly repealed in the present reign. And now every man's property is absolutely at his own disposal. He can pass over all his legitimate children, and leave everything he possesses to his natural child or to his mistress, or to anyone else.

The next question we have to answer is this : Does the present-day law of England, relating to parent and child, succeed in excluding from the ranks of legitimacy only or mainly the children of dissolute and inferior persons? Does it not rather exclude many of the worthy, and include many of the unworthy? If we find that this is so, we shall have good ground for altering the law relating to legitimacy. Take a few instances. Is the man who, years after his wife's death, asks the hand of the loving sister, who has ever since watched over his children and presided over his household, rightly described as a victim of sudden and selfish passion? Or is *she* more likely than other women to be actuated by sordid motives? Again, here is a man whose wife has for years been confined in a lunatic asylum. He meets with a woman in his own station of life, who is willing, in spite of Society's reproach, to share his lot for better or for worse, and to hand down his name and his blood to posterity. Is there any reason to suspect inferior moral qualities in either of these two? Moreover there may be many, there are many, who entertain the strongest conscientious objections to perpetual vows. They will not promise what they may be unable to perform. With every reason to hope that they may be suited each to each through life, they dare not swear as to the remote future. Does this self-possession and scrupulousness indicate a low moral tone? Precisely the reverse. Believers in monogamy, they are not believers in the ability of youth to forecast the tastes and yearnings of maturity. Yet they have sufficient mutual faith to trust one another, and to await with hope the unseen developments of time. Surely none will be found to pretend that the offspring of such unions are likely to inherit unsocial and immoral qualities. Perhaps I should be venturing upon thin ice were I to plead for the youth and maiden who, in the summer madness of love, so far forget themselves as to yield to impatience. It is unnecessary for me to do so. Here, as it happens, they have the support and sympathy of the Law of England—of the very State itself. " For if a child be begotten while the parents are single, and they will endeavour to make an early reparation for the offence by marrying within a few months after, our law is so indulgent as not to bastardize the child, if it be born though not begotten in lawful wedlock." Such are the mild words in which the severe Blackstone essays to whitewash the somewhat lax morality of this Christian State.

And the English law permits of divorce and remarriage, which is a distinct violation of the monogamic principle. And Scotch law is even more unprincipled than either. Then why beat about the bush, and make believe? Let us face the truth boldly. The State has given up all hope of upholding the monogamic principle by force. It recognises the folly of trying to make men moral by law. Then away with all this cant and coercion. The monogamic principle will take care of itself. It is a natural tendency. and not an artificial creation of the State. And what, after all, are these vaunted virtues which the State professes itself so anxious to uphold? And these vices it is so anxious to suppress? What virtues do our present marriage-laws preserve? Patience, self-control, prudence, constancy. Yes ; and what compensating vices do they encourage and engender? Sordidness, life-long prostitution, deception, and secret faithlessness. To what else is due that cesspool of abominations, the marriage-market. Then let the Law leave morality to take care of itself. and restrict its energies to the redress of injuries. and to the doing of justice. In the particular matter of legitimation, let it fall back on the father's acknowledgment of paternity, supported by sufficient evidence, as the one test of legitimacy; and leave the rest to the advancing good sense of sane men and women.

———

CHAPTER XII

MARRIAGE AS SLAVERY

MR. JOHN BADCOCK, JUN., our Corresponding Secretary for London, has published during the year a lecture, entitled "Slaves to Duty," delivered before the South Place Junior Ethical Society. Amongst the duties, the imperiousness of which Mr. Badcock seeks to minimise, are those involved in our system of State marriage. Those duties are, it is true, classed with others which to many readers will doubtless appear to rest upon a different footing. Mr. Badcock writes : " If I choose to fulfil a promise of lifelong marriage, I can do so. If I choose to pay usurious debts to a Shylock, I can do so. But neither the woman nor the Jew should in these cases have any help from the courts of justice, any more than betting creditors have now in this country." Mr. Badcock proceeds to emphasise his objection to the marriage contract, which, as he says, is not free. He writes : " The powers only acknowledge one form of it, and put disabilities upon the offspring from those who have not obeyed the marriage regulations. Therefore the parrot-like, repeated-after-the-official, marriage vows can no more be considered as the voluntary expression of the free desires of both contracting parties than can any other promises that are dictated by public usage and law. Therefore, we are *not* justified in condemning off-hand those who are nonconformists to marriage. When the law threatens, society ostracises, and education produces its bias against those who participate in free natural unions, and against 'natural' children, those who are too weak to openly face the tempest need not be restrained by duties from seeking in secret those satisfactions denied them openly." Mr. Badcock indicates the way of salvation, according to his idea, in the following paragraph : " I do not doubt that the liberation of the means of subsistence from the usurious control of Government will eventually increase the independence of women along with the independence of men. When that comes to pass you may find the duties of a man to support his wife, and of a wife to obey her husband, and of both to remain bound together till death, to have lapsed and gone out of fashion, because superfluous."

CHAPTER XIII

LABOUR AND LEGITIMATION.

THE following matter, under above title, was contributed by the Editor of these *Proceedings* to the *Labour Annual*, 1895 :—

The demand for the economic independence of women implies the slavishness of the stipulation :—keep in perpetuity in compensation for the risk of maternity. With evolved and exalted ideas of a Fair Bargain, the woman of an advanced ethic will scorn eternal payment, compulsorily levied, for transitory service. I doubt if advocates of State-endowed motherhood propose perpetual pensions for every woman who conceives, including vigorous ladies who have children earning back ten years' cost of education in as many months. I presume allowances would lapse with time according to the precedent of the Bastardy Laws, with possible exceptions where prolificacy has resulted in a more or less complete specialization of women as mothers.

The Legitimation League, amongst other aims, making, I hope, for fairness, seeks to provide women who revolt against the slavery of marriage with the means of securing an economic independence which they do not feel is theirs when they are tied for life to an inebriate, a thief, a foul-mouth, a gambler, a drone, an adulterer, a man given to cruelty, or any combination of these except the two last.

The process of provision may be effected by the registration of alliances, fitly accompanied by an assimilation of surnames, and having for meaning on its legal side,—primarily the acknowledgment of parentage in event of issue with all its responsibilities as under marriage, and the placing of offspring in the line of succession; and, secondarily (or reverse the order of importance if you will), the establishment of reciprocal duties as between the contracting parties, entailing financial liabilities, and regulated in respect of the determination of the contract partly upon a physiological basis.

Whilst a woman runs the risk of conceiving, it should be in her power to contract for the wherewithal to save her from wage-earning, and whilst rearing offspring she may surely stipulate for a competence without sacrificing her economic independence. Beyond this, though she has everything to expect from Love, her demands, if embodied in the law of the State as a compulsion-wielding power, are by Favour,—are gains without service. Under such conditions, and under such conditions alone, may woman deem herself a slave.

LEEDS, *October*, 1894.

—

CHAPTER XIV

WHAT IS LICIT LOVE?

I WAS asked by a questioner at the Hall of Science "What is licit love?" Supplementing the brief answer then made, I give the text of an article written for a local periodical, which ceased to exist between the sending of my communication and the time for the publication of the next issue.

Is there anything direly disreputable in licit love, as a phrase, or a propaganda, or in any way? We must first know its meaning. Licit love is love sanctioned by law, all love for which it is sought to obtain legal sanction. But, bar love not brought apparently into the pale of criminality by reason of the commission of seduction and adultery, all love— with a residuum of exceptional cases needless to cite—is licit. I say 'apparently,' because in reality the legal action in the case of these exceptions is civil and not criminal. There is no punishment for seduction or adultery unless an aggrieved party sets out to seek damages. Fornication is not illegal, and, indeed, prostitution itself only comes into conflict

K

with law indirectly. The principal characters are untouched, those who provide the facilities are liable to suffer.

The inference may seem to be that licit lovers, as a school, desire to see all these practices in some way recognised by law. That is not so. Nor do we aim to obtain for them the sanction of custom. All we aim for is to render holy and right—a phrase I will presently explain—all such alliances as the concerned parties are willing to publicly declare, and also perform a further process. This further process is the paying of a fee to the State in registering the name, abode, perhaps also age and occupation, or other needful details concerning the two parties, so that should one die before the other without making a will and the alliance be not terminated, the survivor shall be entitled to rank in the distribution of the intestate's estate. It would have the further effect of allowing the parties to look to each other for financial support whilst allied and during the period for which the notice to part ran. Whether the law should fix or limit that period is another question. At present it fixes it by making it eternal. Possibly the eternal is a fit subject for State cognizance, possibly it is not. Officially, so to speak, I do not assail it. What I ask is that others, who for any reason prefer a temporary contract periodically renewed, or (and the alternative is vastly preferable in every way) a contract indefinite in time and determinable by notice, shall have the privileges which the law grants to the wedded.

Now, to revert to our initial query and to answer it. This may be a direly disreputable idea. I dare say it would be generally voted so. ' Licit Love ' may be as heinously horrifying as ' Free Love,' if by the latter term we meant promiscuity and the breaking up of the system which gives to children more parents than one, or as absolutely abhorrent as seduction or other social delinquencies which men and women commit away from the glare of day in shame and fear. The same adjectives justified by the same adverbs may be applied to all these deeds, but let us not thereby confound or suppose a generic resemblance between two or more widely differing things. Licit love is not legalised liaison. It is open as marriage or the registration of a limited liability company. Weddings are daylight ceremonials. It is usual to publish banns before and advertisements afterwards, and the lady wears a ring. I find no fault with these customs.

CHAPTER XV.

———

THE NEW LEGITIMATION ACT.

THE following communication reached me per book post. It is anonymous, and I have had no subsequent information as to its authorship. It ran to four or five times the length of the extract given below, which forms merely the commencement of the article, which in its developments assumed phases and phrases too obscene for reproduction :—

THE NEW LEGITIMATION ACT.

From the *Skunktown Growler*, in the year 2,000.

A number of cases under the new Legitimation Act came before the Bastardy Commissioner to-day. In some of these the testimony—for it can scarcely be called evidence—was so conflicting, that the judge and jury were totally unable to arrive at a verdict.

The first was the case of Mary Jane Slugs, who claims to be entitled to a share of the large estate left by the eccentric John Slugs, who died a few weeks ago. In proof of her claim, Miss Slugs brought forward her alleged mother, a very stout elderly lady, who acted very much like one under the influence of liquor, but Miss Slugs assured the court that her mother suffered from chronic hiccoughs, brought on by over indulgence in snuff. The lady burst into tears in describing her intimacy with the deceased millionaire, whom she swore was the father of her child, the aforesaid Mary Jane. She was vigorously cross-examined by the judge, who failed to shake her statement that the deceased had met her twenty years previously, etc., etc., etc.

CHAPTER XVI

HONOUR TO WHOM HONOUR IS DUE.

"IRENE," by Sada Bailey Fowler, is an American work of fiction, and has been introduced to the British public through the agency of Mr. Crawford, Larkhall, Bath. The following memorandum appears therein :—

"HONOUR TO WHOM HONOUR IS DUE.

"The Ante-nuptial Contract on page 362, was copied from that of Damon Y. Kilgore and Carrie S. Burnham, recorded in the Office for Recording Deeds in and for the City and County of Philadelphia, in Deed Book D.H.L., No. 8, page 516.

Here is the contract referred to :—

"'Whereas, Edgar Clayton, of the Township of Monroe, County of Mercer and State of West Virginia, and Irene Belham, of the Township of Waverley, County of Essex and State of New Jersey, contemplate entering into the marriage relation with each other, and

"'Whereas, by the laws of West Virginia certain disabilities are imposed upon every woman who enters into this most sacred of all civil contracts, thereby inflicting a great injustice upon women, and manifold evils upon society as the direct and inevitable result of this legal inequality between the husband and wife, therefore

"'This Agreement Witnesseth, that in case the said contemplated marriage between the parties to this contract shall take place, the said Irene Belham shall not be subject to any of the legal disabilities imposed upon married women by the laws of this State, or of any State or Territory of the United States, as between the said parties to this contract ; but that after the said contemplated marriage shall have taken place she shall have ownership, possession, and control of her person, property, and earnings, together with such property as she may hereafter acquire by gift, inheritance, or otherwise, during the continuance of said marriage, as fully and completely as if she were a *femme sole*. And as to third parties, the said Irene Belham shall be as exempt from all legal disabilities as possible under the laws of the land.

"And it is further agreed, that should such marriage result in the birth of any child or children, such child or children shall belong equally to both parents, neither having superior rights to the other in the maintenance and education of their said offspring, all provisions of the Common or Statute Laws to the contrary notwithstanding.

"In witness whereof we, the undersigned parties to this contract, have hereunto subscribed our names and affixed our seals, this first day of

April, in the year one thousand eight hundred
and seventy-one.

"EDGAR CLAYTON [Seal.]
"IRENE BELHAM   [Seal.]

" Signed and Sealed in presence of—
"LEANDER POLLOCK.
"JAMES RUSH.

" Personally appeared before me, Peter
Randolph, a Notary Public in and for the County
of Mercer, State of West Virginia, Edgar Clayton
and Irene Belham, parties to the above contract,
and acknowledged that the foregoing agreement
was their free and voluntary act, and that they
desired the same to be recorded as such.

" Witness my hand and official seal this 1st
day of April, A.D. 1871.

"PETER RANDOLPH,

" *Notary Public.*

[Notarial Seal.]

" Recorded in the office for Recording Deeds
in and for the County of Mercer, State of West
Virginia, in Deed Book I. O. U., No. 9, page 366,
&c.

" Witness my hand and Seal of Office this
First day of April, Anno Domini 1871.

"JOHN GRISCOMBE,

" *Recorder.*"

[Official Seal.]

J. GREEVZ FISHER,
Vice-President of the Legitimation League.

J. C SPENCE,

Vice-President of the Legitimation League.

CHAPTER XVII.

——

A WIFE'S SISTER DEBATE.

A DEBATE was held in the Leeds Law Institute by the Leeds Law Students' Society on Monday evening, the 19th November, 1894. Mr. Edward Fletcher, Solicitor, of Leeds, occupied the chair. The moot point under discussion was as follows :—

"A. and B., British subjects residing in London, went through a form of marriage which, according to the law of this country, did not constitute a legal marriage, since B. was sister to A's. former wife, deceased. Prior to the ceremony, and in consideration thereof, a sum of £20,000 was vested by A. and B. in trustees upon trust (subject to life interests in favour of A. and B. and the survivor) for the children of the marriage. As A. and B. should by deed jointly appoint, and failing such joint appointment, as the survivor should by deed so will, appoint, and failing any such appointment, and as far as any such appointment, if made, should not extend, upon trust for all the children of the marriage, who, being males, should attain twenty-one, or, being females, should attain that age or marry, equally, and if there should be only one child, then the whole to be upon trust for such one child, with an ultimate trust in case there should be no children of the marriage in favour of X. A. and B. have three children and wish to extend their power of appointment, and they are advised that any appointment they might make would be inoperative as soon as there was no marriage between them. The children born to them are not objects of the power, and that the property subject to the life interests of them (A. and B.) belongs to X. But is this advice sound? If so, is there any method whereby A. and B. can prevent the property, the subject of the settlement, passing to X. under the ultimate trust, and secure it for the benefit of their children?"

Mr. A. T. WILLIAMSON opened the debate, and submitted that the children of the marriage were undoubtedly illegitimate, and that the advice given to A. and B., that any settlement made by them would be inoperative, was sound, since there would be no children of the marriage as there was no legal marriage solemnized, and that the ceremony gone through between A. and B. was not such a consideration as would support the marriage settlement as it tended to immorality, but this did not affect the interest of X., since the instrument under which X. benefitted was completed at the time the settlement was made. Mr. Williamson read an extract from Lewin on Trusts, page 118, to show that where a trust is created for an unlawful purpose, the Court will neither enforce the trusts in favour of the parties intended to be benefitted, and will assist the settler to recover the estate. The trust created by A. and B.

tending to immorality, the law would not assist the settlers in recovering the estate, which would therefore pass to X. He also read an extract from Furweller Ruvers, p. 489, and submitted that as both parties must have known that the ceremony was not lawful, the settlement must be construed as a voluntary deed, and that a voluntary deed might be partially valid, and cited the case of the Countess of Strathmore *v.* Bowes, Heselridge *v.* ———, 22 *Law Journal*, 342. He submitted that there was no method whereby the property, the subject of the settlement, would be secured by A. and B. for the benefit of the children of the marriage, as a voluntary deed could not be rectified as X. already had a vested interest, and he quoted an extract from Vaisley on Settlements, vol. ii., p. 1,568, and also cited Platt *v.* Matthews, 22 Beavan, 328.

Mr. WILSON, leading on the other side, urged that the consideration for the settlement was bad, as it tended to immorality, and therefore the settlement was void ; and not only the children of the marriage, but also X. was defeated, and in support of his contention quoted Robinson *v.* Macaulay, *Law Times* Reports, September, 1894. The consideration for the whole settlement was void, and therefore the trusts were inoperative (Ayerst *v.* Jenkins, L. R. 16, Equity 275), and he distinguished Kiddler *v.* Kiddler. Mr. Wilson contended that as there was no marriage, the trusts intended to come into operation in the marriage could not arise, and cited Occleston *v.* Fullalove, 9 L. R., Ch. App. 147. There was a way by which the settlement might be substantially dealt with, and that was by taking proceedings in Chancery could motion a fresh settlement thereof by which they could carry out their intention of benefitting the children of the marriage to the exclusion of X.

Mr. WHITING followed, and argued that although the marriage was illegal, the settlement must be construed according to its intention, which plainly was that the children of the marriage should be benefitted before X. He quoted the case of Ayerst v. Jenkins, to show that the settlement was a voluntary deed, which, he urged, could be rectified, as both the settlers had equally made a mistake; and he read an extract from Vaisey on Settlements, vol. ii., p. 1,573, to show that in such a case the deed could be rectified.

Mr. JACKSON argued that Ayerst v. Jenkins might well be quoted on both sides, but the deed in that case was intended by the parties to be a deed of gift, but the solicitor inadvertently drew it up as a settlement ; but it must be regarded as a deed of gift, and there it was hardly analogous to the present case — that the money was held in trust until the marriage for the settlement, and no marriage taking place, the money resulted back to the settlers, and did not go to X. He further urged that the two cases which were almost identical with the present one, and governed it, were Chapman and Bradley v. Dawson and Brown. In the latter Vice-Chancellor Malins distinguished Ayerst v. Jenkins.

Mr. W. E. FARR urged that if the consideration tended to immorality the contract was void, but only so far as related to the " children of the marriage "; the immorality of the consideration did not affect X. In support of this he quoted Vaisley on Settlements, page 69, and Ayerst v. Jenkins, L. R. 16,

Eq. 273. He urged that the settlement was in V.P. Platt v. Matthews, and that a V.P. could not be rectified in general, and quoted 22 Beavan, 328, and Vaisey on Settlements, vol. ii., page 1,565, and Sayer v. Home, 11 Beavan, 236. A deed was undoubtedly construed according to the intention of the parties, but in this case the parties must have known that the consideration was immoral, as there could be no legal marriage between a man and his deceased wife's sister, and they had the opportunity of proof. It was not a mistake of fact, which could be relieved against, but a mistake of law, which could not be rectified.

Mr. MILNER argued that the settlement could not appoint, as there were no children of the marriage, and that the settlement being entirely void, X. was defeated. He also quoted Ayhurst v. Jenkins, and also discussed Crook v. Hill, and he submitted that a fresh appointment could be made in favour of the children if the mother applied to the court.

Mr. MATTHEWMAN urged that the marriage was void, and the settlement and all the trusts created thereby were invalid.

Mr. WILSON, in reply, relied on Bevan v. Pawson and Clapham v. Bradley to show that the children of the marriage might obtain the property.

Mr. WILLIAMSON, in his reply, urged that the deed was a valid document, and therefore binding on the settlers, and he read an extract in support thereo. from V. V., page 87, and urged that Ayerst v. Jenkins supported his contention.

After the CHAIRMAN had summed up a vote was taken, when twelve voted that the advice was unsound, and that there was a method whereby A and B. could secure the property, the subject of the settlement, and thus preventing it passing to X., in favour of the children ; and three voted that the advice was sound, and that X.'s right could not be defeated.

Chapter XVIII

THE WOMAN AND THE LAW.

A paper by Mr. C. H. Pickstone, of Radcliffe Bridge, Lancashire. was read at the 21st annual meeting of the Incorporated Law Society, held at Bristol, in October, 1894. The writer's aim is to show that woman has, notwithstanding her rebellion against it, the best of the bargain in marriage.

"It is as easy to realise one's just demand against the assets of the ordinary man as it is to get on the Poor Rate book; it is as difficult to realise a like demand against a married woman as it is to get on to the Parliamentary Register. Thanks to the law's anxious care she is well-nigh invulnerable. Even if we successfully dodge the pitfalls which the indulgent law places in the path of the pursuing creditor and obtain judgment, the serious trouble has only commenced. For after you have with infinite pains traced into her possession separate estate you will in all probability find it incased in that execution-proof armour, the restraint on anticipation, which in the case of a man is ruthlessly condemned as against public policy, but which in the case of a married woman is permitted and encouraged as a protection against *herself;* in other words, against the persuasive kick or the seductive kiss of her all-devouring spouse. Under the impervious shelter of this doctrine she can clothe herself in " purple and fine linen, and fare sumptuously every day," however dire may be the straits of poverty into which her conduct may drive her wretched creditors, for the law in its jealous regard for its darling not only refuses to impound the capital, but even denies you the consolation of receiving the income, as our friend Mr. Hood-Barrs has just so dearly learned (Hood-Barrs *v.* Cathcart, 70 L.T. 862). Nay, further, the law in its solicitude for her material comfort withholds that most potent of all levers for bringing to his knees the recalcitrant debtor—the commitment warrant (Scott *v.* Morley), and denies even that forlorn hope, the Bankruptcy Notice (*re* Hannah Lynes, 68 L.T. 739). No, neither Receiver, Bankruptcy Notice, or gaol can reach her. Nor is that all."

Mr. Pickstone then citing Seroka *v.* Kattenburg, 17 Q.B.D. 177, points out how the husband is liable in damage to the uttermost farthing to the party whom his wife defames. Continuing the subject of slander, the writer reminds us how 54 and 55 Vic., cap. 51, pounces " with hungry alacrity " on the person who shall whisper a charge against the virtue of a lady, whilst, on the other hand, " all the illegitimate children in a street may be laid to the charge of a luckless man, and, though never so innocent, he must cheerfully " grin and bear it," since, unless the slanderer chance to " touch him in his business,"—as the law quaintly has it—"she lends a deaf ear."

The Jackson case leads Mr. Pickstone to some amusing reflections. He questions thus: Had the position of the parties been reversed, and *Mr.* Jackson "imprisoned," with his wife as the relentless warder, what relief would the Law have given him? Why, in Smith *v.* Smith, 59 L.J. (P.) 13, when a wife was brought up for molesting her husband *in defiance of the Court's order,* the learned Judge declined to convict. Then again, "if husband and wife together concoct a diabolical felony—short of murder and manslaughter—nay, even though the crime be the sole creation of the wife's fecund brain," the law forgives her, and sentences the husband to ten years penal servitude.

"But the catalogue is not yet full." The last grievance related by Mr. Pickstone is a formidable one, and occupies the half of his pamphlet. Wives who have cruel husbands can obtain a separation from them by going to a court in London. At the same time they obtain maintenance. The Act of 1886 gave the local justices power to grant maintenance *in case of Desertion*—not in case of any other form of cruelty. The reason for this was very clear: the Justices merely possess the power the Guardians had previous to the passing of the Act, only that the Guardians had to wait till the desertion had lasted for two years, whilst the action of the Justices under the Act is more summary. No corresponding legislation designed to benefit man has been devised as a set-off; but this is not Mr. Pickstone's point. He complains that the Act omits to say for what length of time the order is to hold good; and that Justices construe the

Act so that it is made to serve as a substitute for proceedings in London. They are "too ready to assume that because the wife might, in their opinion, have reasonable grounds for refusing to return home," her husband is guilty of neglect to maintain. It is, says Mr. Pickstone, "unpardonable weakness for the Bench to listen to or regard the wife's complaint that she is ' afraid to return.' Do any of us doubt that upon facts," which fail to prove desertion and merely prove cruelty, the Bench, in the absence of a strong clerk, stretches the law in the woman's favour, or rather indeed rules in direct conflict with the spirit and the letter of the law of 1886.

Mr. Pickstone disapproves of this: "The Magisterial Bench is for obvious reasons not the right tribunal to exercise the grave and serious responsibility involved in the relaxation of the fetters of the marital obligation." He is impatient of the new woman and her rebellion against marriage, and his recital of the "'pulls" of the married woman* as against her partner, is in a tone calculated to reconcile her to the institution. Free the married woman from the importunities of creditors, excuse her from bankruptcy, and from doing time for debt; give her special protection against those of evil tongue; leave her free from the necessity of residing under the roof of an objectionable husband; allow her to plan crime in conjunction with her better half, without fear of sharing the punishment—these things excite in Mr. Pickstone a natural humour, and in no place draw forth his explicit disapproval— but the added

* Some of these married woman's advantages are shared by maiden ladies. As to " desertion " and " cruelty," see latter part of footnote to p. 167.

advantage, illegally obtained, of procuring separation without the expense and trouble of taking a case to London, calls forth a distinct note of remonstrance.

Looking to the future – to a transition stage between the present state of the law in relation to woman, and the good time coming when law will leave the woman free—one may picture with the modified satisfaction that appertains to any transition stage, a time when the local magistracy will be empowered to grant separation orders, and every police court be a Divorce Division. The crop of enormities in the way of alimony will work towards further freedom.

Mrs. George Corbett, in an article already referred to (*Free Review*, Jan., 1894), writes thus plainly : "Of the difficulties which cramp and thwart the business capacities of an energetic married woman everybody knows. Those who contend that wives do not labour under injustice or special difficulty by reason of their matrimonial relations will perhaps explain how it is that a single woman, although she may be known to be what is termed immoral, is given the credit and commercial facilities which are denied to an honorably married woman. The old-world tenets of Church and State still hamper a wife's success, and prove veritable millstones round her neck. Theoretically, she is emancipated from many of her legal disabilities. Practically, her power to succeed in her business enterprises is so cramped by reason of her marriage that my contention is again proved to be undeniable. Both Church and State condemn marriage as immoral, since they deny to a married woman those opportunities which they would at once restore to her if death, or divorce, as a result of her own deliberate action, were to place her once more within the ranks of single women.

" If marriage is to be upheld as a moral institution, implying no loss of caste or position on the part of the woman, then the marriage vows must be made precisely similar for both contracting parties, and the term 'married woman,' having reference to a presumed necessity for the enactment of different legal resolutions as to married and single women, must be wiped from our statute books."

An examination of the wife's position before the law is included in the series of historico-legal papers on " The State and the Family in England," appearing in the *Weekly Times and Echo* last year, from the pen of M. J. Farrelly, LL.D., Barrister-at-Law. Amongst the conclusions reached by this learned writer is that the present position of the marriage law is not one of stable equilibrium, and for this amongst other reasons : While the older statutes vied with the Ecclesiastical Courts in enforcing wifely obedience, modern English legislation has set aside all pretence at compelling this fair return for the right of maintenance. Innovation, insists Dr. Farrelly, is ardently required to redress the balance of justice ; and he does not conceal indications as to the lines upon which the innovations should proceed. He would put back the clock a few centuries. There is scarcely an enactment securing the liberty of the English subject which has his approval ; the laws of other times and other countries limiting liberty are universally lauded. The Roman laws of *Interdictio Prodigi* and *Querula Inofficiosi Testamenti*—the plaint of the unduteous will, retained in the law of Scotland—both meet his views, though it is true he admits in the Dower Act of 1833 (which abolished the widow's compulsory share of her husband's freehold land), and like laws, the compensation, a *minor* compensation it is styled, that a man can provide for his illegitimate children and for their unmarried mother. It will hardly need to be pointed out that from the Legitimation standpoint, the several enactments which have had the result of diminishing the State premium on marriage, by reducing the fine payable by illegitimate children, and by paramours to a certain varying fraction of ten or twelve per cent. on the value of the property left them, are to be regarded as of *maximum* importance.

Dr. Farrelly's abhorrence of the liberty legislation which, by permitting mortgages on land, the hypothecating of chattels for the obtaining of credit, etc., may be regarded as one of the main causes of our growth as an industrial nation of fortune-makers, may be noted. This historical recital serves to illustrate the truth of Mr. Donisthorpe's remark that "the law of England has marched forward on the lines of individualism with a thoroughness unexampled in the history of nations," and therefore to encourage the hope that along the same lines will proceed future legislation affecting the relations of the sexes.

The growth of dissatisfaction with the one-sided character of the marriage contract is not entirely confined to its legal aspect. A citation from a recent article by Mr. W. F. Dunton in the *Free Review* may perhaps illustrate the tendency of a coming time, when wives, seeing their paramours have a better claim to constancy than they themselves, will envy them, and envying, imitate. This passage needs no further comment. " The rights are on the husband's side, the permanent and exclusive right to sexual intercourse with the wife, and the right to the control of her children ; and on the wife's side, the right to maintenance for herself and her children at the husband's expense. She has not the exclusive right to sexual intercourse with her husband, the reason probably being that this would leave a preponderance of rights on her side, and would raise the question, 'What does the woman do that she should be maintained by the man ? ' "

Replying to a critic, Mr. Dunton puts forward the forcible argument that " whatever advantage a child now derives from having its parents forcibly kept under the same roof, is, in my opinion, far more than counterbalanced by the risk it runs of eventually being itself compelled to pass the greater part of its life in cohabitation with a mate it is unable to love."

With equal force Mr. Dunton, replying to an argument of his fair critic, Mrs. H. D. Web, in the same *Review*, puts it that disapproval of our present State marriage does not imply rejection of all regulation, which remark he illustrates with the following reference to the Legitimation League :—" Even the staunchest advocate for free love would not maintain that rape should be legalised. Nor would he say that one should be free from social obligation regarding one's offspring ; indeed, most of us would add considerably to a man's present responsibility in this respect. Within the past two or three years a society has sprung into existence to maintain the rights of natural children, the members of which include a good proportion of free love adherents, though free love is not one of its principles. The object of the Legitimation League, as it is called, is to place acknowledged illegitimate children upon the same footing as children born in wedlock, thus giving legal recognition to the obligations of unmarried parents. Readers interested in this question should communicate with Mr. Oswald Dawson, etc."—*Free Review*, November, 1895. I notice with last issue of this valued magazine a change of proprietorship and editorship, Mr. John M. Robertson having given place to Mr. George A. Singer. I take this first early opportunity of thanking Mr. Singer for consecrating a portion of his pages to the defence of that form of freedom which engages the attention of this League, and which cannot always obtain a hearing and fair field.*

---

* An article still more advanced than Mr. Dunton's appears in the same issue and is also in answer to Mrs. Web. Mr. Frederick Rockell, though declaring "Whether under free love monogamy or changing unions would preponderate it were discreet not to prophesy." before he concludes does prophesy as follows : "We are thus led to the conclusion that the future form of the family will be the matriarchal. The mother would be free to conduct her family on her own lines, but would have the advantage of male advice and help from her lover of the time,"—a phrase suggestive of changing unions Mr. Frederick Rockell is very prophetic from the start. as "No one in his senses would dream of advocating free love unaccompanied by that broader economical freedom which will make it easy for all workers, of both sexes, to earn a comfortable livelihood." but he is not prophetic to the finish, for he fails to prophesy that women would have simultaneous lovers, as well as successive ones, which is what I should expect under Soc alism.

The December number contains an article by a lady, E. I. Champness, in which is advocated that women should be free to procreate without apparently being concerned to secure them against desertion by their fathers.

Desertion is held to mean active withdrawal from an existing cohabitation. (See Reg. v. Loresche and Pape v. Pape, in both of which cases it was held that discontinuance of weekly payments under a separation agreement did not constitute desertion under Section 4 of the Act of 1886.) The Act of 58 and 59 Victoria. 1895, Cap. 39. Section 4. provides that any married woman whose husband shall have been guilty of persistent cruelty to her. or wilful neglect to provide reasonable maintenance for her or her infant children whom he is legally liable to maintain, and shall by such cruelty or neglect have caused her to leave and live separately and apart from him, may apply to any Court of Summary Jurisdiction within the district in which the cause of complaint shall have wholly or partially arisen. (Lely's *Statutes of Practical Utility*, 1895.) What might result from such an application I cannot say. It has been ruled that "Mere austerity of temper. petulance of manners, rudeness of language, a want of civil attention and accommodation. even occasional sallies of passion, if they do not threaten bodily harm, do not amount to legal cruelty" "The denial of little indulgences and particular accommodations which the delicacy of the world is apt to number among its necessaries is not cruelty." (Napoleon Argles : *How to obtain a Divorce*, 1895.)

—

Chapter XIX

NATURAL CHILDREN IN FRANCE.

From *The Weekly Times and Echo*, March 30th, 1895.

—

NATURAL CHILDREN AND THEIR RIGHTS UNDER FRENCH LAW.

By Halliday Sparling.

JUST now there is a good deal of discussion going on in France over the position of children born out of wedlock. A number of Socialist Deputies, including MM. Baudin, Clovis Hugues, Jaurés, and Millerand, have introduced a bill dealing with the subject in drastic fashion. They propose to modify the civil code to the extent of conferring the same rights upon " natural " as are now enjoyed by " legitimate" children, and of allowing inquiry into paternity.

At present, it will be remembered, "illegitimates," though much better off in practice, in law are almost as badly off in France as in England. In one way, indeed, they are much worse off, inasmuch as French law carefully guards the man from all responsibility. His name, even, must not be mentioned, nor can any legal claim be made upon him. Of course, there is something to be set against this, and the position of a pregnant girl or woman is much better in Paris than in London, despite the lack of the " affiliation order." She can claim the care of the State on the mere ground of needing it, and she and her infant will be cared for so long as the necessity exists. And, if she will, the child may be adopted by the municipality, to be fed and educated incomparably better than an English "charity child."

But, all the same, the frightful injustice remains of placing the whole responsibility on the woman's shoulders, and leaving the man free as air. Curiously enough, this injustice dates from the Revolution—which removed so many others! The old law knew nothing of such a provision. Indeed, it was practically upon all fours with that obtaining in England, summed up by Plowden in the celebrated dictum which the delicate fastidiousness of modern ears forbids me to quote. It may be paraphrased by, " Who gets the child must keep it." In many ways the French law was even more favourable to the woman than the English. Her oath before a justice was enough to secure a provisional order upon the putative father for maintenance while the cause was pending. Nor was she only *allowed* to follow up the father ; along with the declaration of pregnancy necessary to secure relief, she was *compelled* to give the father's name : this in order that by terrorising her he might not manage to go free.

But, as I have said, the Revolution changed all that. In justice to the revolutionists it must be admitted that the wrong inflicted upon the woman was a blunder committed in trying to do justice to the child. By the law of the 12th Brumaire, year II. (November 3, 1793), natural children were accorded the same rights of succession, etc., as children born after marriage. But in order to preserve some incentive to marriage, a clause was inserted forbidding all enquiry into paternity; so that the only children benefited by the law were those recognised by the father.

The blunder was soon recognised as such, but not before the reaction had set in, and remedy was hopeless. Still a remedy was many times attempted. During one of these attempts it was that Duveyrier made his celebrated onslaught upon the privileged impunity of men: " If," said he, " all enquiry into paternity is abolished outside marriage ; if the mother of a natural child has not even the right to ask for a public sign—I will not say of tenderness or humanity —I will say of the decency of the man who has rendered her a mother, what check do you leave upon human passions, upon disorder, upon debauch? . . Men, guaranteed by the law itself against social responsibility, encouraged by the law itself in public indecency . . will seek, as licentious despots, their pleasures, sometimes shared by, but more often wrung from, the weak and unwary."

That was in 1801. Three years later the clause of 1793 was solemnly confirmed and ratified, and apart from public charity, the un-legitimized natural child has had no rights in France, with the natural, though horrible, consequence that infanticide, before and after birth, has flourished even more than in moral England—if that be possible. Note that, while forty-two per thousand legitimates are returned as born dead, the number among illegitimates is seventy-three per thousand. On the other hand, the proportion of natural births rises steadily. While in 1878 it was seventy-three per thousand, in 1888 it was eighty-four per thousand.

These are the figures for the whole of France given by the latest returns published, those for 1892 :—

	Legitimate.	Illegitimate.
Males	400,260	37,540
Females	381,802	36,245
Total ...		855,847

For the department of the Seine—that is to say, for Paris and her suburbs—the figures are still more striking :—

	Legitimate.	Illegitimate.
Males	30,024	9,565
Females	28,459	9,354
Total ...		77,402

Since writing the above I have received the returns for Paris alone, for 1893, from which I take the following :—

	Legitimate.	Illegitimate.
Males ...	22,418	8,629
Females	21,379	8,599
		61,025

Upon these Paris figures I hope to have a word at another time. Meanwhile, I will only say, that they point to the rise in favour of the "free union" so-called, and hardly at all to any increase in promiscuity.

Anyway, whatever may lie at the root of the increase of "illegitimate" births, that increase is incontestible, and has long called for recognition by the legislature. All the more that the population of France is a falling one, and that it has long been established that "free" families are the more prolific. But this side of the matter requires more extended treatment. So long ago as 1883, M. Gustave Rivet proposed to repeal the obnoxious clause barring research into paternity. Again, in 1890, he repeated the attempt, but on neither occasion could he even secure a discussion upon the subject. Last year M. Alfred Naquet made a similar proposition, again without success, though this time a great and favourable change in public opinion was evidenced.

The present proposition, as befits its origin, is the most far-reaching that has been made ; and, if carried, would place all children upon a footing of absolute equality before the law, whatever the circumstances of their birth. As the preamble of the bill says : " The situation in which natural children are placed by the Civil Code certainly forms one of the most shocking inequalities to be met with in the whole of our legislation ; an inequality all the more unjustifiable, in that it is inadmissible that a human being should be penalised by the law for being in a position which it has not created and has no power to modify."

There is little hope that the bill as a whole will be passed. It practically legalizes the "free union," and removes the last bulwark of hard-and-fast marriage, outside the Church. And public opinion is not yet ripe for that, even in France. But it is almost certain that "Article 340" will disappear from the Civil Code, whereby the country of the Revolution will wipe off one of the blackest reproaches that have ever stained her legislation.

Chapter XX

"THE BAR SINISTER AND LICIT LOVE."

A Lecture.

Reported by Mr. D. Oliver.

ON Sunday Morning, the 24th February, 1895, Mr. Oswald Dawson, Honorary Secretary of the Legitimation League, lectured before a large audience at the Hall of Science, Old Street, City Road, London, on "The Bar Sinister and Licit Love."

Miss Edith Vance, who presided, said at the outset: Friends, before calling upon Mr. Dawson to address you, I should like to make a confession, namely, that I am just about the worst chairwoman that Mr. Dawson could have found anywhere. To those who know me that explanation is scarcely necessary. Generally I regard taking the chair as an unpleasant duty, but this morning it is somewhat pleasing to find myself in this position. That is, perhaps, owing to the fact that I am a lover of reedom,—that I love and cherish freedom. When I occupy this seat, as a rule, I do so in my official position. This morning, however, I preside un-officially, and that is perhaps why I do not mind it so much. Now, we pride ourselves on the occasion of our Sunday morning lectures upon our freedom of thought and opinions of all shades. As freethinkers, we claim the right of liberty of thought and expression, and we always welcome and accord a patient hearing to any defence of the cause of freedom of thought and of action. This morning I am here because the views which Mr. Dawson holds and is about to express to you this morning are also my views ; and if this were not so, I should still admire—as we must all do—the courage with which Mr. Dawson and his wife have tackled this question. He and those who are intimate with him alone can know what it has cost him to advocate and uphold the views he entertains, and the amount of social ostracism to which he and Mrs. Dawson have been subjected on account of the views they honestly hold. There is something else I should like to say. Those who have seen the *Weekly Despatch* this morning will no doubt have noticed that this lecture is announced in its lecture list as " The Bar Sinister." I have noticed lately that this paper, or the editor of this paper, has, in announcing lectures or addresses on anti-theological subjects, carefully eliminated any reference to Christ or God. I now find that any reference to true or licit love is likely to be similarly suppressed, for the second part of the title of Mr. Dawson's lecture, " Licit Love," does not appear. The lecture is simply announced as " The Bar Sinister." I wonder why we should be so treated as to suffer the deletion of the words " Licit Love." Perhaps the editor knows what we mean by that phrase better than we do. I should like to call your attention to some of the literature on our bookstall this morning. There is a verbatim report of the Proceedings of the Legitimation League, containing a good portrait of Mr. and Mrs. Dawson and of the President of the League. Mr. Wordsworth Donisthorpe; also a book by Mr. Donisthorpe, entitled " Love and Law," and our usual freethought literature. The lecture this morning is by Mr. Dawson and not by yours truly ; and, therefore, I will not occupy your time any longer. I call upon Mr. Dawson to now address you on this subject of " The Bar Sinister and Licit Love."— (Applause.)

Mr. OSWALD DAWSON (who was received with applause) said : Miss Vance, and ladies and gentlemen, I believe it is usual at lectures for the vote of thanks to come at the close, but in this case it does not so much matter, because the vote of thanks has not to be made to me on the present occasion, but it has to come from me. I have to thank the National Secular Society in general, but Miss Vance in particular, as being the lady who tendered the invitation to me to lecture before you. I have to thank her for giving me this opportunity of presenting before the secular party some of the views which the Legitimation League sets out to teach. I have long been in correspondence with Miss Vance, and one of the earliest communications of encouragement that I received from anybody was from her, in which she said : " Having read a report of the meeting of the Legitimation League, I am pleased to declare myself in sympathy with the objects of the League. The reception it has met with at the hands of idiots and bigots might have been expected, but this, I am sure, will in no wise deter you from carrying on the good work." That post card gave me great encouragement. and it was followed by an invitation to lecture at some hall of the Secular Society. Subsequently I received a sympathetic letter from Mr. J. M. Wheeler, asking for a few of the prospectuses and publications of the League—I presume for distribution.

The subject of legitimation is by no means a new one. I have brought several books with me, dealing with the subject either wholly or in part. One of our forerunners in this matter is a book which created a sensation some time ago, containing a collection of letters from *The Daily Telegraph* on "Is Marriage a Failure?" In this book, on pages 254, 260, and 261, you will find letters signed by a "Solicitor," writing from Clifford's Inn, and from a "Reformer," and from a lady signing herself "Inward Grief," suggesting various forms of legitimation. Another proposal for legitimation is to be found in a book by "Philanthropus, J.A., LL.D.," in which the author, whose real name does not appear, recommends the adoption of a certain kind of legitimation that pre-vailed in ancient Rome (I quote from page 126 of this volume), "when by the death of one of the parents or by any other cause the marriage cannot be contracted. and consequently the legitimation of the unlawful issue cannot be effected, then, in the absence of lawful children, Justinian established another sort of legiti-mation called *per rescriptum principis*, or by grant of the Sovereign, after express acknowledgment of the child in the will or in some other solemn document. Something of the same kind should be adopted to complete the principle of legitimation." In making acknowledgments to those who have been bold enough to face the sexual question, one must not omit mention of the work that has been done by Mrs. Victoria Woodhull Martin and by Lady Cook. The latter has comparatively recently written a paper on "Illegitimacy," which was printed in several newspapers. With regard to Mrs. Victoria Woodhull Martin, some people imagine that that lady is now less bold than she used to be. This, I think, is an entire mistake, for in the current number of *The Humanitarian*, of which she is the editor, we find a very bold declaration indeed, one which I will venture to read in full. She says: "Marriage laws that would be consistent with the theory of individual rights would regulate these relations, just as they regulate all other associations of people. People should only be obliged to file marriage articles, containing whatever provisions may be agreed upon, as to their personal rights, rights of property, of children, or whatever else they may deem proper. And whatever these articles might be, they should in all cases be equally entitled to public respect and protection. Should separation afterwards come, nothing more should be required than the simple filing of counter articles."

I could give other illustrations of the daring of Mrs. Woodhull Martin did time permit. For statistical information on the subject of Illegitimacy I refer you to Dr. Albert Leffingwell's book of that title in Swan Sonnenschein's "Social Science Series," and also to an article here in the *Agnostic Journal*, which I have permission to reprint in the League's "Proceedings." There is another book I should like to name—

that by Mrs. H. Ellis entitled " A Novitiate for Marriage." I am extremely pleased to find that ladies are so much to the fore in this matter. Numerous novels, and, perhaps I might say still more numerous plays, dealing with sexual matters, have been published during the past year or two, culminating in a recent publication that seems to outvie all others with respect to the audacity of its propositions—I mean Mr. Grant Allen's "Woman who did." His portrait. an illustration of his house at Hindhead, a review of the book—with a full page illustration of the Virgin and Child thrown in as a pictorial antidote--you can see here in the *Review of Reviews*. But I should be neglecting what I consider to be a great duty were I to confine my attention to English writers on these subjects. At the risk of causing a thrill of horror to run through this audience, I shall make bold on this platform to mention aloud the names of Ezra Heywood, now deceased, late editor of *The Word*, and Moses Harman, the still living editor of *Lucifer, the Lightbearer*, and Mrs. Lois Waisbrooker, editor of *Foundation Principles* and author of numerous novels and pamphlets. It has been the privilege of the two first named of these writers to spend time in the same sort of habitation as that in which the President of the National Secular Society passed a year—that is to say, they have been in gaol—and a warrant now hangs over the head of Mrs. Waisbrooker also for the publication of articles that I should certainly not have the slightest hesitation in reading aloud to you to-day did time permit. I have here the photographs of Ezra Heywood, of Moses Harman, and Mrs. Lois Waisbrooker, and those who would like to see them after the lecture will be able to do so. There is another proof of an indirect sort that sex questions are coming to the front. I should take it that free-thought was making headway if more churches were built opposite this hall. If that were so, I should consider that probably secularism was growing, and that it was felt that there was a greater necessity of meeting it. So, when we see what the orthodox are doing in marriage matters, we find an instructive lesson. Down in the county whence I come we have what is called "The Convocation of York." I do not go to those convocations. (Laughter.) I see nothing at all of them save when I happen to be in York. I have observed on those occasions numerous clergymen dining very well and so forth. (Laughter.) We find, according to the newspapers, that they are very anxious to amend certain of the laws relating to marriage, but they want to amend them in an entirely opposite direction to that which we desire. What they want to do—or some of them—is to make it impossible for divorced people to marry again ; not only those who have been guilty of the causes which led to the divorce, but the innocent parties as well. They were meeting only the other day. I have an extract here to which you can refer, and these propo-sitions were boldly brought forward by the Rev. C. N. Gray :—(1) "That the bishops be respectfully requested to consider the propriety of taking common action, so that licences to enable divorced persons to enter into fresh unions may no longer be issued from the diocesan registries." (2) "That this Convocation of York desires to see some legislative enactment which would relieve the clergy of the Church of England from the obligation of solemnising, publishing banns for, or lending the church of which they are the incumbents for the solemnization of the marriages of any divorced persons whatsoever."

The Legitimation League when founded in Leeds in 1893 made some little bit of a local stir. The first stir that it made outside of Leeds was made in *The National Reformer*. The editor of that journal allowed me to answer an article which was contributed to *The National Reformer* over the initial "L." "L.", I may say, is a lady with whom I have been in correspondence subsequently. I mention that because I do want you to realise, almost above all things, that the ladies are to the fore in this matter. Well, my letter to *The National Reformer* dealing with this article, which appeared on August 13th, 1893, led to a somewhat vigorous correspondence. An excellent letter on "Legitimation Rights" appeared from the pen of Mr. John Badcock, Junior, one of the League's corresponding secretaries for London. Another letter which appeared on August 27th, 1893, was from Mr. J. Greevz Fisher, a Vice-President of the League, well known to the secularist as well as to the individualist party. This letter took exception to something that I had said in my communication to *The National Reformer*, namely, that " The League was pledged to legitimate only acknowledged children." The other Vice-Presidents of the League joined in the fray ; and you will find their letters in the further issues of *The National Reformer* of September 3rd and September 10th. I wonder if these letters and this discussion had not appeared in *The National Reformer* in what paper they would have appeared. In that case it is not a lady I have to thank, but Mr. J. M. Robertson. (Applause.)

The storm grew, and Mr. Fisher published a pamphlet entitled " Illegitimate Children : an Inquiry into their Native Rights and a Plea for the Abolition of Illegitimacy." This was issued by the publishers to the League, and it was very widely advertised by me. I thought it very desirable that everybody interested in the question of legitimation should hear what was to be said on the other side. I dealt with Mr. Fisher's paper at a drawing-room meeting held at the house of one of the other Vice-Presidents at Harrogate, and a short report appeared in the local paper ; but the real and effectual reply to Mr. Fisher came from our President, Mr. Wordsworth Donisthorpe. (Applause.) Once again we have Mr. J. M. Robertson to thank for an article which appeared in *The Free Review* for January. 1894, on "Bastardy." Secondly, I have to thank Mr. Benj. Tucker for a further paper by our President. which appeared on the 5th May, 1894, in *Liberty*, a journal published at Boston, U.S.A. in the interests of anarchy. It would be presumptuous on my part— it would be a sort of impertinence—to say that the articles from the pen of Mr. Donisthorpe are well worth reading. I should, however, say this :—If any one is desirous of grasping and mastering the primary questions involved in a study of the "Bar Sinister," it is positively essential that he should study the writings of Mr. Donisthorpe I may add, he need not dig up *The Free Review* for January, '94, although I hope you all have it handy on your shelves, or refer to *Liberty* of May, '94, because Mr. Donisthorpe has re-expressed his views in a recent publication entitled "Law in a Free State," published by Macmillan. Well, the point of the quarrel (of course, I use the word " quarrel " in a perfectly amiable sense) finally hinged upon a question of grammatical construction, and with your permission I will read an extract from one of Mr. Donisthorpe's articles, and afterwards comment upon it. " Nor can I accept Mr. Fisher's amendment of the League's own statement as to its aims. 'The League,' says he, ' has been established with this object—To create a machinery for acknowledging offspring born out of wedlock, and to secure for them equal rights with legitimate children.' He continues : ' These objects would possibly have been better stated in the reverse order, thus : To secure for offspring born out of wedlock equal rights with legitimate children and to create a machinery for acknowledging them.' Now this would amount, not to stating better the objects of the League but to stating quite other objects, objects quite foreign to the intentions of the League. The true aim is to create a machinery enabling parents to acknowledge offspring born out of wedlock, and to secure for them (that is, such acknowledged children) equal rights with children born in wedlock. This is a very different thing from that which Mr. Fisher proposes, namely, that the law shall secure for all bastards equal rights with legitimate children. But they already have equal rights in all respects save one ; hence if he means anything, he must mean that the law shall thrust the bastard by force upon the family of the putative father, with or without the consent of such putative father or his kinsfolk. After this, what is the use of creating a machinery for acknowledging them ? Surely, such a machinery would be a laughing stock. What need would it supply ? In other words, Mr. Fisher proposes a compulsory law, and supplements it by an enabling one." Well, the final issue is that I am permitted to state that, although Mr. Fisher has not withdrawn his pamphlet from circulation, he is convinced by the arguments of Mr. Donisthorpe and retracts from the position he formerly held with regard to the legitimacy of unacknowledged children. Still I was in a peculiar predicament. Here was the object of the League stated very briefly and yet apparently not stated quite clearly, for it was open to two grammatical constructions. We have had an enormous correspondence in relation to this subject, and I have always held out that the League's objects were capable of either construction ; that anybody joining the League was not committed to any interpretation of its objects which the President or anyone else had put upon them as to its grammatical meaning. However, it finally became necessary to arbitrarily decide this grammatical point. At a recent date, Mr. Auberon Herbert wrote and asked me to answer in two or three lines this question : " Do the League propose to put illegitimate children on the same level as legitimate children, as regards property, whether the offspring have been recognised or not by the public act of the father?" I was here in a corner and could not enter into a long correspondence as to the grammatical construction of the objects of the League, and I replied : " The offspring of parents failing to take the necessary steps of registration would be illegitimate, and not entitled to inherit in the event of either the father's or the mother's intestacy." That concludes what I have to say about the Bar Sinister, and the attitude of the League towards illegitimate children.

The question of Licit Love arose very early after

the formation of the League. and was treated by me at a meeting of the Dialectical Society, held in London in the latter part of 1893. I amplified the matter very considerably in an article in *The Modern Review* for April, 1894, and as I have brought some copies of this, anyone who is interested in the matter can procure one to-day. I concluded that article by hinting the desirability of calling into existence a functionary who should rejoice in the post of " Prothonotary of a Licit Alliance League." I had borrowed the word Protho-notary from an article by C. G. Garrison, appearing in the *Contemporary Review*, on " The Limits of Divorce." The idea of a Licit Alliance League naturally suggested itself; but whilst at first blush it appeared a promising undertaking to attempt, the reflection that it meant a fresh League was one to dismay a mortal of ordinary courage, and the feasibility of grafting the apparatus needful for carrying on its function on the Legitimation League was an idea not long in recommending itself. I soon came to think it was the duty of this League to appoint a " Protho-notary," or person to take records of illegitimate children whom the parents desired to acknowledge, and also of the unions of adults. However, we have not been able to determine the exact meaning or suitability of the word " prothonotary " for our purpose, and so for the present we have not appointed anyone with that title. What we have done is this— and it is a practical step—we have appointed Mr. Arthur Cornwell (who is present on this platform), and we have called him a notifying clerk. With regard to the duties of a notifying clerk, I cannot do better than quote a letter I wrote in reply to a recent inquiry. A gentleman wrote from Purley, in Surrey, and asked

me to furnish him with particulars as to the Legitimation League ; I wrote this reply yesterday :—

"   .   .   .   .   .   .   In endeavouring to create
a machinery for acknowledging offspring, it has been
seen to be imperative to take cognizance of the
alliances formed between parents or intending
parents, and it will at once strike you that if any
legislative enactments are to be made, or are to be
contemplated, there must be considerable force in the
motion that whilst the offspring of a union are to be
made legitimate, the alliance of the parents concerned
in the union should be made licit—that whatever may
be the obligations before, the law of legally married
couples should likewise descend upon the parties to
those alliances.

"The League has now appointed a clerk, who
will make a register in the first place of any illegitimate children born whom their parents wish to
acknowledge, and, in the second place, of alliances of
prospective parents.   He will undertake the advertising in the newspapers of all those where the parties
are willing.   He will charge a fee, which fee has not
yet been fixed.   He will keep a register of the officers
of the League, which may be inspected by anybody
on the payment of a fee,—which latter fee is also not
fixed.   He will file all newspaper advertisements
referred to, and send copies to all the officers of the
League, and all such other clerks as may from time
to time be appointed.

"He will register intentions of alliances, will
advertise the same when wished, and will show the
record of the same to anyone applying for information.   He will be entitled to ask the following
questions :—Name ? Address ? Previous name where

there has been a change ? Occupation ? Whether the
contracting parties are either or both of them already
married ? Whether either or both have any illegitimate children whom they acknowledge ?

" He will not be entitled to ask if either or both
have been divorced, or if either or both have any
illegitimate children whom they do not acknowledge.

"The remaining function of the clerk will be to
receive and record notices for the determination of
the alliances.

" It is not for one moment pretended that the
above outlined scheme is anything but crude and
tentative. It is by no means anticipated that it will
meet with any popular response. It is sufficient for
us if it supplies, in howsoever an imperfect form at
the commencement, the need of a few lovers of
liberty.

" I shall be glad to answer any further questions.
" Very faithfully yours,
" OSWALD DAWSON."

The contents of that letter represent the deliber-
ations of those connected with the League during the
past year. I should like to have devoted a whole
lecture to amplifying and explaining the details and
difficulties of any scheme of registration. I may say
that those details and difficulties are positively enormous. For instance, at present our office is at Albion
Walk Chambers. Leeds, and I live near that city ; but
I am by no means so permanent a person as the
State is which registers marriages ; I do not live in a
Somerset House, or occupy such a place as an office.
Suppose we have registration at Albion Walk, Leeds,
what a diminished value it must have if, amidst the
vicissitudes of life, the registers are removed from

town to town—if the notifying clerk to the League has a constantly shifting address. The objections, in fact, to Licit Love and systems of registration are so numerous that I can quite understand a great many people preferring to be entirely anarchical in regard to love relations. By "anarchical" I do not mean promiscuous, or anything of that kind : I mean that a great many of those who go with us would prefer, when forming their alliances, and even when having children, not to care whether those alliances were licit or not, or whether the children were legitimate or not. And there is much to be said for the position of these people. As soon as their children are registered, in walks the vaccination officer. That is one drawback of any system of registration. There are other difficulties. One would suppose that a notifying clerk would arrange his entries on the supposition that the contracting parties were henceforth to bear a name in common. Usually the lady changes her name. Now, it appears from time to time that the point discussed is whether there is any necessity for the lady to change her name ; nay, more than this, we are even confronted with propositions that ladies should persist in being regarded as "Miss" still, although they were married. And, to crown all, we are told the ideal marriage will be entirely independent of cohabitation, that is to say, of a residence common to the two contracting parties. I merely mentioned these matters in passing, in the way of pleasantry, to show some of the difficulties that face us. They take us even further, nay, much further, than the remonstrance against the usage which gives women the style of Mrs. Charles so-and-so, Lady Henry so-and-so, and a vast deal further than the proposition one sometimes meets with, that married partners should occupy separate apartments in the same house. Now let me read to you a short extract from a powerful article in *Liberty*, by Lillian Harman :

"All depends on other factors than the license granted or withheld by the State, on the formula repeated or not repeated by priest or magistrate. The essential verities do not depend for their validity on any such ephemeral things as States and Churches. There is no reason why liberty should degrade love, and no reason why a political or religious machine should legitimatize or sanctify prostitution or invasion, but there are many reasons why liberty should make sane and responsible the relations of the sexes, and why legal and ecclesiastical tyranny should do the very opposite."

The League has been in existence two years now. Its aim has been to make a machine to legitimatize ; yet assuredly some of us are apt to despise all these seals of State approval equally with those of the ecclesiastical type. The second volume of our proceedings, called "The First Biennial," will be published in due course. There has been such a demand that we should take some practical step, that I felt it was really necessary we should start keeping a register, even if it comes to be simply a mere matter to be laughed at.

As a few minutes remain of the hour allotted to me, I will briefly allude to—or rather I will illustrate —certain remarks of Miss Vance in opening the proceedings to-day. She referred to what people have to suffer who indulge in these principles of Licit Love and that sort of thing. Well, I could give you

sundry illustrations of this, and I certainly think that
it is wise for me to illustrate to you some of the
difficulties which do beset the paths of those who seek
after righteousness of this particular kind. It is,
indeed, very rarely that chapter and verse can be
given and the scientific character of the evidence
placed on a sure foundation. Here, however, we
have a specific matter.

The Leeds papers have recently had reports of a
County Court case—Naylor *v.* Dawson—of which I
have here a full shorthand report. The plaintiff in
this case said in open court that he had tried to get
me out of one of his houses which I had taken from
a certain tenant of his. He further stated the cause
of this—or rather his solicitor did. Hear these
extracts,—the Plaintiff's Solicitor is addressing his
Honour—"When Mr. Dawson purchased the property
from Mr. Gomersall these gates were then there, and
Mr. Dawson used them for some time, until that
arose which caused dissension between these two
neighbours, which I shall call your Honour's attention to. Mr. Dawson was in the habit of visiting
Mr. Naylor's house, and was received there as a
guest and a friend, and in consequence of a statement
made by Mr. Dawson, in regard to a certain League,
called the Legitimation League, and having regard
to his connection with a certain person, whom I shall
not name, Mr. Dawson was asked to leave the house
and not to annoy Mr. Naylor with his presence or
any member of Mr. Naylor's family. After that had
happened, Mr. Dawson seems to have proceeded in a
most extraordinary manner, and one which I wish I
could excuse, as no man in his right mind would have
acted in the way Mr. Dawson did. He broke down

these gates personally. . . . I submit to your
honour, to have these gates is only a reasonable
thing, and especially is it reasonable when this man
knew of it--did not complain of it until that dissension took place which I have already reverted to."
My Counsel, on the other hand, said: "I take it,
your Honour, it is sufficiently clear this is merely a
case of right. This suggestion of spite————." His
Honour: "I think so. If it was a case of spite. It
is a right of property." Counsel: "I think it is a
mistake, your Honour." His Honour: "I take no
notice of it myself." Then in due time came my
turn. I addressed his Honour, commencing: "With
regard to the Legitimation League————." His
Honour: "If you want to explain anything to me
with regard to the Legitimation League, take my
advice and leave that alone—treat it as if there was
nothing in it; if we discuss it————." You see,
ladies and gentlemen, I stand charged with doing
acts in consequence of a dissension arising out of a
"statement with regard to a certain League." What
I wished to point out to his Honour was, that the
date of Mr. Naylor's letter to me was the 28th of
April, 1893. That letter brought the defendant's
acquaintanceship and his visits at plaintiff's house to
"a very abrupt end"--a very abrupt end. Well,
now, it was not until the 9th of September that I
complained of the gates, as a letter of that date
already read in the Court had made clear; the latter
date being, as the letter itself showed, the day after
I obtained the deeds. You will agree, I think, with
his Honour, in taking no notice of this absurd
charge; you will agree, I think, with me in condemning this allegation of vindictive action on my

part, some months after the occasion which was supposed to inspire the action. to be most prepos·terous. But you will, I am sure, agree with me that we have in it an instructive illustration of the way a thing like the League may be used against anyone concerned with it, or be sought to be so used, to pre-judice a case in a manner wholly gratuitous, having regard to the circumstances.*

* These are given in "Notes of an Interview," in Waddington's *Guide to Ilkley*, *1895*, in these words :

" Calling upon Mr. Dawson the other day, we enquired how he came to locate himself in a spot where there was promise of such a harvest of litigation. It appeared that driving from Ilkley after the conclave when the League was first formed, the question of a residence at some convenient distance from the city arose, and the proprietor of the conveyance in which the party were driving offered to let a cottage at Seacroft for some months. A lease was taken almost on the spot. To make a long story short, Mr Dawson bought and built there. In the deed of conveyance a right of way for carriages was granted with the land, and in the plan endorsed on the deed the road measured to scale some 16 to 18 feet wide. The actual carriage road, however, was but 10 to 12 feet, and was encumbered with gates not provided for in the deed. The vendor having received £150 an acre, and having imposed upon the purchaser an obligation to keep in repair another road on the estate (some hundred yards long and a continu ation of the road in dispute), 18 feet wide—indications that the property was of a distinct category from mere farm land – Mr. Dawson, acting under advice, repeatedly unhinged the gates obs'ruct-ing this so-called road for carriages. and finally smashed one. At the hearing it was urged that these and other acts were done out of spite, visiting terms between plaintiff and defendant having ceased. at the request of the former, owing to the formation of the Legitimation League. The defendant lost the day on points of law, no notice being taken by the County Court Judge of these allegations of vindictiveness."

It affords me great pleasure to append the following letter.

Mr. Naylor, I must tell you, is a County Councillor

written by the plaintiff at my house on the 2nd May, 1895, and here published with his authority :—

" I hereby state that I have this evening visited Mr. Dawson on some private business, and I wish to state that although I had thought he took the above house, called Harman Villa, or built the same out of *spite* to me, I believe, after his explanation to me this evening, that I have misjudged him, and that his building this house was in no way connected with me.—I am, yours,

" B. NAYLOR."

In case some may think that the *spite* was on the other side, I have pleasure in stating that I believe an action would have arisen even had there been no dissension arising out of the Legitimation League, or any personal matter between us. I shall be glad at any time to hear from those who are interested in the question of obstructions (other than impossable ones. where the right of road is a disputed matter), placed where there is a right of way It seems to me. as it did to my solicitor, perfectly absurd to suppose that a right of way for carriages should not be an unobstructed way ; whilst other persons. on the other hand, would argue that if a stile may exist on a footpath, a gate may exist on a carriage-road. In my opinion there is an obvious difference. and I think a bill should be passed giving the holders of rights of carriage-roads power to " enfranchise," that is, to do away with gates upon payment to the owner of the land through which the road runs a sum of money sufficient to fence off the road, with a percentage added for loss to the owner of the land of the road-side waste. Of course I consider this proposal to be entirely in accordance with the policy of individualism ; and I trust the reader will kindly forgive my introduction of an idea quite foreign to the general objects of this book at this point.

N

and Justice of the Peace. I had taken a short lease of a cottage next door but one to his house, and let by him to a tenant—a short lease from February to the end of June—and for the same period the hire of a conveyance from the said tenant, who was the keeper of a livery stable in the City of Leeds.

Our occupancy here was objectionable, though not in consequence of any particular " statement " in regard to the League ; nor was I ever asked to leave Mr. Naylor's house. I will read you that gentleman's letter to me, to make these points clear.

*   *   *   *   *   *   *   *

I may mention that I lost the day and that an appeal is now pending.* I have explained to you that the superior landlord tried to get us out of the house by requesting his tenant to get rid of us. This is how the tenant went about his duty. He wrote me this letter :—

" 27*th May*, 1893.—Sir, I write to inform you that from the strained relations between you and Mr. Naylor, and the unpleasantness that exists on all sides partly arising from your principles and mode of life, and partly from the dissatisfaction that exists in the treatment of the pair of horses, which are badly treated in their being driven so fast while they have banged their front shin bones, and are very much swollen in consequence and in all probability may soon go lame ; now from all these causes I feel it to be my duty to write to you and let you know my

---

* "That appeal case decided last week, adversely to Mr. Oswald Dawson, is just the sort which is far more interesting to those ' in the know ' than to people who only hear what is stated in court."
—*Armley and Wortley News.*

opinion on this matter." And he hopes that I will " give up possession of the cottage as soon as possible, for the welfare of Mr. Naylor and his family, and the comfort of his home and its surroundings." (Laughter.) My answer was—" In reply to yours of to-day's date, I decline to terminate the contract. As to the horses not being properly treated, this is the first complaint I have had ; and it is very curious it should come just at the time you have another reason, of a sentimental kind, for wishing to terminate the contract, which I decline to do."

Later on my landlord wrote :—" To inform you that I have sent for my veterinary surgeon to-day, and he certifies the mares unfit for work and advises me to give them a six weeks grass run at once. Therefore I cannot comply with your request to send them down, and I have none others to knock up." I merely replied to that by stating that the matter would be placed in the hands of my solicitor, and that there would be a claim for expenses. Well, the upshot was that we did not go out of the cottage, no, nor even out of the stables. We stayed in the cottage until the termination of the contract on the 30th of June, and we were supplied with a fresh pair of horses in place of those which "in all probability may soon go lame."

Another illustration of the persecution to which we are subjected is afforded in relation to our occupancy of rooms at Albion Walk Chambers, Leeds. They put on pressure there too. I have here a letter addressed to the landlord protesting against " the Company for 'legitimatising illegitimate children'" continuing as his tenants, and "more particularly now after seeing the placard in the window,"—this was an advertisement of *The Rights of Natural Children* and *Love and Law*—and winding up with the protestation that "when we signed the lease for these offices we, at all events I, expected to have some respectable neighbours," etc. I do not need to give any name, as this particular matter has not been made the subject of a lawsuit, or got into the papers.

Our announcements have been the cause of other troubles besides this petty one. A few of you are aware that some of our difficulties in obtaining a hearing, even by advertisement. are already matters of history. They are dealt with in the early part of the " Rights of Natural Children." I shall not allude to them now, not even by name. I will give you another illustration, which I think you will consider rather amusing. I received this letter from the *Liberty Review* :—

"*October* 30*th*, 1893.

" Dear Sir,—As your subscription to the *Liberty Review* has expired, we shall be glad if you will kindly fill up and return to us the enclosed form with a remittance for one year's subscription.

" We beg to call your attention to the enclosed scale for advertisements, and we shall be happy to provide a good place for the publications of the Legitimation League, a review of which will be given in an early number of the paper.

" Awaiting your early instructions, we are, yours obediently, WATTS & Co., Publishers."

I replied, and sent them this document. It is several advertisements : one of the League's officers and objects, one of the " Rights of Natural Children." Mr. Donisthorpe's " Love and Law," and Mr.

Fisher's " Illegitimate Children," while there are also advertisements announcing the publications by our corresponding secretaries, Mr. Badcock and Mr. Dupont respectively, entitled " When Love is Liberty and Nature Law," and " The Evolution of Marriage." In addition to these I sent the personal advertisements of Mrs. Dawson and myself when that lady announced that she would take my name. ·These advertisements were to occupy respectively half a page, an inch, and the eighth of a page, ·cost £4 12s. 6d. I got this answer :—"*November 1st*, 1893 Dear Sir,—We acknowledge with thanks receipt of advertisements for forthcoming *Liberty Review*, and also a quarter's subscription to paper. As to the position of advertisements. we guarantee that they shall face matter, or be on outside page at top. When sending proof we hope to be able to enclose ' dummy.' We thank you for your offer to advertise further with us. Faithfully yours, WATTS & Co."

So far so good. Then came a letter to say that they were very sorry, but the advertisements of the Legitimation League did not suit them, and they could not accept them. So I wrote to Mr. Millar for an explanation of this, understanding that he was the proprietor-editor of *The Liberty Review*. Mr. Millar is also assistant secretary to the Liberty and Property Defence League, and I may also mention that he is well known on the secular platform. This is my letter :—" *1st December*, 1893. Dear Mr. Millar,— Having promised you to advertise in your new weekly, I ought to let you know that I drafted three advertisements of ¼-page, ½-page, and inch respectively, and sent them to Messrs. Watts & Co., with their own order form duly signed by the Treasurer agreeing to pay £4 12s. 6d. for their insertion in your first issue. I have this morning received from that firm a letter saying 'We regret that we are unable to insert your advertisements, which we accordingly return.' I think it not merely friendly, but fair, that you should have immediate notice of this procedure, so that you may be in a position to take steps, as early as possible, as proprietor of *The Liberty Review*, to rectify the matter. I enclose the advertisements, the order for which may hold good for your second issue if you care to persuade Messrs. Watts to reconsider their decision.—Believe me, very faithfully yours, OSWALD DAWSON."

Mr. Millar wrote to me saying that Messrs. Watts were joint proprietors with him of the paper, and that they had absolute control over the publishing and advertisement department; and that he had forwarded my letter to Messrs. Watts with a request that they would communicate with me. Mr. Millar added that he had written a short notice of the League's publications, which would appear in an early issue of *The Liberty Review*. There was a notice of the publications in the *Review*, and a representative of the paper was sent to the annual meeting in London. An article appeared in *The Liberty Review*, further particulars of which you will find in the forthcoming volume detailing the proceedings of the League. Messrs. Watts wrote to say "The advertisements which you were good enough to offer us would not be consistent with our interests in the paper, and we therefore decline same." Well, anyone taking up legitimation, or licit love, or the like, must be prepared for things of this sort. Although we may win in the long run we have to put up with little annoyances in the interim. If I may be permitted to give what I may call advice, I should advise anyone taking up this cause to be extremely circumspect in his mode of life. I will illustrate this remark. At the place where I have built my house, the man who lived in the lodge did a little horse dealing, and he put up a number of stalls —more stalls than were necessary for my purpose. That has for some time past led to my keeping a horse or two on sale ; you can all realise how easy and innocent a thing it is for one to drift into enterprise of that kind. Well, would you believe it, people who would have thought little and said less about the pursuit of this " fad " found ready occasion to manufacture double-barrelled insults and mix up the two things together—horse dealing and legitimation. But, mind you, I do not hear these things. As is the custom of society at large, the man is let alone (I am speaking now of vulgarities such as the passing of remarks which it is intended you shall overhear), and all the insults and innuendos fall upon the lady. (Shame.) You, Miss Vance, have been kind and bold enough to preside over this meeting this morning, and have expressed your sympathy with the objects of the League; but Mrs. Dawson will tell you that of the social obloquy which attaches to legitimation and licit love there are phases which affect or fall only, and fall heavily, on the woman. (Shame.) That is my last note, and I find I have occupied the hour allotted to me for my lecture. I sincerely thank you for your kindly attention. (Cheers.)

The Chairwoman : Now is the usual opportunity for questions and discussion. I am sure that Mr.

Dawson will be very pleased to answer any questions that may be addressed to him. I should like to tell him before I sit down that I am prepared to take the consequences of the fearful crime I have committed in taking the chair this morning. I am already used to working for causes that do not pay, and if this Legitimation League pays no better than Secularism, the rewards are not enticing. Secularism does not pay, as we know to our cost. I should like to correct one little error into which Mr. Dawson fell. He told us that Mr. Millar was well known on secular platforms. I am not quite sure whether that is so. I am quite sure that Mr. Millar is not now a member of the National Secular Society. I do not know whether he ever was a member, he has certainly not been a member in my time.--(A voice : " Years ago.") I do not think he is quite so well known on the secular platform as Mr. Dawson seems to think. Let me again remind you of the publications of the Legitimation League, which are to be had at the bookstall at the other end of the room. Our National Secular Society friends will be glad to know that the Benevolent Fund will, through the generosity of Mr. Dawson, benefit by the purchase of these pamphlets. Are there any questions? I will take the questions first if there be any.

Various questions were then put to Mr. Dawson by different persons in the Hall, and answered by him as under :—

Q. Does Mr. Dawson seek to render illegitimate children legitimate so that they may inherit the property of their forefathers?

A. Yes, *legitimated* children would inherit the property of intestate parents, or any collateral relations, just in the same way as children born in wedlock would.

Q. What is the definition of licit love and illicit love?

A. Licit love is the union of two people under these terms : That if one dies without making a will the survivor shall have the same title to the deceased's estate, or part thereof, as husband and wife have, and, similarly, that all the other attributes of husband and wife should be transferred to the parties concerned in the licit alliance, such as mutual support, responsibility for debts, and so forth.

Q. Did I understand the answer to the first question to be that illegitimate children would come into the property of their parents in the same way as children born in wedlock ?

A. If they are acknowledged by some process of registration.

Q. Would it not be better to have some process or method of acknowledgment by swearing or by affirmation? Would not that be a sufficient acknowledgment without leaving the father to take steps to get his natural child registered? In the plan proposed by the Legitimation League, the majority of children born out of wedlock would have no acknowledgment until the economic condition of society—which is at the root of the whole thing—is changed, there is a very poor chance of getting illegitimate children acknowledged.

A. I do not agree that there would be few or no acknowledgments at all. I should think that most of those present—men as well as women—would be prepared to acknowledge their children. Married people usually acknowledge theirs, in a social sense.

and I take it that decent people living together unmarried would do the same, even if they did not formally register them.

Q. Is it not a fact that many people do not, and would not, acknowledge their illegitimate offspring?

A. Well, if they don't I am sorry for them, and I am sorry for the children. Indeed, I am sorry for lots of things. I am sorry for the present economic conditions of society, though I do not happen to have any particular remedy. I accept individualism as a system, but that may be merely a pious opinion.

Q. Does not the present economic condition of society bear so hardly upon the average man, who has responsibilities in relation to children, that he is often constrained to shirk his obligation through insufficiency of means? Does not the robbing system in vogue involve these other evils to a very great extent?

A. I think you will have to show, as I have no doubt you are perfectly prepared to do, that you can remedy the present economic system, and bring about a system under which people would be able to support their children, or all the children they might have. I do not doubt that an attempt might be made in this direction, but I do not know of any system under which so many children could be supported as under the individualistic *régime*.

Q. Is not Malthusianism a remedy? Prevent the children coming into a world which has no need of them under present conditions.

A. But I say we want the children, and we want to acknowledge them. (Hear, hear.) I love children. We want them, sir.

The Chairwoman : I am afraid our friend's question is not in order, but I am reluctant to interpose, as I do not wish to appear desirous of burking discussion.

Q. Does Mr. Dawson's system of licit love apply to people already married?

A. The answer to that is very decided indeed. It is no matter to me whether a person is married. If I wish to form an alliance with a lady it is no matter to me whether she is married or not by law. But I should expect and wish that she privately divorced herself, gave notice to her husband that she was not going to live with him any longer, just as I should expect private notice being given to me of any similar change. We certainly do not wish to shut out all the unhappily married people from the benefit of our scheme of licit love, far from it. In fact it is intended as much for them as anybody else.

Q. I would ask Mr. Dawson how his scheme would work where a woman had lived with several different men? Where would the property consideration come in?

A. I don't see where the difficulty comes in. We will suppose a given lady over forty years old who has, during the last three decades of her life, spent them with three different men, entering into a licit alliance at the commencement of a decade, and terminating it at the end of that period. About the man's property. If the man dies in the ten years without making a will, she benefits. If he dies after the alliance is broken off, and the woman forms a fresh alliance, there would be no benefit. While the contract is on if either party dies, provision would be made for the lady if she were the survivor, and also for the children of the union. I do not recommend a change every ten years. As a mere matter of law, however, I should say that people would be entitled to change every five years or less.

Q. Suppose children to result from the three alliances the hypothetical lady might enter into, I presume that those children—if legitimated—would be entitled to inherit from their several fathers, even though the alliances might be broken off?

A. Yes, that is so. The fathers would be compelled to support their legitimated children until they had reached the age of self-support ; so, similarly, if dying intestate, a share would descend to each child, even though the contract with their respective mothers had been determined ; while, on the other hand, if a man form a licit alliance with a woman who already had legitimate children, and he died intestate, such offspring would rank as to inheritance in precisely the same position as a step-child now occupies. In a word, legitimation seeks to incorporate the claims, the responsibilities—perhaps even some of the abuses of wedlock—with the qualifying proviso that it will recognise no limit to the number of alliances any person may form, and that the limit in point of duration of any contract shall not be eternal. That, ladies and gentlemen, is the idea of the Legitimation League as I understand it. (Cheers.)

The Chairman : I thank you very much for your attendance, and declare the meeting closed.

The proceedings then terminated.

Chapter XXI

MR. MILLAR ON MARRIAGE.

MR. FREDERICK MILLAR is editor and proprietor of *The Liberty Review*. An unsigned article on " The Limits of Divorce " (Feb. 24th, 1894) effectively criticises Mr. C. G. Garrison's article of the same title in the *Contemporary Review*, and then proceeds to administer a mild rebuke to Individualists, charging that it has not met with the reprobation at their hands which it seems to deserve, and contending that they ought not to allow that a bargain which, expressly, is speculative, and may turn out for the worse, is not within the contractual capacity of adults. I took exception to these opinions in a letter sent to the paper, and to which " The Reviewer " replied in courteous terms. The correspondence, besides any inherent value it may have, was useful as indicating that Mr. Millar did not regard the topics discussed as outside the province of his columns. Nor must we omit to note that shortly before (Jan. 6th, 1894) " The Rights of Natural Children " was briefly noticed in Mr. Millar's paper, and the opinion expressed that "in agitating for the amendment of the law which is responsible for much grave injustice with regard to natural children, the Legitimation League will be doing a good work. Beyond this it would, in our opinion, be unwise to go."

Lapse of time brought about change in the tone of comment the *Review* assumed toward the League. A representative attended the first annual meeting and furnished a report thereof under title "Among Free Lovers, Neo-Malthusians, Bastard Legitimisers, etc." The questions which Mr. M. D. O'Brien asked at the meeting are here repeated, together with some preliminary abuse and a final forecast of "imperial downfall and racial extinction" should our principles prevail. The report, however, is not without argument, and, therefore, apart from the fact that Mr. Frederick Millar is responsible for the insertion of the article, and that it appeared in an Individualist journal, it claims notice here. I therefore try to present the argument. The living man has power to will his property as he wishes. On the State devolves the duty of distributing an intestate's wealth. As the deceased could have used his own judgment in the matter, but failed to exercise it, and as the State now stands in his stead, it follows that the latter should not be "bound down by a league of bastard manufacturers," *whose wants are not the measure of the infinite*, as the probate laws are, inferentially, represented to be by this Individualist. This critic, by the way, calls the State a funny abstraction, and hence styles the third party who arranges property matters between a deceased man and his relations, Cæsar, "for the sake of clearness." This Cæsar is a supreme individual administrator of law, and it is asked, "shall freedom be denied to him who acts in the father's place?" The existence of this Cæsar is said to be "a very awkward truth for those who dislike autocracy." I do not see that. Paternal administration is less hopeless when you have to get one supreme man to change his views as to what is fair than when you have to pass a bill through a democratic Parliament to rectify wrong. If there were such a person as this Cæsar, it might be worth while to debate amongst ourselves whether the League propaganda should any longer be complacently regarded as outside the pale of practical politics ; or whether, on the other hand, it might not be desirable to press upon him the claims of offspring who have been acknowledged by the League machinery as suitable recipients of the wealth of intestate kindred.

In an unsigned review of Mr. Badcock's "Slaves to Duty" it is remarked—"No one is obliged to marry, or is taxed if he does not marry. The State simply says that, if parents desire to have children legally recognised, these children must be born in wedlock"; and the fairness of this is then dwelt upon. I take it that if the State simply said that it would adopt the principle of primogeniture in all inheritance of real and personal property, it would be fair. If not, why not?

I have extreme pleasure in noting that the issue of *The Liberty Review* enunciating this doctrine contains the second and concluding portion of Mr. Spence's article on "Law and Marriage," which forms as complete a refutation of the preceding pronouncement as can be conceived. (Dec. 8, 1894.)

On March 23 there appeared what at first sight seemed to be a review of Mr. Donisthorpe's " Law in a Free State." but which was in reality an independent article bearing these words as sub-title. It forms one of a series of " Insoluble Problems," since reprinted in book form. In its first paragraph we read : " I should never have dreamed of giving the Marriage question, or that of the Status of Children, the position they occupy in this book ; not that, as a whole, I dissent from his views, but because they seem to me inopportune in the present state of the public mind. So long as the overwhelming majority of women continue to regard marriage in no other light than that of a status supernaturally enjoined, the question has not yet become a question of freedom. It can wait until the principle of freedom has been accepted in cases where the Indeterminate Co-efficient of supernaturalism does not affect the problem. It will be time enough to raise the cry of Free Marriage when we have got rid, for example, of ' free. compulsory education.' " I submit that this Indeterminate Co-efficient is a factor which may rightly be ignored by Individualists. Indeed, its recognition appears to be highly dangerous for any purpose other than Parliamentary ones. Our teaching is to fearlessly speak the highest truths, and expound them regardless of their poor prospect of favourable reception. Besides, if the overwhelming majority of women do regard marriage as supernaturally enjoined, it is still a question which is the better way to combat the idea : to attack supernaturalism wholesale and direct. or to insist that this particular subject should be regarded supernaturally by those so disposed, otherwise by those otherwise inclined, and decidedly otherwise by the State as having no rightful official cognisance of supernatural affairs. Moreover, if an overwhelming majority of women do so regard marriage, and if in consequence they are to be left alone, there are still two other classes of persons to be reckoned with—the men and the new women. The position taken seems to presuppose the inadaptability of theology to changing social needs, which is by no means absolute. Let us, after citing the argument of a great theologian of a past time, John Milton, who writes in these words : " For all sense and equity reclaim that any law or covenant, how solemn or straight soever, either between God and Man, or Man and Man, though of God's joining, should bind against a prime and principal scope of its own institution, and of both or either party covenanting,"—take for example the analysis of the expression : " Till Death us do part," by Mr. F. H. Rochester, in a pamphlet on " Marriage : is it an ecclesiastical function or a divine ordinance ? " He deems it to be morally on a par with the salute, How glad I am to see you ; the former expression being in reality " put into the mouth of, and not invented by, the couple who present themselves to be married," and, therefore, presumably even more empty of meaning. Yet Mr. Rochester writes from the orthodox standpoint, and as a subscriber to the *Church Times* since 1871. He further writes : " To object to ' divorce ' on the ground that ' what God hath joined together no man may put asunder,' is really an argument that tells in its favour, unless we are guilty of profanity, and deny God's omniscience. In the case of a justly-opposed or ill-assorted match, it is nothing less than infamous to say the man and woman are joined together by God." In capital letters Mr. Rochester adds the declaration : " It is a scandalous profanity and a barbarism to allege that a life of married misery and wretchedness is of necessity more pleasing to Almighty God than the severance of a bond contracted without his sanction or approval "

The authorship of " Insoluble Problems " is not traceable to Mr. Millar himself. A recent anonymous pamphlet issued from the *Liberty Review* office, and entitled " Socialism and Marriage." may or may not be his composition. In vigour of language it excels, and is open to be regarded as reflecting little credit on the critical accomplishments of the Individualist camp. A treatise on "God's England or the Devil's ?" by George Brooks, in attacking the position taken up by Socialists on sexual questions, acknowledges indebtedness to the *Liberty Review* as rendering yeoman's service in this connection. Having therefore hinted at a doubt concerning the desirability of indulgence in railery and vehemence in sexual criticisms by Individualist leaders, I take the opportunity of showing that this doubt is not shared by every writer who is opposed to Socialism. Whether that cause loses or gains by it I leave as an open question. A signed vindication of the existing order of things appeared in Mr. Millar's notice of the Inaugural Proceedings of the League in the *Agnostic Journal*, 28th October, 1893, where the inviolability of the tie is insisted upon on the ground that it is woman's " only safeguard against aggression.' and that " the one and only duty of the State is to prevent aggression."

CHAPTER XXII

STATISTICS OF ILLEGITIMACY.

I have referred the student of this subject to Dr. Leffingwell's admirable little treatise. I am here able to reproduce a brief statement by " Agnosco," from *The Agnostic Journal*, December 1st, 1894, by kind permission of " Saladin."

THE occupations of 10,010 unwed mothers in Scotland during the year 1883 are thus tabulated by the Registrar-General :—

Domestic Servants	4,706
Factory Girls	2,442
Farm Girls	985
Seamstresses	607
No occupation (chiefly daughters of working men)	831
Daughters of professional men	54
No information (chiefly widows)...	385
	10,010

From which it is seen that domestic servants are responsible for about 47 per cent.—nearly one-half—the total number of illegitimate births, and girls

employed in factories for 24 per cent.—nearly one-
fourth—these two classes alone being responsible for
more than 70 per cent. of the entire number. Much
the same report has been given independently and
more recently in England—in the metropolis itself, in
fact; for at a meeting of the Hackney Board of
Guardians (reported in *London*, August 2nd, 1894) it
was stated that during the year ending June, 1894,
80 per cent. of the admissions into the Infirmary
of unmarried women in confinement were domestic
servants, 15 per cent. factory hands, while the remaining 5 per cent. are said to have lived at home. The
two classes to which attention is here drawn may be
set down as pre-eminently urban, and that notwithstanding the indictment brought against country life
by Richard Jefferies and by Emile Zola in "La
Terre." Still, we must remember that many prospective mothers leave their rural homes and enter
town life, taking up situations as domestic servants,
or finding employment in factories. The country
exclusively has 10 per cent. laid to its charge in the
case of farm hands. The number of births attributed
to the daughters of professional men is remarkably
small—only about half per cent. It would be interesting to know how far this is obtained by successful
concealment of birth, and how far by false registration
as legitimate births. Indeed, the present writer has
known more than one case in which the " the wife of
——," as the announcement read in the local newspapers, was an unmarried woman. In one case both
the young woman and her " husband " belonged to
the " unco' guid "; their parents were leading lights
at a certain church in a well-to do suburb of a
northern city; they themselves were Sunday-school

teachers, communicants, and examples of what Christian believers should be ; while the notice in the newspaper was inserted by the father of the unwed " bride "— a prominent local preacher and class leader ! In other cases the parties have been unmarried at the birth of the child, but have subsequently been privately united in a distant town or village. Such a child is illegitimate in England, although quite legitimate in Scotland, the Isle of Man, and many Continental countries. Truly, in this respect the English law is far from synonymous with justice. Here, indeed, the custom of *bastard ainé et mulier puisné*—borrowed, it is said, from mediæval canon law, and having nothing in common with old English common law — might entitle the child to rank (but only after making formal claim to that effect) with his legitimate brothers and sisters by the same parents. Otherwise he would be *filius nullius*, nobody's child—a being having no existence in law.

But, be the cause what it may, the wide disparity in numbers between unwed mothers among the daughters of professional men and those of working men is most strikingly significant.

Illegitimate births are thus locally distributed in Ireland per 1,000 births of both descriptions :— Connaught 7, Munster 17, Leinster 22, Ulster 40. The disparity between Connaught—poor, wild, miserable, and Roman Catholic – and Ulster—wealthy, arrogant, prosperous, and Protestant—is remarkable. Some explanation seems necessary why the counties which are ultra-Protestant and ultra-Presbyterian, and which include that most godly of cities, Belfast, should have the proud heritage of eleven times as many illegitimate children per annum as ignorant and degraded Mayo! Pious Ulster has almost as many bastards as the whole of the rest of Ireland put together.

In certain cities in Great Britain the percentage of illegitimate births is as follows:—London 38, Birmingham 45, Liverpool 58, Glasgow 83, Edinburgh 85, Dundee 104, Aberdeen 106. The lowest rates in England are 34 in Essex, 35 in Middlesex, 38 in London, and 40 in Surrey, the highest being 58 in Lincolnshire, 59 in Nottinghamshire, 60 in the North Riding of Yorkshire, 62 in Cornwall, 70 in Westmoreland, 74 in Norfolk, 76 in Hereford and Cumberland, and 82 in Shropshire. The following rough classification shows the distribution of the rate in relation to geographical position:—11 Southern Counties (English Channel), 45; 10 Midland, 48; 8 North Eastern (east of Pennines), 53; 7 East Anglian and East Midland, 55; 3 North Western (west of Pennines), 63; 4 Welsh Marches, 63. Average for England, 51·74.

Monmouth approaches most nearly the South Wales rate, whereas Hereford and Shropshire exceed that of North Wales. Cheshire nearly approaches the English average. These rates are:—Monmouth 42, South Wales 45, Cheshire 52, North Wales 69, Hereford 76, Shropshire 82. In the essay above referred to it will be remembered that I described border-lands as productive of genius and crime; it is here seen that they are likewise prolific in illegitimacy. On the Scottish border Westmoreland and Cumberland have a rate of 70 and 76 per 1,000; while Northumberland is slightly above the average; Berwick has 103, Roxburgh 108, Kirkcudbright 146, and Dumfriesshire 147 per 1,000, nearly 15 per cent. of its births being illegitimate.

Scotland is divided into 8 registration districts :-
North Western, 64 ; West Midland, 65 ; South
Western, 68 ; Northern, 77 ; South Eastern, 78 ;
East Midland, 89 ; Southern, 139 ; North Eastern,
141. Only 3 Scottish counties have rates below the
English average—to wit, Shetland (48), Ross and
Cromarty and Dumbarton (50). The highest rates in
the British Isles are, in addition to those already
mentioned as border counties, Caithness (115),
Aberdeen (132), Elgin (152), Banff (168), and
Wigtown (182). Surely there is a vast distance
between Mayo with 5 and Wigtown with 182 illegitimate births per 1,000. In the latter, one person in
every five is a bastard !

It is noteworthy that in London the highest
illegitimacy rate should be found, not in the 'savage'
East-end, but in the civilised North-west, in the
land of peers and painters. In the registration sub-
district of St. Mary's, in the parish of St. Marylebone,
more than two-thirds of all the births are illegitimate,
the astounding rate of 406 per 1,000 being reached. In
the Rectory sub-district of the same parish nearly
one-fourth (247 in 1,000) of the children born are
nobody's bairns. In the entire parish of St. Marylebone the rate is 168, whereas in Whitechapel it is only
27 ! Curiously enough there is a similar peculiarity
in the distribution of lunatics in these two parishes.

The illegitimacy rates in 1889 of a number of
European countries were as follows :—Russia, 27 ;
Ireland, 28 ; Holland, 33 ; England and Wales, 46 ;
Switzerland, 47 ; Spain (1870), 55 ; Italy, 73 ; Norway,
74 ; Prussia (1870), 79 ; Scotland, 79 ; France, 84 ;
Hungary, 85 ; Belgium, 88 ; Denmark, 93 ; Sweden, 101 ;
Saxony, 125 ; Bavaria, 141 ; Austria, 147. (In the case

of Switzerland, Prussia, and Bavaria still-births are included in the totals given.) Most of these nations showed a distinct decrease ; but in Austria and Hungary an almost uninterrupted rise has gone on since 1870 — in the latter country to the extent of 5, in the former 17 per cent. The most noteworthy falls have been—in Norway of 22 per cent., in Scotland of 24 per cent., and in Bavaria of 27 per cent.

The poetic description of spring as the season of love has, as was remarked in the original text, a physiological justification. The number of conceptions among mankind, both legitimate and illegitimate, is greatest during the warm months of the year, at which season the breeding period of other animals usually occurs, while at the same time the vegetal world orders itself towards the same end.

These conceptions have been thus classified in France, Holland. Norway, and Sweden, according to the season of the year :—

		Legitimate.	Illegitimate.
December-February	...	24.25	23.81
March-May	..	27.11	23.65
June-August	...	25.36	26 61
September-November	..	22.59	25.31
		99.31	99.38

From which it is evident that legitimate unions are most numerous in spring, fewer but still numerous in summer, and rarest in autumn ; while illegitimate unions are commonest in summer and fewest in winter, the second place being taken by autumn.

The influence of the seasons upon conduct is thus very evident ; yet there still remain people who deny the rational physical theory of morality, and who are now. as ever, willing to absolutely ignore all the facts of the case, and to pretend that morality has had a divine and heaven-inspired origin, and that it is directed towards the well-being of humanity—not in this world, which is most concerned in it, but in a land beyond the skies.

CHAPTER XXIII

NATURAL CHILDREN AND PERSONAL RIGHTS.

A MONGST the further services rendered by the President during the past two years was the starting of a series of articles on " Natural Children " in *Personal Rights* (July, 1893). Mr. Donisthorpe contends against the granting of affiliation orders, an interesting question, but aside of our purpose here. In the following month the editor follows with an article arguing against that contention, stating the position which the Association and the journal have taken up, and ticketing it the Individualistic standpoint from which "neither is likely to swerve by a hair's breadth." This entertertaining reading is, however, also quite foreign to our subject. What is germane, however, is Mr. Donisthorpe's explicit declaration in *Personal Rights* that acknowledged children should be legitimated, and that " no exception should be made so as to exclude the offspring of adulterous and incestuous unions." Here was the gauntlet flung down with a vengeance! Would this be ticketed anarchy by the Editor of *Personal Rights?*... or was it not so much as a hair's breadth from the Individualist position? The two-columned reply contained no word about the matter. The doctrine that NO EXCEPTION SHOULD BE MADE SO AS TO EXCLUDE THE OFFSPRING OF ADULTEROUS OR INCESTUOUS UNIONS was passed unchallenged by the Editor of *Personal Rights.* Was it so obviously Individualistic that he felt it would be a superfluity to express his acquiescence?

October brought the third instalment of articles on Natural Children, running to four and a half columns, with contributions by Mr. E. Sellon, Mr. J. C. Spence, Mr. F. Evershed, and the Editor. Mr. Sellon advocates the "irresponsible private ownership" of children—a thesis unconnected with legitimation; Mr. Evershed asks, could not the gains of legitimation be secured by bequest? They could not. Children born out of wedlock pay ten per cent. on legacies not exceeding £100, and twelve on sums over that amount, whilst legitimate children. in cases of the largest fortunes, under the new Death Duties pay no higher than seven and a half or eight Besides that, whilst it is so easy to bequeathe (though from the faults of their neglect and procrastination, inherent in frail humanity, people often fail to do so), it is so easy also to make a vitiated will, or to lose it by carelessness, misadventure, or fraud.

"Mr. Spence's arguments need but few comments," writes the Editor in his general reply; and he volunteered none on the righteous declaration which Mr. Spence makes in these words: "The laws which enforce perpetual marriages, or none at all, that ignore all matrimonial settlements, except those of the regulation type, are certainly barbarous, and should receive the unqualified opposition of all those who value liberty."

Allusion to "the proposals of certain quasi-Individualists in England" occurs in a leaderette in *Personal Rights* of March, 1895. A bill to be laid before the French Chamber, "giving illegitimate children the same rights as those born in wedlock," but re-affirming the famous maxim *La recherche de la paternité est defendu*, is declared to bear a striking resemblance to the proposals in question, and to be appropriately introduced by a Socialist. In the issue for April, Mr. Greevz Fisher wrote a letter, printed by the Editor "with some hesitation and much regret," stating a doctrine of parentage editorially declared to be "not the Individualistic but the Anarchistic one," the compulsory maintenance of children being the question on which there is supposed to be a divergence corresponding with this classification of thinkers. The topic is, of course, distinct from that of legitimation and the relations of adults, and Mr. Fisher kept it so, not only in the letter quoted, but in a further one appearing in May *Personal Rights*. Nevertheless, Mr. Levy, after closing the correspondence in the words, "and here the matter must rest for the present," adds: "We decline to discuss the Free Love doctrine, which is altogether beyond the purview of our paper; but it may not be uninstructive to our readers to have a glimpse of that theory of 'free parentage' which is one of the most important corollaries." Mr. Fisher replied disclaiming having introduced the subject of Free Love, but in the editorial dissection of his letter, which occupied the greater part of a column in June

Personal Rights, this remonstrance was entirely suppressed. I caution the reader against accepting as corollaries doctrines entirely dissociated.

At the annual meeting of the Personal Rights Association this year, Mr. Henry Wilson "asserted that that Association, being founded on Individualist principles, was bound to take the course it had taken" on a certain matter involving the Legitimation League. Further, "he always liked to meet opponents on principle." (*P. R.*, March, '95.) This challenge led to a correspondence between Mr. Wilson and myself, which will be published at length in my *brochure*, "Personal Rights and Sexual Wrongs." As Mr. Wilson upholds State marriage with argument, and was met by argument, this would be a proper place to reproduce the letters. Seeing, however, that what is deemed by some to be a personal question is involved and treated of therein, I ignore the discussion altogether in this volume.

In the following month (April) Sir Roland K. Wilson, reviewing Mr. Donisthorpe's "Law in a Free State," dwelt at length upon our President's chapters on Marriage and the Status of Children, expressing himself as follows: "We are at one with the writer as to the anomaly and hardship of enforcing a contract of life-long partnership," adding. "In point of fact, since the Matrimonial Causes Act, 1884, and the Jackson case, 1891, only the negative part of the contract can be said to be enforced specifically." I take this to mean that State interference with married persons is confined to the punishment of bigamy. Yet surely magisterial orders for maintenance have little of the negative character about them ; whilst suits for the restitution of conjugal rights have not been unheard of since 1891. Sir Roland Wilson then proceeds to give reasons which "the wiser apologists of the existing system" adduce for the support of marital coercion —the consideration of the children, of the woman cast off after losing her charms, and a third reason, "the danger to domestic peace from the fact of each partner being able innocently to contemplate a future change of partners, and to make personal comparisons from that point of view." This presupposes a domestic peace to be endangered by some change, whereas there is much testimony for a wide prevalence of domestic warfare which would give place to peace if the State would act on Individualist lines and no more concern itself with domestic peace in this matter than it does in other domestic affairs where the law of liberty is not invaded, as, for instance, where a tyrannical mistress rings a curfew bell, prohibits all kitchen visitors, and shows a supreme contempt for the eight hours movement alike in matters of work and sleep.

The difficulties as to children, and the other difficulty, are just the ones the League seeks to meet by the devices of legitimation and licit love, and I am happy to note that Sir Roland Wilson is "quite open to conviction as to the possibility of adequate safeguards being devised against the dangers already hinted at."

Treating of the status of children, Sir Roland Wilson remarks: "No man need die intestate, and anyone can provide by will for his illegitimate child, even to the exclusion of his legitimate children, if such be his pleasure." That is so, but men do die intestate, and some wills are invalid and some are lost, and the illegitimate child, when he does benefit under a will, has to pay a higher rate of duty. Besides which, in the case of entailed estates, he cannot reap the advantage of the paternity to which, as the acknowledged son of a father, he might be entitled. Herein is a vital difference between legitimation and adoption, which Sir Roland Wilson regards as having equal logical claims for embodiment in any proposed change of law. Whatever may be the historical explanation of our probate laws (and laws, said Mr. Justice Stephen, ought to be adjusted to the habits of society and not to aim at remoulding them),—howsoever far from true it may be that they " are based upon observation of what is usually done by persons who make wills "—it nevertheless will not be doubted that the possessors of fortunes have evidenced earnest desires to transmit their wealth to their blood-relations. frequently from generation to generation, in perpetuity ; and that the State, when it has not enforced this method of bequest. has acquiesced in it. Sir Roland Wilson says of adoption that " at most it would involve a slight change in the terminology of wills and settlements " ; but it is conceivable to me it might also involve " danger to domestic peace " in a form aggravated in comparison with that prophesied as likely to ensue from the legitimation of offspring. Sir Roland Wilson pronounces on Mr. Donisthorpe's argument that it proves a good deal more than was intended.—inasmuch as it proves the justice of adoption. At this rate it may prove that his own argument also proves too much. " No man need die intestate, and anyone can provide by will for his illegitimate child." Quite so ; then what becomes of the Legitimation by *Subsequent Marriage* Bill espoused by the Personal Rights Association? Must it not be dismissed as a superfluous measure? If it be answered : No, its design is not so much to affect succession as to establish parental relationships, and to give status to the offspring,—then, very good, for that too is our primary aim. In fine, adoption, legitimation, and affiliation, may be left to severally stand or fall on their own merits.

Chapter XXIV.

AT THE BEDFORD AGAIN.

Reported by D. OLIVER. 22, Theberton Street. London, N.

ON Monday evening, the 25th February, 1895, Mr. and Mrs. Oswald Dawson entertained at dinner at the Bedford Hotel, Covent Garden, W.C., the friends and supporters of the Legitimation League, and personal friends of the host and hostess. Mr. Oswald Dawson, the Honorary Secretary of the League, presided, and Mr. J. G. Fisher occupied the vice-chair.

THE CHAIRMAN said: Ladies and Gentlemen, I give you all a very cordial welcome here as my personal friends. At the same time it is a circumstance that we are now holding two informal meetings. It may be rather out of order to hold two meetings at the same table. However, according to the terms of your invitation here, that is what we are doing. On the one hand and at the lower end of the table, you are dealing with a very disgusting problem (at least that is the way I view it, and I may be allowed to give expression to such adjectives as suit my views), of my expulsion from the Personal Rights Association. You are all members of that association at the lower end of the table. (A voice: "Minus myself.") You are invited to attend to-morrow the annual meeting of that body. The second meeting—the one that is being held at this, the top end, of the table, is a meeting of the officers of the Legitimation League. Of that body I happen to be the honorary secretary. I have nothing very particular to say to you, except that I want you to confirm the remarks and statements I made in a lecture which I delivered yesterday morning at the Hall of Science. I may say—in case anyone present does not know that hall - that it is the building in which the National Secular Society hold their usual weekly and other meetings. The circumstance of my lecturing there does not in the slightest degree commit either the National Secular party, or any individual member of that party, to the views of myself or the Legitimation League ; but as I said yesterday morning, our thanks are certainly due to the Secular party for allowing the Legitimation League to send a representative to lecture there— (hear, hear)—and especially to Miss Edith Vance for taking the initiative in inviting a representative of the Legitimation League to lecture there. Well, what I have to ask to-night is your support, in a general way, and in a general way only, of the remarks I made yesterday at the Hall of Science. The leading feature of those remarks, in my opinion, is this : the Legitimation League was formed to create a machinery for doing a certain thing. That was two years ago. Now, at the end of the two years, I announce that we have created that machinery. We have appointed Mr. Arthur Cornwell to register the alliances of the parents of illegitimate children, born, or possibly to be born ; and I introduced Mr. Arthur Cornwell to the audience at the Hall of Science yesterday morning. I have pleasure in doing the same at the present moment.

I believe he is quite prepared, while in my service, to carry out any instructions in relation to those questions of legitimation that are given to him, and to carry those instructions out in a perfectly scrupulous manner. I make these remarks in his presence, and if this is not so, he will be open to resign his post to-night if he should think fit. We have appointed Mr. J. C. Spence a Vice-President of the Legitimation League—(hear, hear)—in place of Dr. F. A. Lees, who has resigned for reasons which I do not think it needful to enter upon now.

I have just received by messenger a note from Mr. Evan Streachan, advertising contractor, 295, Strand, established 1855, that he will be pleased to be appointed an advertising agent to the Legitimation League. I met Mr. Evan Streachan this morning, and explained to him exactly what he might be called upon to do, namely, to advertise unions of persons who might possibly be the parents of illegitimate children, but who desire to acknowledge them. This sort of advertising, you will readily agree with me, could not be so well conducted without a London agent. We want to get a foothold among the births, marriages, and deaths, and not to belong to the Agony colum. (Laughter.) I call upon Mr. Cornwell to say a word or two now.

Mr. ARTHUR CORNWELL : I am not very good at

making a speech. Indeed. this is my first attempt at it. As regards my being notifying clerk to the Legitimation League, I have to say that I am willing to do my best in that office, and to help in any way required. (Hear, hear.)

MISS EDITH VANCE : I claim that I have the toast of the evening, for it is my intention to propose the Legitimation League. I shall leave the aims and objects of the League to be spoken of by more capable speakers than myself. My desire is to speak of the League in relation to one important point, or rather one important person. To me (if Mrs Dawson will forgive me for saying so), the League is Mrs. Dawson She has been fighting for the League—for you and all its members—the whole time, and only reasonable, thinking men and women can understand and realise what a deal she has been doing for you and for it. The moral of the song to which you have just listened [a comic song by Mr. Banks, illustrative of the contempt of the higher-priced dolls of Lowther Arcade for the lower]. has some bearing on my theme. Respectable marriage is 2/3, and the League is decidedly 1/9. (Laughter.) I was rather amused that Mr. Dawson, in the course of his lecture at the Hall of Science, should have thought it necessary to apologise to me for what I might have to endure because I took the chair on the occasion. As I said then, I can bear it. I have borne worse. I did not know until I had a talk with Mrs. Dawson afterwards, what a very great deal she has to endure. It is very easy—perhaps it is fun to you gentlemen—to be twitted with your connection with the Legitimation League. You can bear it with fortitude, and perhaps rather like it than otherwise, and if the conversation get too bad, you can knock the man down, or threaten to do so, but Mrs. Dawson is not in a position to thus deal with her slanderers, men or women, and in most cases the women are the worst.

However, we are coming into the daylight and, perhaps, this time next year we shall be better understood. The meeting yesterday at the Hall of Science was more pleasant and favourable than the meeting here last year. I think Mr. Dawson felt yesterday that he had a very good audience, and a very patient hearing. People are already beginning to think over and talk about the aims of the Legitimation League, and there is, I am sure, more tolerance in store for it. I think it only wants advocating and knowing to be better appreciated. The public need to be shown that we are not the disreputable beings they imagine we are. I ask you to drink to the success of the Legitimation League, and with it I couple the health of Mrs. Dawson. (Applause.)

The toast was heartily received.

Mr. WORDSWORTH DONISTHORPE: Mr. Chairman, Miss Vance, ladies and gentlemen, I have myself to tolerate a good deal of chaff. I will not say more because, as Miss Vance pointed out, what is cruel to a woman is mere chaff to a man. I have been told that this League is, if not exactly a criminal association, at all events a despicable and improper association, formed for the purpose (as an *Athenæum* reviewer said one of my books was written for the purpose) of promoting and excusing butterfly relationships. The fact is, I loath butterfly relationships, believing them to be in all respects unsatisfactory, and I do my best to advocate monogamy. I believe in monogamous unions really and truly so called

—unions that are really and essentially unions of hearts and not merely of hands. But the belief prevalent among our enemies is that we favour butter-fly relationships. We do not favour these relations, and it is our own fault that we allow this view to become prevalent.

Mr. JOHN BADCOCK: I should like to say a word or two, if I am not out of order. Mr. Donisthorpe's remarks appear to me to draw the line rather hard and fast at butterfly relationship. Now the principal thing I like about the Legitimation League is that it is on the side of toleration, and that it seeks to make respectable relationships that are outside ordinary conventional relations. Why should we, in trying to extend the respectability to unorthodox opinions, draw the line at butterfly relationship? I am not certain that butterfly relationships are ideal relationships between the sexes, but in any case I look with equal respect upon butterfly as upon any other sexual relationship. We should not draw a line between those relationships—butterfly relationships—and any other sexual relations. As long as the two parties to the relationship agreed, and no force was used, I would maintain butterfly relationships as equally-- in my eyes at all events, and I can only speak for myself—as equally respectable with other sexual relations, and as deserving to be upheld and tolerated and not despised.

THE CHAIRMAN: By the rules of procedure I would advise that Mr. Donisthorpe has the right of reply if he choses to say anything in answer to Mr. Badcock.

Mr. DONISTHORPE: Well, Mr. Chairman, ladies and gentlemen, I am not sure that I have any right of reply in an after-dinner meeting like this, but I should like to say that I, personally, have no objection whatever to butterfly relationships, provided they are confined to those for whom butterfly relationships are sufficient. I have no objection to the arrangements made by the cats on the wall—(laughter),—but I think in the scale of civilized humanity we have risen a few rungs above that ideal. I honestly believe that the tendency of mankind is towards something in the nature of a monogamous union as long as it is a tolerable one. When that union is found to be a mistake, when it is productive of nothing but disagreement, discord, and misery, then I think the time is ripe for dissolving that particular union, and bringing the relationship to a close. I am sure, however, that Mr. Badcock will not pretend that the arrangement by which parties enter into a monogamous union is or should be made of short duration. Those arrangements are intended to be permanent, and in the case of the most highly civilized nations those unions tend to become more and more permanent. I can only say that we, as members of the League, favour monogamous unions, which are the tendency of the age, and desire to remove the fetters that prevent the true union of the sexes.

The Chairman : I have now to call upon Mr. Fisher, who is, and has been from the commencement, the vice-president of the Legitimation League, who has been mixed up with what we may call its squabbles—perhaps what we may call its petty squabbles, but who, throughout all these, has not only perceived but boldly declared that, underlying these, there was a great principle of liberty, which was not to be overshadowed by them. ("By what?")

By those petty squabbles. He has stuck to us faithfully throughout. He has opposed us. As I explained yesterday morning, he has issued a pamphlet in opposition to our principles. But Mr. Fisher has since adopted our principles—principles that are in diametrical contradiction to the views that Mr. Fisher then held. He has recanted, but has not in any way publicly acknowledged his recantation. I do not ask him to do so to-night, but he is here to-night, and I shall ask him to speak, and leave it to him as to what he shall say.

Mr. GREEVZ FISHER : Mr. Dawson, ladies and gentlemen, my natural modesty has been subjected to a fearful strain by the observations that Mr. Dawson has chosen to make in introducing me. I wish, in the first place, to state that I have no objection to any publicity being given to my acquiescence in the statement that I wrote the pamphlet on "Illegitimate Children" under a misconception, which I attribute to my want of knowledge of the law. And I believe that Mr. Donisthorpe will excuse my saying that he owns that the remarks which he made at the inaugural meeting of the League at Leeds were somewhat misleading. Speaking as a barrister and member of the Inner Temple, he uttered certain observations that were calculated to lead a mere layman like myself into the supposition that an illegitimate child was saddled with serious legal disability. The real position, as I now understand it, is that the illegitimate child is not altogether an illegitimate person ; that although the illegitimate person cannot be the son or brother to anybody, because the law does not take any cognizance of his coming into the world in regard to inheritance, yet he may be a legitimate father, and in all the other functions of life a legitimate person. Having set off with a mistaken idea, I elaborated it in a pamphlet, which has been in every respect a mistake. With regard to the position of this League, let me say that I am sorry that Mr. Donisthorpe was so much hurt by the phrase "butterfly relationship," because, on the whole, I think butterflies are rather pretty things. (Laughter.) I do not think we ought to protest against butterflies and their doings. but at the same time I thought that Mr. Badcock's exposition in reply to Mr. Donisthorpe was absolutely uncalled for, on this ground : that it is inconceivable to us that butterflies could acknowledge their children, legitimate or otherwise, and seek to have conferred upon them the status of legitimacy, or that they could record their arrangements to provide for the maintenance of offspring yet unborn; and these are amongst the things which the Legitimation League proposes to do. I am very glad we have had a notifying clerk appointed. I am, unfortunately, lawfully married—(laughter)—and have got four children, but I do not see why I should not acknowledge them in the manner prescribed by the Legitimation League ; and when it has a form of acknowledgment drawn up, it is my intention to acknowledge these children whom I know about and believe to be mine. I am only waiting until Mr. Dawson gets the forms prepared, and my children shall be 1, 2, 3, and 4. Then we have to consider whether the League should require that those who acknowledge their children or register their unions, should consent to the publication of the unions. With respect to this, I think that having regard to the relationship that would be entered into, it would be beneficial on the whole to have them made public, but at the same time I do not think that it would be wise for this League to dogmatise. Some of my children are not registered in the Government books. Some of them are, but others are not, and I prefer to rely upon private individuals registering than upon Government registration--registration being, as I consider, a function with which Government has nothing whatever to do. (Applause.)

Mr. Crawshay: I wish to say a word or two about the Legitimation League. I think the scope of the legitimation proposed is too narrow. Although two individuals have a right to enter into any relationship they choose, yet in the present state of public opinion the consequences of their union entail hardship. The nature of their alliance throws a certain amount of obloquy upon, and an obstacle in the way of, the offspring they bring into the world; and the League, I think, seems to be mistaken in not trying to do away with the social ostracism that attaches to illegitimacy, so far, I mean, as the children themselves are concerned. The very word "illegitimate" is objectionable in many ways, that is to say, any one called "illegitimate," or "bastard," is looked down upon—not so much. perhaps, now as formerly. It appears to me that the League proposes to retain the word "illegitimate" as a description of all children not acknowledged in the way the League prescribes, which happen to be born out of wedlock. (The Chairman: Hear, hear.) I think it would be helpful to the children of such unions if we—that is, the League—tried to introduce some other words, and dispensed with the objectionable terms "illegitimate child" and "bastard."

Mr. Ashdown Jones : So far as I can see, the League does not wish to cast any stigma upon children because they happen to be born out of wedlock. It is rather the other way : the League wants to acknowledge them and legitimatise them. If you ask a Frenchwoman who has a child "Are you married ?" or " Is that child born in wedlock ?" she will go for you like a tigress. She will indignantly reply " No, but he is acknowledged ! " She regards that as enough, and considers her child legitimate. She does not look upon her child as under any social stigma whatever. Since my attention has been more forcibly directed to this subject by the writings of Mr. Donisthorpe, I feel myself bound to admit that in the present state of public opinion many people—more especially the feminine part of the community—have a great objection to risking their reputation by embarking in a sort of connection that they regard as an uncertain union. But that objection could be got over if, before a lady formed a licit alliance, she had a contract drawn up recognising her union, and providing for any possible or probable offspring according to the terms decided upon. If you had the unions under contract the people would know what they had to expect, and what they would have to face, and these contracts, like any other contracts, would be liable to be rescinded by mutual agreement.

After several conversational speeches dealing with the topics discussed during the evening, the company dispersed.

CHAPTER XXV

THE SECOND ANNUAL MEETING.

A Shorthand Note was taken by Mr. HARRY TOOTHILL, of the
Leeds School of Shorthand.

THE Second Annual Meeting of the Legitimation
League was held at the offices, Albion Walk
Chambers, Leeds, on Saturday afternoon, 30th
March, 1895, Mr. J. GREEVZ FISHER, Vice-President, in
the chair. The Hon. Secretary read the letter con-
vening the meeting, and apologies for absence from
the President and others, including one from Mr.
Badcock having intimate bearing on the aims of the
League. Mr. BADCOCK expressed himself as follows :
" I have just read Grant Allen's *The Woman Who
Did*. It is the finest thing I've read on the subject.
I fall in absolutely with Herminia Barton's ideas. No
legitimating, no registering, nor anything of that
kind. It is a matter of privacy, with which the
outside world has nothing at all to do. The cere-
monising, even the advertising in the papers (the
latter a great advance upon bowing down to compulsory regulations, but nevertheless a kind of
voluntary binding, from which. having been made
public, a withdrawal is mortifying and perhaps
impossible), is an affront upon the purity, the sacred-

ness of the bond of affection. Hence it appears to me that mating should be absolutely severed from all officialism. and children should all be 'illegitimate' (in the sense in which that word is used now)."

Mr. J. C. Spence, whose visit to Leeds was unavoidably postponed until a later date, wrote in a counter strain of the work in question. He said " . . . . . . For my part the lofty sentiments of Grant Allen are simply loathsome. The idea that we are to share the woman we love with other men is repulsive. If children are to be dropped into a foundling hospital for the parish to look after, as per Bellamy, or looked after by the mother, as per Grant Allen, then promiscuity is the only rational consequence, but I can see nothing lofty in it. It is a reversion to an inferior and beastly type: If parents are to share responsibility in children. as I think they ought, then definite relations must be formed between the parents. I believe there are only two possible or practical methods for this—privacy in a harem, or publicly acknowledged relationship."

Mr. Fisher: I am certainly at variance with Mr. Badcock. The whole object of the Legitimation League is to try to arrange for acknowledgment of the family ties without being subject to the life-long bond which, in a great many instances, produces injury, both to parents and also to the children ; instead of realising the blessing of family life, it really converts family life into one of the greatest possible curses. We do not in our objects express that as one of the things which we aim at, but it undoubtedly would imply that in any attempt to acknowledge children that there shall be some relationship of constancy between the parties, therefore to accept Mr. Badcock's suggestion would be tantamount to disbanding the League. It would have no purpose whatever in existence.

The Hon. Sec. explained that copies of these letters had been sent to each member of the League, and from several of these and from strangers he had been asked to give his opinion of *The Woman Who Did*, and therefore, after the report had been presented and the balance sheet read by the Treasurer, he would attempt a criticism of that book

The report showed that the membership had doubled since 1893. No canvass for adherents had been attemped. Mr. Arthur Cornwell had been appointed Notifying Clerk, and the announcement already made to every member, that the League was now open to register alliances with or without the publicity of newspaper advertising, would shortly be made public. A cheap edition of Mr. J. C. Spence's book on the *Dawn of Civilisation*, containing a chapter on Marriage, would be issued simultaneously with the First Biennial Proceedings of the League, and sent to all members who paid their subscriptions of 1/6 and upwards for the year then past. In relation to the income of the League, a large sum had been spent in advertising. The proposal to form a fund, with a nucleus of £200, offered by the Honorary Secretary, had been abandoned, having been found to involve insuperable difficulties, and the money paid had been devoted to the general purposes of the League, which forthwith would pay a nominal salary annually to its notifying clerk. The Report was adopted, and it was agreed that a copy of the report be sent to every member of the League.

Mrs. Oswald Dawson, Treasurer, then presented the balance sheet, which was as follows :—

LEGITIMATION LEAGUE.

Balance Sheet, April 1st, 1894, to March 31st, 1895.

RECEIPTS.	£	s.	d.	EXPENDITURE.	£	s.	d.
By Balance in Bank, April 1st	26	1	10	Advertisements … …	67	2	10
,, Cash in hand … ..	0	7	0	Printing and Stationery …	17	2	10
,, Subscriptions … …	238	19	8	Shorthand Writer's Charges	13	7	0
				Books—*Dawn of Civilisation*	15	0	0
				Notifying Clerk's expenses to London … … ..	4	0	11
				Law Students' Society— Leave to take note …	0	10	6
				Bank Charges … …	0	3	6
				By Balance … … …	148	0	11
	£265	8	6		£265	8	6

Bankers—
The London and Midland Bank, Kirkgate, Leeds.

GLADYS DAWSON, *Treasurer.*

Mr. Oswald Dawson then spoke as follows :—

Ladies and Gentlemen, *The Woman Who Did* bore in title so striking a resemblance to *The Woman Who Dares*, by Ursula Gestefeld, that when I first saw it I, as it were, automatically anticipated a novel which would delight our transatlantic comrades, and such a book we indeed have in *The Woman Who Did*. Its terrific meaning was soon perceived by the English critics. Mr. W. T. Stead met it with a full-page illustration of Botticelli's "Virgin and Child." Of these two the child gave up his life as a sacrifice not specially for the mother's sake. In *The Woman Who Did* the woman immolated herself solely for the child's sake.

Mr. G. W. Foote, who is known not to favour the theological training of children in order to spare them social trouble, is quite sympathetic with Herminia's daughter when she protests against her illegitimate origin, and he considers Herminia's answers ineffective, though word for word with what he would commend to a free-thought mother. "How could I foresee you would turn aside from your mother's creed?" I apologise—Mr. Foote would not have commended any such question in reply. He would advise a mother to teach a child the truth, whatever she foresaw.

There is another leading comment of the critics which does not appeal to me. Grant Allen is blamed for the suicide of the heroine. I regret this in so far as it associates *felo-de-se* and "free love" in people's minds ; but, having regard to the motive of the act, it identifies disbelief in marriage with self-sacrifice for children. Above all it shows that reformers are human, even when they are women.

Herminia Barton was guilty of one gross remissness.   Herminia Barton, I say—not Grant Allen, for he has given us a picture of humanity with its inevitable fallibility, and this book would have appealed far less keenly to us had the heroine been ideally logical, ideally strong, and ideally right in every way, and therefore infinitely less like ourselves—and that remissness was in keeping secret, from her daughter, the mystery of the latter's origin.   One day Dolly asked her mother, "Did you marry your cousin?" She had noticed the identity of her mother's and grandfather's names.   Herminia's reply was : "Your dear father was not related to me in any way," given in a tone that closed the discussion.   Then we read, " In time Herminia sent her child to a day-school," and here the enquiries as to her antecedents became to her a source of anxiety.   Still she dares not question. How painful, how probable, how pitiful, how true; the moment for disclosure never to come, though the days came and seasons changed, and years rolled on. Not until her lover had exhibited some slight change of demeanour, having learned something "about her family," does Dolly appear to raise the question again—then to learn of her illegitimacy.   Dolly's intense horror and distraction, on solving the problem, and her resolution not to marry whilst Herminia lives, because "she could not think of burdening an honest man with such a mother-in-law," with the resultant suicide of Herminia, may partake of the licence of fiction.   Licence there may be, but it is the licence of exaggeration only, not psychological distortion.   In their frailty mother and child are alike human.

If we recognise this we shall see what eminent service the book renders in serving to shew the kind of persecution we of the Legitimation League may expect to meet. It is not simply a question of ranking at a disadvantage with regard to inheritance, nor even of occupying some invidious position in the classification of parish registers of the Poor Law Authorities, if you come to want their services. It is not merely that one's friends and relations will not cultivate your company. The boycott ramifies.

Herminia's father was Dean of Dunwich, and "people said he might have risen to be a Bishop in his time if it hadn't been for that unfortunate episode about his daughter and young Merrick." Young Merrick died, and in ten years' time Herminia fell in love with Harvey Kynaston. He wished to marry, she declined. She would be to him all that she had been to Alan Merrick, but not his wife. Well, what does Harvey say? He loves her, and " in theory " he " accepts her points of view," but he " couldn't consent to take her her own way. His faith was too weak, his ambitions were too earthly." " He was a brilliant economist, with a future before him. He aimed at the Cabinet." Now this young man certainly had a head larger than his heart ; he realised that to climb into the Cabinet required the practice of respectable connubiality, and they who wish to get within sight of a See will find the same thing.

And this brings me to a consideration of considerable importance as affecting the "characters" of persons who eschew the legal ceremony. I have been assured by the solicitor to the League that the applicant for a licence under the liquor laws of this land would stand no chance of success if the " free " character of the alliance he or she had formed were not strictly concealed. Howsoever entirely competent, sober, and otherwise respectable a man or woman might be, however dependent upon hotel management as upon the one business to which he or she had been brought up, however much the needs of the neighbourhood call for an hotel, however old the licensed premises might be, and choose what the applicant might have paid for the goodwill or the freehold, the bar to earning a living as an hotel-keeper is erected against him or her. One can appreciate the fact of the State refusing to elect as master and matron, at any of its institutions where this dual control is needed, persons living out of wedlock. There is at least the pretence that the servants advertised for thus in double harness will be wanted to work together in perpetuity, and that if unmarried there is greater likelihood of the dual service discontinuing, and so occasioning the inconvenience of a change of employés. But this line of argument will scarcely apply to landlords and landladies of the only licensed house within a radius of ten or two miles. This disability is the more unfortunate from another point of view. Mine host and hostess at an hotel, with their visitor's book, might be eminently fit persons as a class to assist in the notification of alliances. This I merely throw out as a suggestion, to any development of which there at once arise conceivable objections from the business point of view.

When the hero and heroine of *The Woman Who Did* journeyed to Italy, "Alan entered their names at all the hotels where they stopped as 'Mr. and Mrs. Alan Merrick, of London.' That deception, as Herminia held it, cost her many qualms of conscience; but Alan, with masculine common sense, was firm upon the point that no other description was practically possible." At a Milan hotel, when a clergyman, turning to Alan, remarked, "Your wife is a very advanced lady," " Herminia longed to blurt out the whole simple truth, ' I am not his wife,' etc., but a warning glance from Alan made her hold her peace." For hotel purposes it has always seemed to me right and proper that couples should pass as man and wife. That false representation is involved only a stickler for verbal truth would contend. Neither the hotel proprietor nor one's fellow guests would thank you for going out of the way to explain anything about legitimation or licit love, or anything of the kind, and in common conversation the use of the terms husband and wife will be found a convenience about which few will share the scruples of Herminia Barton ; though the enthusiast will not unwisely renounce them, except in parlance with entire strangers,—where the promulgation of heresies might be deemed unpolite aggression,—as having legal connotations which he hates, and insist as far as possible on those with whom he comes in contact using the expression paramour, or other word, partly by request that they will oblige by so doing, but principally by the force of example in employing that or other agreed upon term whenever reference is to be made to the reputed husband or wife. The objection is intelligible enough —for these terms have a meaning at law, and it is no secret that I myself systematically eschew them, " except for hotel purposes "; but the like does not apply to the use of the term " Mrs." That is a courtesy title not occurring in statutes, and it is one for which there is no synonym. Its convenience arises from the fact that in a general way, that is to say, except in the case of widows, it indicates that a woman is not open to advances. Men cease to be "Masters" and become "Misters" without regard to their marital relations, but whether they gain by so doing I know not. So long as men hold purse, so long will they do the wooing, and so in their case there is less need to have a warning-off "handle" to their names. This is the best reason I can give why a master is transformed into a mister by the simple process of attaining maturity, and the mere fact that it happens to be the custom, seems no sufficient reason why a miss should become transformed into a mistress without better cause. On the other hand, if, as often happens, an unmarried lady, for purpose of dignity or other reason, elects to be styled by the maturer term, the worst that can be said about her is that she is probably trying to deceive people into thinking that she has not been left behind in the matrimonial race.

After Alan's death, "Herminia was known to the friends, who by and bye gathered round her, as Mrs. Barton." No one, so far as I know, contends that a man ought to take the woman's name, so the issue is not which partner shall surrender, but whether there shall be identity or no. It is a fortunate occurrence that in the novel there is a child, Dolores Barton, who took her mother's name. Now if there be anything in a name to indicate ascendancy, the conferring of the mother's name on the child surely points to a form of matriarchal *regime* which may or may not be commendable to feminine or to masculine feeling or reason, but which is certainly not contemplated in the objects of the Legitimation League. No one can be more thoroughly conscious than myself that those objects do not represent the length and breadth of needed sexual reforms, —but that by the way. I suppose what my correspondents wish to know is in what respect the alliance of Alan Merrick and Herminia Barton falls short of my ideal. Personally I dissent from the retention of either the maiden name or the maiden prefix for a " paramour," or " reputed wife." Yet in relation to other innovations advocated in this book, this matter of nomenclature has a comparative unimportance. Alan and Herminia do not reside together. To do so would be to encourage a "simple ancestral notion derived from man's lordship in his own house." Unfortunately Alan dies before Dolly is born, so whether Herminia would have found it necessary to surrender her liberty to live apart—as she had yielded in the matter of her name whilst on a continental journey,—when there was a child, who was to be " half hers, half his, ' or whether the child would have divided her time at the two residences, one cannot tell.

If couples are not to live together—if the wife is to cease to do the house-keeper's work—it is obvious that some portion of her husband's money will be diverted from her. She may be earning as cook or companion, or otherwise, at home. but if she is to receive from him a series of presents given by usage and equivalent to an income or allowance. in the average of cases the parental supply will tend to cease. If she is not to receive such presents constituting an allowance, what is to become of the sum which the average man ceases to contribute—or partially ceases to contribute—to the maintenance of another class of women when he takes a wife ? Herminia continued to teach at school till her condition made it necessary for her place to be vacated, her future intention being to turn to literature for a living. Now this may have been Herminia Barton's fancy--with a dash of principle thrown in—but it was not by any means her full philosophy. We are clearly told that the independence of women is to be brought about, not by tuition or literature, nor needlework, nor nursing, but by collective support of woman, " by the whole body of men who do the hard work of the world." So that the surplus income I have referred to will be wanted for taxes. The question will then arise : What option of occupation will be afforded to woman? and parenthetically I should like to enquire how the problem of prostitution is to be dealt with when woman has been nationalised. Has not our economic excursion brought us back to the point whether the monogamic marriage with a residence in common is not the highest form—even though the man pays the tax-gatherer and the tax-gatherer pays the woman ? It is in answer to this important question that Mr. Grant Allen is not perfectly clear. In denunciation of legal marriage *The Woman Who Did* is magnificent. That comes in chapter 3. In chapter 17 come fierce denunciations of monopolies, including " the monopoly of the human heart, which is known as marriage." ' Not by levelling down, but by levelling up," is the moral equality of the sexes to be brought about. The level of men obviously needs to be defined. Pre-marital lapses we may assume to be normal and excusable. Are women to indulge likewise? The new woman, whose ideal of a life work is not the enforcement by legal process or moral suasion of an equal standard. will know that she has to reckon with the developments of Neo-malthusianism for other cause than that they are possibly subversive of prevailing ethical principles. The creator of Herminia Barton doubtless realises this, though *The Woman Who Did* is destitute of allusion to this transcendentally important factor in the fermenting ethical code.

In what way, then, one has to ask, does Herminia Barton's alliance differ from the conventional one? Her whole recorded life shows her chaste and without suspicion. We are assured that she and Harvey Kynaston, for all the years of their acquaintanceship, were "loyal friends—no more." Even in her relation with Alan she was as precise as any Quaker: "We must say to one another in so many words, I am yours, you are mine," she said, and she was alarmed lest in the absence of such contract they should "slip by degrees into some vague arrangement they hardly contemplated definitely." Though for six months she resided in Chelsea, and he in Lincoln's Inn, subsequently she lived with him by sheer force of the circumstance that they were together on the Continent till his death. She took his name and the title of "Mrs." She probably would have retained these on their return. The journey to Italy was not a honeymoon. It was undertaken as a discretionary measure conceived by Alan for the avoidance of scandal at home, and one which by no means commended itself to Herminia, who, however, gave in.

It is not recorded that Herminia objected to the institution of the honeymoon, but she did object to any social functions answering to a wedding; indeed, "publicity of any sort was most odious and horrible," and so the alliance was not advertised or otherwise recorded. Had the Legitimation League effected its objects in a Parliamentary sense, doubtless Alan would have persuaded Herminia to register their alliance, if only for the gain to their children; and seeing that the former died without signing his will, the wisdom of this step would have been fully demonstrated. But I, for one, cannot admit the alleged privacy of marital unions, though agreeing that it should not be compulsory to advertise them—which is not quite the same thing as recording them. Residuary legatees and others entitled to benefit under wills may have a direct interest and title to enquire as to the descendants of any person. But pending the Parliamentary progress of the principle of legitimation—an idea altogether too chimerical to be entertained in this generation—the desirability of recording alliances is a point upon which stress should be laid. The way to effect a change in the law, in the sentiment which leads to change in the law, is to shew that there is a public need for such a register. Again, the possibility that the Act might be retrospective in character may be mentioned if it be profitable to dwell any further on the legislative side of the question. Apart from that aspect, the following claims in favour of the registration, and even the advertising of alliances, may be put forward. If it makes the snapping of the tie more difficult, if it mortifies, this surely must be set down as a gain if we have still trust in monogamy. Most people, again, regard the entering upon conjugal relations as a matter for congratulation, and therefore desire the fact to be more or less widely known. Is it not well for this pride to be encouraged? Whilst illicit love is common must not registration serve a useful purpose in distinguishing those who have bared their heads to the image of the goddess of Constancy from those who are serving convenience without risk of "mortification" from an act of change?   Or is every man to pass everywhere with whatever woman he happens to be living with or have "in keeping" away from his own home?   How useful, again, is a record in enabling those who are approached to ascertain what other ties may bind the candidate for the favours of love.   Or are we to say that this is best left to personal enquiry, based on high trust in human veracity for expectation of a true reply? or upon trust in an effectual working of a law dealing with those who have coupled their bigamies with fraud? Without advertising, or at least recording, how is the light of the Women Who Do to shine, are their brave deeds to leak out by vague report, and become differentiated from fragments of scandal only by investigation of their motives?   I apprehend that we are rather more likely to move in a contrary direction, and perhaps express our faith in monogamy, qualified by freedom, by some symbol, which may at one and the same time indicate the fetters and the freedom.   What this should be, without being fanciful or misleading, it would be difficult to say; but as a fancy which might, however, mislead, I have often thought a splinter-bar an emblem worth a vote.   It instantly conjures up the matrimonial state of being in "double harness," and it may be taken as also pointing to the fact or condition of being separable with ease.   How important is registration for statistical purposes!   Or shall we contend that the number of alliances formed, and their duration, are matters of no concern to the sociologist.

The extra-legal advantages, direct and incidental, of registration are many and great, and the drawbacks—what ? The constraint that is placed on ill-assorted couples in the speedy dissolution of their bonds—in reality a gain ; and an offence against decency in proclaiming to the world a change of habit involving matters of delicacy. One most respected officer of this League, in a letter read to-day, has characterised this objection as cant. I consider it a hyper-sensitive objection to which no recrudescence of Puritanism is likely to give countenance. Announcements of births might be similarly objected to, whilst the custom of reporting celebrities *enciente* would vanish, and the practice of making known engagements be ruled indecorous. If the morality of the future is to develop on the lines foreshadowed with appalling bareness of detail in *The Woman Who Did*, and women are to " henceforth be the equals of men, not by levelling down, but by levelling up ; not by fettering the man, but by elevating, emancipating, unshackling the woman "; then I apprehend that the publication of alliances will become more popular than ever, and more extensive in scope, affecting those also who are merely " engaged." But, after all, let it be recognised that with " unshackling " of the character indicated, this League is unconcerned, though any review of *The Woman Who Did*, from the reformer's standpoint, would be woefully incomplete which ignored it altogether.

Chapter XXVI

THE ADVERTISING AGENT'S VIEWS.

AN intention to advertise is one thing ; to advertise an intention is another, and quite a different affair. On page nine of this volume, an announcement appears to which I sought to give newspaper publicity.

On the 28th September, 1894, Mr. Evan Streachan, Advertising Contractor, 295, Strand, established 1855, wrote me, having noticed that the League had spent £220 14s. 6d. in advertising, pointing out certain advantages of transacting such business through an agent, and asking to receive our orders in the future.

On the 25th February, 1895, Mr. Streachan wrote as follows :—

"I shall be pleased to be appointed Advertising Agent to the Legitimation League, and will at all times do my best for same."

Mr. Streachan made very good use of the money I entrusted to him to advertise my lecture in the Hall of Science, and I was proud to place his name in an official way on the League. I announced Mr.

Streachan's willingness to undertake the office at the last Bedford dinner, and added "I met Mr. Evan Streachan this morning, and explained to him exactly what he might be called upon to do, viz., to advertise the alliances of persons who might possibly be the parents of illegitimate children, but who desired to acknowledge them."—(See page 227).

On the 26th August, 1895, I wrote instructing Mr. Streachan to insert the Dunton advertisement, and the Prelude to it, in four London papers, viz., *The Times, Pall Mall Gazette, Weekly Times and Echo*, and the *Freethinker*.* Mr. Streachan replied with thanks, and regretted that not one of the papers mentioned would accept the advertisement. Thinking that there might have been some hitch in consequence of the restrictions placed upon the price and space, I re-wrote to Mr. Streachan respecting these points. On the 29th of August, 1895, I received the following letter. "Dear Sir,—The Papers will not insert either of your advertisements at any price. I therefore again return your matter." (The two advertisements referred to relate to the Dunton announcement and the prelude thereto). Considering this rather curious, Mr. and Mrs. Dunton, who were staying with us, wrote to each of the papers named, and from each received a reply that the advertisements had never been submitted. On the 6th of September, I wrote to Mr. Streachan thus,—"Dear Sir, I enclose copies of the following letters (1) Letter of Mr. and Mrs. Dunton to each of the four papers alleged by you to have refused the advertisement I sent you; (2), (3), (4). (5) copies of

---

* Certain restrictions were laid down as to space and price, but they are immaterial to the question at issue.

the replies from these papers. I have now to ask you whether you can give me any explanation." The following explanation duly came to hand. "Dear Sir,—In reply to yours of 6th inst.—As one of the oldest Advertising Agents in Great Britain, I exercised my discretion on behalf of the papers named, and replied to you that they would not accept your advertisement for insertion. I admit I did not try, but acting on long experience, I was confident the order would be refused, and I did not desire to give unnecessary trouble. It was to my interest to have the advertisements inserted, as by their non-appearance I lost my commission. Yours faithfully, Chas. Evan Streachan."

I then submitted the advertisements direct to the papers. The *Weekly Times and Echo*, and the *Freethinker* accepted them without curtailment or any modification. The *Times* and *Pall Mall Gazette* refused them; so when next in London I called at their respective offices and discussed the matter. Both agreed to re-consider. Mr. Dunton sent the following advertisement to the two papers. "Births.—Dunton, on the 4th February, 1894, the reputed wife of W. F. Dunton, of London, of a daughter. Millicent Louisa, acknowledged before the Notifying Clerk of the Legitimation League, Albion Walk Chambers, Leeds, on the 19th July, 1895." Both again declined. The announcement was then submitted in the following form as being probably slightly milder than the preceding notice of birth. In an accompanying letter I said, "It aims to be as mild as possible, consistent with the serving of any useful purpose whatever from our standpoint." "Marriage.—Dunton-Briggs. 12 November, 1893.

William F. Dunton to Emma M. A. Briggs, both of London, without legal ceremony. Recorded before the Notifying Clerk of the Legitimation League, Albion Walk Chambers, Leeds, 19th July, 1895." The *Pall Mall Gazette* accepted it ; the *Times* refused it. The Prelude and the original announcement appeared in the *Leeds Express* and *Leeds Daily News*, of the evening papers, and in the weekly *Leeds Times* and *Skyrack Courier* ; whilst the Prelude appeared as news in the *Owl*. It was refused by the *Leeds Mercury* and *Yorkshire Post*, and by the *Yorkshire Evening Post*. The copy sent to the last-named paper was headed " Declined by the *Yorkshire Post!!* (Morning)" —which may in some way have accounted for its non-appearance. It was declined by the *Evening Post* for the same reasons as the *Yorkshire Post*, as contained in the latter's reply. Those reasons were that the proprietors were advised by the Directors to decline insertion. As this seemed, perhaps, a reasonable answer, but hardly an answer giving reasons, I quoted it to the *Evening Post*, and enquired : " Have I to understand that the fact of the Directors having advised, in a given manner, itself constitutes the reasons referred to, or are there reasons of a less general kind with which your letter presumes that I am already acquainted, but of which I know nothing ? " I received no reply to this enquiry. The *Mercury* declined for the reason that the proprietors " do not consider the advertisements suitable for insertion."

The *Weekly Times and Echo*, as I have said, inserted the announcements, which were duly ordered on Sept. 8th, a quotation for price having been obtained. Intimation was sent that prepayment must be made, the note-paper bearing a printed notice that "the first edition is published Thursday afternoon." A cheque for something over five guineas was posted on the Wednesday, in time for first London delivery. The advertisements did not appear in the first edition, which, I understand, has a large sale in the country, and is, in fact, the only edition of the paper seen by many thousands. I called at the office and expressed my opinion of the unfairness of this method of conducting business, and was assured by a gentleman in charge of the advertising department, that it was all in order, and that I should gain nothing by appealing to those above him.

The shorter advertisement of Marriage without legal ceremony, which was accepted by the *Pall Mall Gazette*, for some reason or other did not appear in the early editions of the issue of the first day for which it was ordered (Saturday). I wrote, bringing the fact before the notice of the Advertising Manager, who responded that the announcement would appear in all editions of the day following the expiration of the order to make up for the omission. Thus do the ethical notions of business differ amongst London journals.

The precise lesson of the latter part of this chapter it is difficult to draw. The most prominent truth seems to me to be that we must not be impatient of the methods of the Press, having regard to the fact that the Fourth Estate is worth all the other three put together to those with a mission for reform. We must remember by what network of difficulties. too, all, or almost all. newspapers are surrounded—their multiple proprietary. their sensitive readers, their advertising custom, the appalling rapidity of their processes, rendering decisions ordinarily instantaneous, etc., etc.—and, bearing these in mind, must be thankful for net gains, which are no small mercies, without enquiring too closely whether any particular paper has been faithless without clear cause, or whether its business methods are in precise accord with our own notions of scrupulous fairness.*

As to the position of an advertising agent, I prefer to leave the correspondence given above without comment. Let him excuse who can.

* I should like to add another illustration of the peculiar nature of the newspaper trade. In the evening papers, which come out sometimes before noon, and continuously up to six or later, it is nothing unusual for news to appear in one edition and not in another. But one would hardly expect this in a morning paper. Yet the first edition of the *Leeds Mercury* of November 18th, 1895, contained an excellent report of a League meeting held in London on the 16th; yet this report I was unable to trace in the later editions circulating in the City itself. Whether the people of Leeds, and roundabout, have an expurgated edition of the *Mercury*, or whether the report was cut out to make room for more important and later news, I do not presume to say.

CHAPTER XXVII

THE GREAT LANCHESTER CASE.

THE Dunton advertisement, as printed in the *Pall Mall Gazette*, was soon to be repeated. It came about in this wise. Miss Edith Lanchester, a lady of 24 summers, and daughter of a Fellow of the Royal Institute of British Architects. a candidate at a recent School Board Election, a winner of honors in the science studies of the schools. and who had matriculated at the London University, an ex-teacher in a training college (from where she removed, or was removed, owing to her advanced opinions), a clerk in a Gold Mining Co., and earning her own living, a well-known leader of the Socialist group in Battersea, had come, as the result of her reflections, to regard the married woman as the chattel of her husband. Her doubts about the wisdom of wedlock had crossed her mind, so she assures me. before she had adopted the Socialist creed, and she had debated the matter with her family at home for a prolonged period. In Mr. James Sullivan she had found a partner of her own way of thinking, and they had mutually arranged to live together. She acquainted her family of their intention. Their alliance was to commence on Saturday, 26th. 1895. At breakfast time on the preceding day, Miss Lanchester was seen by George Fielding Blandford, M.A. and M D. (Oxon.), F.R.C.P., a specialist in mental diseases, and the author of books and articles on this subject. After a conversation with Miss Lanchester, which Dr. Blandford says lasted half-an-hour, at the house of Mr. and Mrs. Gray, 72, Este Road, Battersea, where Miss Lanchester lodged, Dr. Blandford gave a signal. That signal meant that Edith Lanchester was to be removed to a lunatic asylum. By force exercised by Mr. Lanchester, her father, and two of her brothers, she was dragged from the room, one of her brothers pinioning Mrs. Gray at the foot of the stairs in the meanwhile, and thrust into a brougham, her hands tied ; she resisted, but ineffectually. A window was broken. For some time she felt the effects of the rough handling. She was conveyed to the Priory, Roehampton, near Barnes, a house licensed for the reception of the insane.

On the following morning, Mr. James Sullivan applied to Mr. Cluer, the Magistrate sitting at the South-Western Police Court, London, and stated the circumstances, informing him that they did not intend to conform to the present marriage laws. Mr. Cluer said " What ! do you mean to go to a Registry Office ? " The applicant answered, " No, sir, we do not believe in the marriage laws at all as at present constituted." Mr. Cluer replied, " The parents would naturally raise an objection." He said further, " It's no use coming to me, you had better go to the High Court of Justice." The applicant :

" Would it be any use consulting a solicitor ? " Mr. Cluer : " Certainly, if you can afford it." The applicant : " I shall get the amount, if it cost me my life ! "

Inferring from the last remark of Mr. James Sullivan that probably an introduction to a solicitor would be of service, and thinking we might be of other possible use as well, Mrs. Dawson and I went to London on the Monday, and called at 72, Este Road. Awaiting the return of Mr. and Mrs. Gray till the small hours of the morning, and meeting them at their door, we learned that the whereabouts of Miss Lanchester had been ascertained from an anonymous letter, and that they had missed their last train home from Barnes, having been to the outside of the Priory with a cornet player, who had rendered " The Marseillaise," " The Roll Call," and " All for the Cause," in the hope that Miss Lanchester would know that her comrades had found out her whereabouts, and were on the watch. By appointment next morning, we met Mrs. Gray and Mr. James Sullivan, and went with them to see Messrs. Radford and Frankland, Solicitors, 40, Chancery Lane, to whom Mr. Sullivan had been introduced before our arrival. It appeared that the Lunacy Commissioners had visited Roehampton about 5 p.m. the previous evening, and had ordered the patient's discharge. At 2 p.m., the Lanchester family medical man, Dr. W. E. St. Lawrence Finney, had visited Edith, and had an hour's interview with her, and he found it to be his duty to sign a second certificate—the purpose of which could have been no other than to render possible the patient's permanent detention in place of the week's detention following an urgency order. At 3 p.m Mr. Lanchester called and took the two certificates to a Magistrate, who, however, was not at home. An impression prevailed that Miss Lanchester was liable for detention until the first of November, but whether she could have been legally detained till then or not is not very material, as, apparently, the asylum authorities did not wish to keep her. On the contrary, on the Monday night she was removed from the wards of the asylum to the private apartments of the proprietor.

Mr. John Burns, M.P., who had, it appears, for some time been an adversary of Miss Lanchester over questions of local socialistic organisation, or similar detail, had exerted himself to secure her release. He had written to the Home Secretary and the Chief Commissioner of Police. He had then called upon the Home Secretary, and then made his way to the Lunacy Commissioners who informed him that they had made an order for Miss Lanchester's release. He then witnessed her release at Roehampton, accompanying her to Mrs. Gray's house in company with Mr. Sullivan. Shortly after reaching there, Mrs. Dawson and I made her acquaintance and heard her story. Whilst we were there, the Marquess of Queensberry called. The *Star* of the same evening gave the following :—

"Two new figures appeared on the scene this morning which effectually remove the fight from the region of Socialism into that of women's politics, and the social and personal liberty of the citizen. The sensational news from Battersea only reached Mr. Dawson, the secretary of the Legitimation League, at his country home, near Leeds, yesterday afternoon, and Mr. and Mrs. Dawson hurried to London last night to take part in the contest. 'We are prepared,' he told the *Star* man in Chancery Lane, 'to finance the movement up to a certain extent, and to go anywhere and do anything that may be required of us in this battle. It is not a case of Socialism. The fact is that we are individualists of almost the most extreme type. We don't go so far as Mr. Auberon Herbert, but we object to taxation for anything beyond national defences, police, and highways. Now we have arrived at precisely the same conclusion as Miss Lanchester, though starting from precisely the opposite pole. We do not look at her Socialism ; that is nothing to do with us. We find a young lady carried off and treated as a lunatic, merely, to all appearances, because she holds one of our principles, and we are going to fight it for all we are worth.' The Legitimation League, by the way, is the body of which Mr. Wordsworth Donisthorpe is President. The *Star* man suggested that the present case was absolutely unique. Unique Mr. Dawson admitted, in that no such case had come before the Courts, but not in respect of the character of the marriage. By a curious co-incidence, precisely such a marriage was advertised in the *Pall Mall Gazette* of 19, 21, and 22 October. Thus runs the announcement : Marriage — Dunton-Briggs, 12th November, 1892. William F. Dunton to Emma M. A. Briggs, both of London, without legal ceremony. Recorded before the Notifying Clerk of the Legitimation League, Albion Walk Chambers. Leeds, 19th July, 1895. 'We sent the announcement to the *Pall Mall* and the *Times*.' said Mr. Dawson, 'but the *Times*, good, respectable, old *Times*, wouldn't have it at any price.'

'In this case,' he added, 'the parties had been living together for some years, and there was a child which they fully recognised.' 'And you want a law to legitimise such offspring without further legal ceremony?' 'Well,' Mr. Dawson answered. 'we don't look so much to laws, we want to influence public opinion.'"

The Sun said the League had "taken occasion by the hand and bravely coming out." *The Globe* styled it an "egregious body," and Miss Lanchester it also pronounced "egregious."

The Leicester Daily Post wanted to learn the "thrilling career" of the Notifying Clerk, whether he was an identical person with myself, and whether I was "a prophet hiding his light under a bushel in his own town." It surmised that when the Lunacy Commissioners "heard that Mr. and Mrs. Dawson were on the war-path, they perceived the necessity for prompt action." *The Yorkshire Evening Post* considered that "it must be a sincere sorrow to Mr. Oswald Dawson that he entered the lists as Miss Lanchester's champion, just as the foe showed the white flag."

An appointment was made for the following morning, for a further interview with the Solicitors. This having taken place, a conversation between Miss Lanchester and Mr. Sullivan, Mrs. Gray, and ourselves, led to the decision to convene a meeting of friends and sympathisers, under the auspices of the Legitimation League on Thursday. This was duly held at the Great Eastern Hotel, Liverpool Street, at 8 p.m. A report of the proceedings follows in the next chapter.

Chapter XXVIII

THE GREAT LANCHESTER CASE—(*Contd.*).

THE FIRST LEAGUE MEETING.

LADIES AND GENTLEMEN,

AS I have convened this meeting, it will perhaps be fitting if I explain, in the first instance, how I come to be connected with the Lanchester case. For the benefit of any person who may not know anything about the Legitimation League, I may explain that the organization aims to secure equal rights for acknowledged offspring born out of wedlock, equal rights, that is, with legitimate children. Of course, if it can be ruled that you are a lunatic at law when you form an alliance that the law calls illicit, it is a matter of serious consequence to the Legitimation League in general, and to certain members in particular. Our main idea in coming to the rescue is two-fold. In the first place, having read from the reports in the newspapers that Mr. Sullivan would consult a solicitor " if it costs his life," we thought that probably he was a poor man, and a prompt offering of money and introduction to a

London solicitor—and having had recent litigation here, I happen to know of a firm in London—might be useful to him. I saw that Mr. Sullivan was a socialist, but I was unaware to what extent the local branch of the Social Democratic Federation was either able to assist or willing to be mixed up in the case.

Our second object was to see if the solicitor, when consulted, thought that it would be well to set about marshalling of witnesses to come forward and testify that adoption of such practices, as that for which Miss Lanchester was sent to an asylum, was sufficient indication of insanity.

I am thoroughly alive to the fact that the issues involved in the Lanchester case are not in any way confined to the interests of the Legitimation League, and I am sure you will agree that anyone who has the liberty of the subject at heart, would be doing right to call a meeting to consider what action should be taken—even if they only viewed the case from the point of view of the rights of the citizen, or the standpoint of the Lunacy Law Reformer.

I may mention that I myself was for many years a member of the Personal Rights Association, and that until expelled from that association on account of certain circumstances arising out of the formation of the Legitimation League, I was on the Lunacy Law Committee of that body.

We reached London on Monday evening, and driving to Battersea, we saw Mr. and Mrs. Gray, and talked to them until two in the morning. They had received an anonymous letter in which was conveyed the information that Miss Lanchester was at an asylum at Roehampton. Next morning we went with Mr. Sullivan to the solicitors in Chancery Lane, but without being privileged to take any part in effecting release, this became an accomplished fact. We were advised Miss Lanchester would be released as to-morrow, the first of November. Mr. Radford was about to visit the Lunacy Commissioners. We were to call again on his return. The order for Miss Lanchester's immediate release had been given, and that afternoon I had the honour of making her acquaintance—a free woman again.

Now, many of you may think that our work was done, but that is not the view I took of the case, and. acting in conjunction with Mrs. Dawson, Miss Lanchester, Mr. Sullivan, and Mrs. Gray, we arranged yesterday morning to hold a meeting under the auspices of the Legitimation League in this room. I then went down to Leeds and consulted the solicitor to the League, Mr. B. C. Pulleyne. I will summarise the conversation we had. The probabilities are that in any action for damages which may be taken against the father and brothers of Miss Lanchester and Dr. Blandford, we should win the day. An action against the proprietor of the asylum would in all probability fail, if the documents upon which he received Miss Lanchester were all in due form. If the doctor did not use reasonable care and professional skill, and if he did not act in every way *bona-fide* and honestly, the latter being also characteristic of the action of the relatives, the jury, to protect the general public, will think it their duty to give exemplary damages ; but there would have to be reckoned with a possibility of a jury whose sympathies with the father, whose daughter was going to live in an immoral relation, getting the better of their judgment as to the *bona-fides* of the action, and giving vent to their prejudices by awarding a farthing, or it might be £5. damages. There is another legal point involved as to committal to an asylum. It is necessary to obtain the signature of two qualified medical practitioners, unless there is reason to apprehend immediate danger to the patient or others. Now, it is not suggested that Miss Lanchester has exhibited any homicidal tendencies ; she has not, for instance, been known to rush at Mr. Sullivan with the bread knife in hand, and, therefore, the point arises as to whether, even if her action in proposing to go and live with him was a symptom of insanity, it was also a symptom of insanity about which there was immediate danger. And I understand it to have been known to Miss Lanchester's relations for some time before that she contemplated marriage of the character in question, and, therefore, seeing the practicability of getting two medical men to examine her only leads one to suspect there may have been a gross illegality in getting only one prior to her removal to the asylum.

With regard to Miss Lanchester's father, my own inclination is to advise that we resolve to recommend her to take no action against him. We of the Legitimation League set out to teach that the family virtues—conjugal and filial love—can be fostered without the use of force, as exercised by the State in its meddling with matrimony, and, therefore, it is hardly to be expected that we should advise a girl to prosecute her own father if the same gain can be obtained by other means. In this instance we shall gain quite enough if we can successfully prosecute the medical man. You will agree with the view that much depends upon the *bona-fides*, and you will also, perhaps, agree to give credit for *bona fides* to the father and brothers ; but with Dr. Blandford the case is different. I am not aware that he is related to Miss Lanchester, or that he has any special interest in her welfare. He was merely a professional man doing a job for a fee, and I tell you I am a little suspicious of doctors when it comes to a question of fees—they are too fond of fees. They want fees to vaccinate you, and then you know they want to vaccinate you twice. Then there is that Notification of Infectious Diseases Act ; they want fees for notifying your illnesses as well as for curing them. Still Dr. Blandford may not be one of these ; but whatever his position may be, I am sure that he does not appear to me to make much of a case for himself in his statement as it appears in the newspaper. Here we have some very ridiculous talk about " Social Suicide," and the Doctor probably would lead one to think that Miss Lanchester was the first lady who objected to legal marriage. Now to my mind it is utterly impossible that such views as he found Miss Lanchester held are new to any medical man. I cannot conceive that he has never heard of " The Woman who Did," and the doctrines advanced in it, even though he may have the misfortune to be unfamiliar with the Legitimation League. If Dr. Blandford is at all acquainted with Socialism he must have been aware of the prevalence of dissent from the conventional views amongst persons professing that political system. Certainly, if his knowledge of Socialism is derived from the Rev. George Brooks, who has recently been made the recipient of a bounty of £200 for his services to literary politics, he will know that many Socialists are heterodox on the marriage question, for Mr.

Brooks is not sparing in the use of vigorous language applied to this heterodoxy. By no possibility can I persuade myself that Dr. Blandford really entertained the idea that he was sending an insane person, dangerous or otherwise, to an asylum. I think he was acting to suit the convenience of the father.

The next point is as to whether an action would lie against the brother who pinioned Mrs. Gray at the foot of the stairs, whilst Miss Lanchester was dragged out of the house. This was an assault upon a woman in her own house. and unless she was doing something corresponding to interfering with the police in the execution of their duty, it seems to me that an action must lie. But here again we are confronted with the difficulty of the jury. Would an English jury, either fathers or others, decide that the brother exceeding the law had acted as no respectable brother could refrain from acting, and award nominal damages?

Before inviting discussion I beg to offer a couple of suggestions—firstly, that if damages are offered without going to law, I should say accept them; but let them be substantial damages, and let there be no secrecy about the arrangement. Looked at from the advertising point of view, by this means we shall obtain a sufficient amount of publicity to satisfy us with complete satisfaction, by obtaining tangible admission in writing on the part of the aggressors. Next. as to the Marquess of Queensberry's offer of a wedding present of £100, on condition that Mr. Sullivan and Miss Lanchester will go through the marriage ceremony and then protest and repudiate it. Well, this is really an affair of the parties concerned, but looking at the matter from an advertising point of view once more, and venturing to treat on a delicate matter, I advise that this offer be accepted, and that Mr. Sullivan and Miss Lanchester give me permission in writing to frame a repudiation and publish it in such way as I think fit, as an advertisement of the Legitimation League.

I will now read the resolution which I wish to put before this meeting : —

"That this meeting expresses its sympathy with Miss Edith Lanchester, with Mr. James Sullivan, and with Mrs. Gray, and admiration for the pluck they have shown in this matter, and urges Miss Lanchester to take legal advice as to the advisability of proceeding against Dr. Blandford, as having acted in a manner obviously not *bona-fide*; and also urges Mrs. Gray to take advice as to proceeding against the brother who forcibly interfered. The meeting further resolves that a fund be started to defray the costs of a prosecution, if such course be decided upon, and that in any case a fund be started to defray the cost of obtaining legal advice, and to recoup Miss Lanchester, Mr. Sullivan, and Mrs. Gray, their out-of-pocket expenses incurred in connection with the case."

Mr. J. C. SPENCE (Vice-President of the Legitimation League) seconded the resolution.

Mr. JOHN BADCOCK, Junr. (Corresponding Secretary of the Legitimation League for London), coincided with the Chairman's view that if any party was to be selected for attack that party should be the Doctor. He had no right to take any interest in the case save a professional one, and it was not the province of the physician to save people from social suicide. As to Lord Queensberry's advice, he was unable to agree with the Chairman's recommendation. If they went through the form of marriage they would be married before the Law, no matter how much they repudiated it afterwards. To follow his Lordship's advice would be giving up the game.

Mr. BARNIVELT, who said he had come as a listener and a learner, said that Miss Lanchester was quite *compos* and conscientious, and that any violence towards her should be resented. As to the principles advocated by her, however, he thought that the nation was not ripe for them, that the people were not educated up to the required point. He advocated the marriage of the parties for the sake of the family.

Mr. HERBERT BURROWS reminded the meeting that their business that night was not to give a definite decision as to the course of action to be taken. All that they were summoned there for, as he understood, was to decide what course to recommend Miss Lanchester to adopt. With regard to the remarks of the previous speaker, he would say it would be quite impossible to progress at all at that meeting, if they allowed themselves to drift into discussion of the moral question involved in Miss Lanchester's mode of living.

Mr. W. F. DUNTON said he could not in any way agree to regard the offence of the father and brothers as a light one. Miss Lanchester was not a minor, nor was she in the custody of her parents, nor dependent upon them, but was living in lodgings and earning her own living.

Mr. H. SEYMOUR was the next speaker. He held that this was a case for the Treasury to take up, that a grievous offence had been committed under the Lunacy Law, and the prosecution of the Doctor and other offenders should be conducted without regard to cost by the Treasury.

Mrs. GRAY spoke of the noble character of Miss Lanchester. She felt sure that Miss Lanchester was quite unwilling that proceedings should be taken out of vindictiveness, but she and Miss Lanchester alike saw that the matter had been raised above the level of a family row, and become one of public interest. Miss Lanchester's nobility of character had been put to the test, and she had agreed to leave the country with Mr. Sullivan, purely out of regard to the feelings of her family. As to Mr. Lanchester, she must speak of him frankly. He and his sons had tried to worry his daughter into madness for about a week. They had been pestering her—persuading her not to form this alliance, but she was resolute, and they thought to silence her by force and strategy. Their plans had failed, and she (Mrs. Gray) would stick to Miss Lanchester to the last, and would fight for her to the last. There was the question of money ; she herself was a working woman. In her opinion the only honest people were working people, so they would have to have assistance in the fight, but that was forthcoming and there was no reason to fear.

Mr. GEORGE BEDBOROUGH pointed out the necessity for moving cautiously, inasmuch as it would be damaging to the League which had organised this meeting, if an action were to fail, or if the successful result was merely the reward of a farthing or £5 damages. It was possible that Mrs. Gray, a lady who had been assaulted and forcibly held in her own house, might have a better ground for action than

Miss Lanchester would have against those who dragged her from the house. On the other hand, it might be argued that Mrs. Gray was interfering to prevent the performance of a perfectly legal act, and in which she would have no valid ground for redress. If it had been the case of the murder and the arrest of a murderess under warrant, Mrs. Gray would have had no right to interfere with the police in the performance of their duties. The speaker urged the necessity for convening a larger meeting in London.

Miss MORANT denounced the tyranny of the Lunacy Laws. The main point about the present case was the administrative ease with which anybody who is offensive to relations may be dragged off to a lunatic asylum, and it would not always happen that there was a *furore* about the case, and consequently persons of perfectly sound mind were left to linger there sometimes for very long periods.

After some remarks from another speaker—Mr. Anderson—the CHAIRMAN said as follows :—

Ladies and Gentlemen — Passing over the observations of my friends Mr. Spence and Mr. Badcock, who are officers of the Legitimation League, I must assure Mr. Barnivelt that I am in entire accordance with him as to the debatability of the ethical aspect of the contemplated alliance of Miss Lanchester and Mr. Sullivan, but at the same time, interesting as a debate of that question might be, there is really no time to enter into it to-night, as Mr. Herbert Burrows has remarked. The latter gentleman is quite right in saying that the business of this meeting is not to give a definite decision, but merely to advise Miss Lanchester as to the course to pursue. My friend

Mr. Dunton is in disagreement with me as to the relative culpability of the father and the doctor. I thoroughly see the force of what he had to say as to Miss Lanchester being of age, and not even in the custody of her parents. At the same time, if it was sufficient for our purpose to go for only one of the two, I suggest the doctor, for he could have no family feeling in the matter. He was simply called upon to give professional—that is. or should be, true and sound advice. Mr. Seymour is anxious the Treasury should take this matter up, but for my part, I don't think I should hand the management of an affair of this sort to any Government Department. I have no great faith in Government Departments, and I don't think Mr. Seymour has. I am glad we have Mrs. Gray with us this evening, and I have no reason whatever to doubt that her testimony to the nobility of character of Miss Lanchester is correct. I can assure Mr. George Bedborough that if he can get up a larger meeting than this in London, he will be doing a great service to the cause. I cannot agree with Miss Morant that the Tyranny of the Lunacy Laws is the chief point involved in the Lanchester case. I consider the fact that you can find a medical man—and an expert in his own line—willing to use the machinery of the Lunacy Laws for the suppression of heresy, and that heresy an offence against sexual freedom, is the greatest scandal and wrong of the present case. I will now re-read the resolution which I wish to put before this meeting.

It was unanimously adopted.

Mr. HERBERT BURROWS moved that a Consultative Committee be formed.

Mr. Dunton seconded.

This resolution was also unanimously carried.

This Meeting was widely reported in the press throughout the country. The Consultative Committee met on the following Thursday, at the Great Eastern Hotel, when Mr. Herbert Burrows was elected Hon. Sec., and Mrs. Dawson, Provisional Treasurer.

Mr. Herbert Burrows read the minutes of the previous meeting, and reported that he, with Mr. and Mrs. Dawson, had called upon the Solicitors, and had read copies of the certificates upon which Miss Lanchester had been seized and taken to the asylum. He testified to the apparently false character of many statements contained in these certificates. It had been decided to take the opinion of Mr. Asquith, the ex-Home Secretary, and the facts of the case had already been put before him in conjunction with Mr. Corrie Grant. Unfortunately, that opinion had not yet come to hand.

The Chairman (Mr. Oswald Dawson) said he could support what Mr. Burrows had said as to the false character of the certificates, one of the most farcical points about which was the evidence of the family Doctor. He might be the Doctor of the Lanchester family at Kingston, but he was not in consequence family Doctor to Miss Lanchester, who for some time had been living away from Kingston. It was unfortunate Counsel's opinion was not before them that evening. They were beginning to have experience of the Law's delay, but whilst delayed there was plenty to do in the shape of collecting money. There were two funds, one for the out-of-pocket expenses of Miss Lanchester, Mr. Sullivan, and Mrs. Gray, and the other to carry on the prosecution if that was decided upon.

Miss LANCHESTER then addressed the meeting. She expressed strong objection to prosecute her own family, but was quite willing the Doctor should be prosecuted if the funds were sufficient, if they were advised there was a case. In this respect she quite endorsed the resolution passed at the previous meeting holding that it was advisable, conditions being favourable, to prosecute Dr. Blandford. With regard to the Law's delays, Mr. Radford had told her that proceedings would probably last till February or March, and the prospect of this was not altogether agreeable, but she was prepared to act as stated if Counsel advised that they had a case against the Doctor, and if the money was forthcoming.

Mr. BURROWS then proposed that an Executive Committee be formed, and Mr. BEDBOROUGH seconded.

The CHAIRMAN proposed Mr. Burrows as Honorary Secretary.

Mr. BADCOCK seconded, and he was unanimously elected.

Counsel's opinion not having come to hand, the Committee met again on the following Thursday at the same hotel, under the same chairmanship. Counsel's opinion, the nature of which had already unfortunately become known, was then considered. By a majority of twelve against three (the Chairman not voting), it was decided to refer the opinion back for consideration on certain points. Press representatives were present at both these meetings, and reports appeared in the news papers. The second meeting of the members and friends of the Legitimation League was convened for

2.30 p.m. on Saturday, the 16th November. A report of the proceedings appears in the course of an ensuing chapter.

Chapter XXIX

THE GREAT LANCHESTER CASE—*(Contd.)*.

DR. BLANDFORD'S BACKERS—AND THE LEAGUE'S.

IN the meantime the sensation had grown. Mr. Lanchester and Dr. Blandford each appeared in print. Mr. Lanchester played the trick of the card up the sleeve. He expressed the belief that had the Commissioners "put themselves in possession of all the facts known to the family, the result would have been different," and "that a more prudent course for the Commissioners would have been to have allowed a certain time to elapse for further evidence to be taken," which opinions may be all very well in their way, but why was not the further evidence given in the original document, and why was it not given now? There was talk of Mr. Lanchester pursuing his case against the Commissioners, but this appears to have dropped. Dr. Blandford, in his recital, expounded the now famous doctrine of social suicide. Had Miss Lanchester, he argued, contemplated suicide, a certificate might have been signed without question; and he considered he was equally justified in signing one when she expressed her determination to commit social suicide. The *Lancet* perceived a difference, pointing out that whilst the attempt at suicide was a penal offence, the "living together" unmarried was not of the category of crimes. Dr. Blandford was interviewed by the *Westminster Gazette*, and when asked was there anything curious in her manner he replied, "No; she was merely a self-possessed young woman, evidently used to speaking."

But as a matter of fact the Doctor had something against Miss Lanchester besides heresy on marriage matters. He had asked her how she would regard his annexing some apples which were lying on the table. She told him that in his case she would hold it to be theft, but she would not so regard the act if committed by a starving man. The *Fulham News* remarks hereon: "She actually believes that a starving person is morally entitled to steal apples! Dr. Blandford may be surprised to learn that this is one of the fundamental social doctrines of the Roman Catholic Church. Is the Pope a madman? Ought Cardinal Manning to have been sent to an asylum for expounding this very opinion?" Mrs. Lanchester was seen, but said nothing new about Miss Lanchester's lunacy. One of her brothers was also interviewed, and he has placed on record that his sister is "highly intellectual, but extremely impressionable."

Numerous letters in defence of the father's course of action appeared, but the one embodying the greatest argument appeared in the *Daily News* of November 5th, signed "A Father." An answer thereto was sent signed "A Mother," but, I believe, never saw the light. The latter pointed out the "fallacy involved in assimilating sacrifice in sustaining the marriage tie, in spite of trials with sacrifice in going to war for one's country in spite of risks," pointing

out that " the resemblance is really to conscription.'
" The Father," having apparently admitted a considerable amount of personal trial and injustice as resulting
from the marriage laws, lays it down that early marriage is responsible for the wrongs which, he says,
cannot be righted by any weakening of the marriage
laws. Upon this " A Mother " asked " If marriage involves personal trial and injustice in these days when
late marriages prevail, how, by extending in time the
matrimonial life of married people, are we likely to reduce the amount of personal trial?" " A Father" begins
his letter by asking if a young lady insists on jump-
ing out of a third-floor window to please her lover,
are not her parents justified in taking certain steps?
whereupon " A Mother " pointed out that " either ' A
Father ' was inadequately acquainted with the facts of
the Lanchester case, or was indifferent about giving
a wrong impression,"—it being well known that Miss
Lanchester did not act as she did to please her lover.
" A Father " having appealed to history : the history of
millions of fallen women—which fate he prophesied
as certain for everyone who refuses the protection of
marriage,—was asked to back up his historical appeal
by a case where the girl had notified her relations of
her contemplated change of status when she had been
going to live with a man, and argued the *pros* and
cons of the move with them at leisure. He was also
asked, Does he wish to represent as history that every
woman who goes to live with a man ends up as a
fallen woman, in a technical sense, in which he uses
that word ? and does he think the children of all unmarried women are " friendless"? ' A Father " was
then asked to apply his arguments in the following
terms : " Even if every woman who goes to live

with a man as assuredly becomes a fallen woman as the one who jumps from a third-floor window is past physical redemption, it behoves "A Father" to state whether he would be willing to bring the Lunacy Law to bear upon the girl who gave out her determination to join the ranks of the fallen at one fell swoop. If not it seems rather odd that he should acquiesce in the application of that law to experiments which merely lead to the fallen condition."

The Birkdale Association for the Care and Protection of Young Girls saw its opportunity to bring about a rescue. Kate Ryley and Helen H. Rimmer, on behalf of the association, wrote to the *Southport Visitor*. It was not often they came to the rescue of girls of the educated or higher circles of society, they said, but in the present case they would do so. They were trying to heighten the responsibilities of fathers who were indifferent to them. So, said they, may we ask Miss Lanchester: "whether she has considered the trouble and expense that are now constantly gone to in order to recoup to innocent children that status in society which the absence of a legal father has deprived them of?"

A comrade gave an opinion of Miss Lanchester. He thought she had a whole hive of bees in her bonnet. She wore her hair short, and walked with her hands in her jacket pockets. *Justice* objected to the question being raised publicly in an acute form by an official member of the Social Democratic Federation, without any conference whatever with any other comrades—an instructive example of Socialist subordination of liberty to solidarity. But the Individualist *Liberty Review* eclipsed all contemporaries. Here is its humour: "In the actual prosaic Lavender Hill

case the hero is an Esquimo gentleman called Sullivan, a reputed capitalist, and a well-known zoophilist.
When the O'Sullivan perambulates Lavender Hill with
his stock-in-trade, numbers of cats follow him, mewing
and looking up in his face. That is because he is a
Problem."

A " British Woman," writing to the *Woman's Signal.* urged that " If Miss Lanchester cannot conscientiously marry according to law, then let her sacrifice
herself to her convictions, and altogether abstain from
the union she desires, and so proclaim to the world
her opinions and utter her protest ! "

Some papers took exception to the characteriza-
tion of wives as chattels by Miss Lanchester, and to
my phrase of the chattel slavery of wives. They contended that, inasmuch as a wife is not the absolute
property of her husband, she is not his chattel. This
will not hold. A man's bull is not a man's absolute
property, inasmuch as he may not practice bull-baiting
with it. And, etymologically, chattel is derived from
cattle, which formerly was a more comprehensive term
than it now is, and as chattel is now a more comprehensive term than cattle. Will the *Leeds Mercury* and
other papers objecting to the application of the term,
tell us whether a man may administer chastisement to
his wife. Can he compel her to stay indoors, or prohibit her having any visitors ? Can he compel her to
emigrate with him against her will ? Has a married
woman an absolute right over her own property, or
are there some important qualifications—not only as
to her property in general, but also as to her
" separate " property ? Has she freedom to vote at
municipal elections, or does she lose it on marriage ?
Can she exercise an equal power of will with her

husband, and can she give away articles given to her by him if he says he wants them back himself? Can she call her body her own, or is she at the mercy of the carnal appetite of the man she has chosen at all times and without regard to the state of her health, or any other considerations. This slavery of compulsory cohabitation is surely chattel-like, or nothing will deserve that name, and until a woman who is a wife can say, at least at certain times, either "I wish to sleep alone;" or make a proposition which will answer the same purpose, she can never consider herself free. If for intrinsic reasons peculiar to such a case the law cannot be adapted to enforce her right, she should be free to go. That is all. I am aware that precise answers to all these questions cannot be readily given. In many cases one has to reckon with the element of contradictory magisterial decisions, but I say that when all allowances for such, and for ambiguities in the law, have been made, the net result is to justify the application of the figurative term chattel to wives; whilst looking at the position of the wife from another standpoint, namely, her privileges, some of these are of a type which reduce her to a lower level than that of a chattel. Married women have to obtain the leave of a judge and to give security for costs, before they can defend an action for the enforcement of contract alone, without their husbands. even though they are carrying on a separate business with their own money. If guilty of atrocious crimes in conjunction with her husband, providing it is not a crime of violence, she can claim an acquittal. In case of fraud or libel committed by a wife the husband may be made a co-defendant, even though the parties may be permanently separated. The precise legal import of the Jackson case may not be fully determined, but if it gives the wife the power of remaining with her husband or not, according to her fancy, it cannot be held to be a privilege which will comport with the ethical notions of the day. Women will not be satisfied to be even winged chattels, who can fly from the consequences of their deliberate acts, or escape the vengeance of justice when they have committed crimes.

Mr. Dunton took up the cudgels in the *Star*. He pointed out: "Mr. Sullivan and I could be legally compelled to do quite as much towards bringing up our illegitimate offspring, as we should were we to marry in the usual way." "With regard to the position of the woman," continues Mr. Dunton, "here there is a considerable difference between marriages and free unions, but it is surely in favour of freedom. The woman is bound, in return for her keep, to live with the man, and be true to him, whilst he is free to have as many other women as he pleases, so long as he takes the precaution not to combine this conduct with cruelty. Some women might feel no hardship in such a life, but to any woman worth considering, there could be nothing more intolerable."

Mr. George Bedborough also wrote to the *Star*, urging persons interested to communicate with me. His letter was copied by the *Birmingham Daily Post*, and brought numerous enquiries from that place.

Mr. Larner Sugden, of Leek, wrote, fearing that the Personal Rights Association would be slow to take the case up, and urging Mr. Grant Allen to form a rescue committee. Miss M. E. H. Colson, Secretary of the Personal Rights Association, wrote in reply to that, saying, " I do not know what right persons have to call upon us to do work, who contribute nothing to the means by which that work is to be done, and who indirectly cause the evil which they call upon us to abate, by their advocacy of the doctrine of force." She states, however, " that the committee would not be influenced by the fact that Miss Lanchester was a Socialist, in endeavouring to secure her personal rights." So we are led to wonder whether the said committee would be influenced by the fact that Miss Lanchester is a disbeliever in marriage. The notice taken of the Lanchester case in the November issue of *Personal Rights* was confined to the foregoing correspondence, and to an allusion to the Socialistic awakening to Personal Rights, embodied in a dozen lines, and expressing the greater satisfaction the editor would have felt " if the rights to whose defence they have been roused were not their own. Even the Czar would go so far as this."

The South-Western Personal Rights and Anti-Compulsory Vaccination League was not slow to set its namesake an example. Prior even to Miss Lanchester's liberation it held an open-air meeting, Mr. F. Longman, Hon. Sec., in the chair, and unanimously carried the following resolution : " That this meeting views, with great indignation and abhorrence, the harsh, brutal, cruel, and inhuman treatment that Miss Lanchester was subject to, and calls for immediate reform of the Lunacy Laws." At a subsequent meeting, Mr. Longman promised £5 towards the prosecution.

Messrs. Alfred Slade and C. W. Jones Harper, agents in England of the Grand Order of Emorians,

U.S.A., wrote to *Reynolds Newspaper*. They proposed that "a certain part of each morning might be set apart in our police courts for the public proclamation of unions. A form would be filled, a fee paid, the union registered, and by virtue of this the future offspring legitimised." Mr. Allan A. Durward suggested to the *Star*: "Should not the public acknowledgment of a child by its father render it legitimate? I am prompted to write this as an individualist."

Mr. Gerald Massey contributed the following lines :—

> " In every battle some must bravely fall,
>   'Tis only thus great victories are won !
>   The dash of blood and brains upon the wall—
>   A woman's, too —may make the conq'ring call
>   That leads the sappers and the miners on !"

Another poet wrote these lines to the *Star* :—

> "The woman who isn't insane
>   Doesn't reason, but does as she's bid ;
>   She who thinks for herself must be mad,
>   As is proved by ' The Woman Who Did.' "

The *London Illustrated Standard* not only blossomed into rhyme—and an inclination to kick Mr. Sullivan and duck him in a horse-pond—but into pictures, one representing a lady, who as " a member of the Legitimation Society," bade a gentleman keep his distance, " spare her shame," and " not brand her, in the eyes of the world, as a married woman."

One of the most important letters appearing was that of Mr. F. Dever-Summers :— " Sir,—As the employer of Miss Lanchester, I can say without the slightest hesitation that if ever a person were sane, no one could be more so than she. In her work I have always found her most methodical and exact, and any doctor certifying her insane would furnish unmistakable evidence of his own aberration. My experience of Miss Lanchester extends over a period of four years, and I feel so strongly the injustice that has been done her, that I am willing to subscribe liberally to any fund for the purpose of taking legal proceedings. I should have written on this subject earlier, but I only returned from Paris yesterday."

The Principal of the Maria Grey Training College, Brondesbury, wrote :—" I have never had the slightest reason to suppose her to be insane, or likely to become insane. Members of the staff have always spoken of her as a remarkably intelligent student, and of her high moral character."

The Marquess of Queensberry offered a wedding present of £100 if the parties would marry and then protest. An esteemed correspondent of mine was at the pains to draft such a protest. Mrs. Elizabeth Blackwell wrote to the *Chronicle*, and reproduced a protest signed by her late husband and his former wife, Lucy Stone, and issued at the time of their marriage.

A correspondent of the same paper contributed some extracts from Dr. Blandford's work on " Insanity and its Treatment," which, as the editor remarked, " could hardly have a more pointed bearing if Dr. Blandford had been invited to condemn the procedure " he took part in at Battersea. He guarded students against the necessity of making allowance for prejudices in persons giving information about alleged lunatics, he dwelt on the unconcern of the alienist with things immoral, and his concern merely with things irrational. He cautioned his readers that extraordinary political or religious views were not signs of insanity, etc.

Mr. Herbert Burrows, writing to the same paper, suggested the formation of a committee of men and women apart from any special organization ; and this, as we have seen, was formed at the close of the meeting reported in the last chapter. Other Socialists also took an active part in the rescue and other work, whilst a lengthy correspondence arose in *Justice*, an organ of that political school. Mr. Burrows was duly interviewed by the *Star*.

Mr. Sullivan and Mrs. Gray were also interviewed, and were the recipients of funds. The representative of the *Evening News and Post* sought out Mrs. Dawson, who, as provisional treasurer, opened an account at the London and Midland Bank, Cornhill, and deposited therein over £50 collected from members of the Legitimation League, the Social Democratic Federation, and others.

CHAPTER XXX

THE GREAT LANCHESTER CASE—(*Contd.*).

THE SECOND LEAGUE MEETING,
NOVEMBER 16TH, 1895.

ON the motion of Mr. J. C. Spence (Vice-President), seconded by Mr. John Badcock, Junior (corresponding secretary), Mr. Toleman Garner (joint corresponding secretary) was elected Chairman.

The CHAIRMAN pointed out that the present meeting was a meeting of the Legitimation League. His first duty was to report that he had had handed to him a telegram from Mr. Wordsworth Donisthorpe, the President of the League, expressing his inability to be present—being indisposed, and away from London. A meeting of the Executive had been held that morning, but he had nothing to report as to the course that was likely to be pursued by Miss Lanchester and her friends. He supposed some reform of the Lunacy laws would be a necessary outcome of this case, for it would appear that it was within the power of anyone to incarcerate a relation in an asylum at five minutes' notice, on the strength of being able to demonstrate to themselves and to a learned and kindly doctor that the ideas of the

T

patient were irrational, and that he or she could not
be made to see their irrationality. The business of
the meeting was to give a *resumé* of the Lanchester
case and to pass a resolution, and he called upon the
Hon. Sec. of the Legitimation League to address it.

Mr. OSWALD DAWSON said :—

Ladies and Gentlemen : I am in entire accord
with my friend the Chairman that there is evidently
need for some reform of the Lunacy Law. At the
same time I can but reiterate what I said at the
previous meeting convened by the Legitimation
League, and held at this hotel, that the issues
involved in the great Lanchester case altogether and
entirely transcend the province of Lunacy Law Reform ; and reflection has shown me an initial difficulty
in this connection. It seems to me that the urgency
order is a needful form of order, and though it may
not be safeguarded in an absolutely efficient manner,
I am bound to say for one that I cannot lay my
finger upon the precise spot where the Lunacy Law
is wanting and say " See here, it is this that requires
reform." Be that as it may, I submit that from
among the various issues which are focussed in the
great Lanchester case, there is one that has a pre-
dominance over and above any question of Lunacy
Law Reform—the issue to which I allude is that of
marital freedom. It is highly important that we
should remove every obstacle – it is still more highly
important that we should remove every legal obstacle
—erected against the ability of persons forming their
marital relationships as they think wisest and best.
In some states of America the "living together"
without the legal tie is a penal offence. In England
here you are liable to be thrust, not into gaol, but

into an asylum. We intend that that shall not be so. But I ask you to bear in mind that this consideration as to the penalties or dangers of "living together" unmarried does not cover the whole ground of possible difficulties which beset us. You will know that in that immortal book—the work from which Edith Lanchester has popularly, but erroneously, been supposed to derive her notions—Herminia Barton lived in Chelsea, whilst "her husband" lived within easy reach of the Law Courts. Now what is there to show that at some future time, should the system foreshadowed by Mr. Grant Allen prevail, the ladies who, owing to their notions of independence, elect to live away from their reputed husbands instead of "living with" them,—what is there to show that they will escape the penalties attaching to the frequenting or keeping .of disorderly houses, as the law defines that term? But this does not complete our list of difficulties.

It is an interesting circumstance that in this morning's papers there appears a report of a meeting of the Vigilance Committee of Soho,—a meeting in which I notice a clergyman took a prominent part. At this meeting an interesting point was raised, and that was as to the liability of hotel keepers—and a special point is made of the fact that the keepers of large hotels, as well as the keepers of small hotels, -are to be brought under notice,—being held responsible to the police authorities that their guests, when coming in couples, should possess, if not produce, their marriage lines. Now, ladies and gentlemen, I submit that it would be a very inconvenient thing if Miss Lanchester and Mr. Sullivan, when they start their honeymoon, or at any time on their travels

—if they should alight from their cab at the door of an hotel, and entering with their luggage find that, not being able to produce any marriage lines, they were bound to hail back the cabby and tip the porter to reinstate their luggage on the cab, and drive elsewhere where they might not happen to be known. I say this would be a positive inconvenience, and yet it is one which is not so absolutely extravagant to anticipate, having regard to the agitations which are taking place around us, and to which I have referred in detail. Moreover, it would be very awkward for an hotel proprietor if, without it being incumbent upon him to ask for marriage lines, it were his duty to refuse his hospitality to all couples whom he might have, from any cause, reason to know were pursuing the line of action favoured by Edith Lanchester and James Sullivan. At present the difficulties which beset the path of reformers in this direction have not reached this stage ; but even now I am assured by the Solicitor to the League it would be quite impossible for a couple whose aversion to the legal ceremony was practical, and a matter of common knowledge, to obtain a license to carry on the business of hotel proprietors. A test case, so far as I know, has not yet arisen, but I hope the matter may be tested some day.

I have here a new book. It is a work by Mr. Grant Allen, and in the same series as " The Woman Who Did." It is entitled " The British Barbarians." Now, in the opening chapter of this book you are introduced to an English gentleman in a village who comes in contact with an alien, and the alien proves himself a little bit puzzled with the English system of coinage. He cannot see why twelve pence instead of ten pence should make a shilling, and he cannot see why twenty shillings should make a pound, and is even still more bewildered as to what a guinea can be. Whereupon our English gentleman comes to the conclusion that the alien must be a madman. Any body who was convinced that the metric system of money reckoning was the best, must, according to this English gentleman's idea, be a madman; and that was simply because the English gentleman knew nothing about the metric system of money. Now, to Grant Allen the English gentleman was a British Barbarian. Applying the language of the book, George Fielding Blandford is a British Barbarian. He could not understand Miss Edith Lanchester's system of marriage. He was wedded to the conventional ideas of her country, which are no more sane than our system of currency, and so he pronounced Miss Lanchester insane; only the unfortunate part of the business was that it lay in his power to do more than merely express a pious opinion—he was able, in conjunction with the father, to consign her to an asylum.

But the calling of Dr. Blandford a Barbarian will not gain us as much as we desire. We want on this occasion to do something practical, and what I propose is that after having examined the certificates upon which Miss Lanchester was committed to Roehampton, we should pass a resolution bringing the Doctor's conduct before the notice of the President and Council of the Royal College of Physicians.

Now, as to the certificates. Before considering them and Dr. Blandford, it will be profitable to notice a statement signed by Mr. Henry Jones Lanchester, Architect and Surveyor, Salvadore, Kingston Hill, her father. He gives his daughter's age as 24 years. Her age at first attack was about 22, and the duration of existing attack about two years. It was " the first attack," and her residence at or immediately preceding the date hereof is given as Salvadore, Kingston Hill. At the same time, during this protracted period of illness, and when his daughter, according to his account, was residing with him, the name and address of the usual medical attendant of the patient was " none," which is at least a little singular. Though residence at or immediately preceding the date hereof is set down as Salvadore, Mr. Lanchester's certificate sets forth that he last saw his daughter at 72, Este Road, Battersea. Now I am assured that in every sense of the word as used in common speech, Edith Lanchester " resided " at and immediately preceding the 25th of October at Battersea, and that her connection with Salvadore was strictly in the character of *visits* there, in every sense in which that word is used in common speech. I am informed that Miss Lanchester had never removed all her books and sundry belongings from Salvadore to Battersea, but that is neither here nor there. She lived in lodgings in Battersea—that was her commonly known postal address, and on the occasion of her *visits* to Salvadore, she had not removed her belongings from Battersea, or in any manner or form changed her address from Este Road to Kingston Hill. Miss Lanchester is present, and will correct me if any of these statements are not absolutely accurate. One particular in the certificate to fill in is " Religious Persuasion," and Mr. Lanchester, whose daughter resided at Salvadore so recently, and about whose mental state he had known for so long a time, answered that question by writing opposite the words " religious persuasion " the word "unknown." That also seems a little singular, does it not ? Then he is asked the supposed cause of insanity, and the answer is " over-education." Whether subject to epilepsy; " No." Whether suicidal ; " Doubtful." I do not know in what sense this is doubtful, and I do say it is most strange that Mr. Lanchester, who has appeared in print in defence of his conduct, has had nothing to say in elaboration of this doubtful answer. We do indeed know—many of us know—how an editor is liable to pare down our contributions, but I cannot believe of any single journal in London that it has on its staff any responsible person who would take upon himself to curtail any document signed H. J. Lanchester in such a way that any statement that gentleman might have to make as to the indications of suicidal tendencies in Edith Lanchester, should not appear. Now comes the question whether any near relative has been afflicted with insanity. It was so —the particulars are filled in : " Grandmother imbecile in old age." Now, ladies and gentlemen. I have given these details of Mr. Lanchester's certificates, not with any view of urging that the question of proceeding against him be reconsidered. These answers interest us in this wise—that upon them Dr. Blandford may be presumed to have acted in conjunction with his diagnosis, made at the request of the author of these answers. In Dr. Blandford's certificate one of the headings is " Facts communicated by others," and the " others " who supplied Dr. Blandford with facts, include, and. in fact comprise Mr. H. J. Lanchester, and he alone ; and in Dr. Blandford's famous letter no other informants than Mr. Lanchester and two of his sons are dragged on to the scene, and from them, apparently, the

Doctor had learned that there was an insane uncle in the family besides the grandmother, and possibly insane in the same way, "imbecile in old age." Dr. Blandford examined Miss Lanchester at 72, Este Road, Battersea, the same address as where her father last saw her, and he came to the conclusion that she was a person of unsound mind on the following grounds :—

    (*a*) Facts indicating insanity observed by myself at the time of examination, viz., She says she is going to live with a man below her in station because marriage is immoral. This she argued in a wholly irrational manner. She thinks it more independent to live like this, but she fails to see that if she has a family and is deserted, she will not be independent at all. She persists that she will go and live with this man, and go to Australia.

    (*b*) Facts communicated by others, viz., Her father, Mr. H. J. Lanchester, tells me that his daughter cannot be persuaded of the irrationality of all she proposes to do.

Now let us examine seriatim, Dr. Blandford's grounds. The sentence " She is going to live with a man below her in station because marriage is immoral," is not entirely clear as to meaning. Is it because marriage is immoral that she is going to live with a man, and is it for the same reason that she is selecting a man below her own station, and did she say that the man she was going to live with was below her own station? "This she argued in a wholly irrational manner." That of course is the Doctor's pious opinion. The irrationality of a course does not necessarily prove the insanity of it, but the conduct contemplated in this case was " wholly irrational." " She says it is more independent to live like this, but she fails to see that if she has a family and is deserted, she will not be independent at all." The word independent is here used in two independent senses, and the sentence is perhaps designed to approach the level of a pun. Dr. Blandford interviewed Miss Lanchester for the space of half an hour--so he assures us in his letter. I do not know in what wholly irrational way Miss Lanchester argued with him, but it does not seem to me to be wholly an irrational supposition that a woman can be as independent without marriage to a man as if she had wedded him. If Miss Lanchester is deserted in the course of years, and should have, say, a family of five children, she can obtain affiliation orders for their support if Mr. Sullivan can be found ; and if Mr. Sullivan cannot be found, then, married or otherwise, she cannot obtain maintenance for herself and family. As to her position under marriage— providing always her husband allows her shelter under his roof and a bare subsistence of food—she will enjoy an independence of a sort, but it is wholly irrational to contend that it will be an independence worthy of the name. "She persists that she will go and live with this man, and go to Australia." Here is some more superb grammar. Did the insanity consist in persisting in the idea of living unmarried, or was some part of the alleged insanity assignable to the fact that she would go to Australia? Now most of us know how this intended journey to Australia came about. Miss Lanchester was a girl to whom the highest feelings of filial love and sacrifice appear to come naturally. There was no inducement to go to Australia, so far as is known, no special prospect of worldly gain, no hidden motive.

nothing save and except a desire to show the utmost consideration for the "respectable" susceptibilities of her family, and to make her actions fit in with that wish.

But even if the Doctor were victorious in the argument as to the relative independence of wives and women who are not wives, he has to establish another proposition besides the rationality of his own views. before bringing to bear upon an opponent the force argument of a lunatic asylum. The State has not, so far as I am aware, ever expressed an intention of taking charge of those who take steps which may lead to a loss of their independence. If Dr. Blandford's methods are justified, then every woman who, for any reason, refuses a settlement at the time of marriage should be consigned to an asylum, for is she not failing to take a precaution against possible loss of independence? Nay, indeed, is not every woman who does not press for a settlement in all cases where such is attainable by pressure, guilty of insanity, and in need of care and treatment? I say it is not the aim of the Lunacy Law to keep people independent, and still less, if anything, is it the aim of the Lunacy Law to suppress heresies, whether of a religious or a sociological order. At the pre-vious meeting of this League I dwelt at some length on the extraordinary unlikelihood of Dr. Blandford being ignorant of the fact that the course which Miss Lanchester proposed to adopt was no original course —no very remarkable course—but a course which found expression in contemporary fiction, particularly in Grant Allen's "The Woman who Did," of the nature of which work I presumed it to be impossible for Dr. Blandford to be unacquainted. I also submitted to that meeting my opinion of the unlikelihood of Dr. Blandford being ignorant of the charges frequently brought against Socialism, that it sought to abolish our system of marriage, even if he should have the misfortune to have heard nothing of the attack on marriage from the Individualist side; but whatever may or may not have been the extent of Dr. Blandford's knowledge, I submit that it must have been impossible for any man who was "wholly rational" himself, to have talked with Miss Edith Lanchester for half an hour, and not to arrive at the conclusion that in consigning her to a lunatic asylum, howsoever irrational the way she talked, he was not assuming the function of a suppressor of sociological heresy. At the meeting referred to, a resolution was unanimously passed urging Miss Lanchester "to take legal advice as to the advisability of proceeding against Dr. Blandford, as having acted in a manner obviously not *bona fide*." Some forty to fifty persons voted for that resolution. Now you know that advice was taken, and what it was. Counsel considered that "In the case of Dr. Blandford, his certificate itself frankly setting forth facts which are not irreconcilable with sanity, is some evidence of good faith; his enquiries elicited the facts to which he certifies, and those facts are admittedly true. It may be that he was wrong in his deductions from those facts; if so, he committed an error of judgment; but an error of judgment is not actionable, unless it proceeds from a want of reasonable care and skill, of which we see no sufficient evidence. In an action for libel against Dr. Blandford, Miss Lanchester would have to prove that the certificate, which is clearly a privileged document, was false, in fact, an allegation in which she would fail." Now it may be presumptuous for me to say so, but I cannot concur in all these remarks. But our discussion this afternoon is not whether Miss Lanchester should proceed or not. A meeting of the Executive was held this morning, and I read then some extracts from the Act of Parliament, which appear to take the matter very much out of Miss Lanchester's hands. I will re-read the sections of the Act now.

"55 Vict., Ch. 5.

Sec. 317.—(1) Any person who makes a wilful mis-statement of any material fact in any petition, statement of particulars, or reception order under this Act, shall be guilty of a misdemeanour.

(2) Any person who makes a wilful misstatement of any material fact in any medical or other certificate, or in any statement or report of bodily or mental condition under this Act, shall be guilty of a misdemeanour.

(3) A prosecution for a misdemeanour under this Section shall not take place except by order of the Commissioners, or by the Attorney-General, or the Director of Public Prosecutions.

Sec. 328.—A Secretary of State, on the Report of the Commissioners or Visitors of any Institution for Lunatics, may direct the Attorney-General to prosecute on the part of the Crown any person alleged to have committed a misdemeanour under this Act."

It seems to me, therefore, that the best thing that can be done would be to bring Dr. Blandford's conduct before the Commissioners, possibly with a request that they will report to the Secretary of State.

On the point of wilful misstatement I have myself
nothing to say, I merely press what is contained in the
resolution. which is the disbelief of myself and of those
who vote for the resolution, that Dr. Blandford can
have supposed that in Miss Lanchester he had a patient
merely subject to morbid idiosyncrasy or monomania,
inasmuch as it is quite impossible for me to believe,
unless we have his express assertion to the contrary,
that he thought that this lady was unique in disbelief
in marriage. And I further think that the Doctor has
lent his services to the suppression of a sociological
heresy, in a manner not contemplated by the Lunacy
Act, for, I take it, the Lunacy Act does not contemplate such suppression at all ; and I and those who
vote with me further express the opinion, after most
careful analysis, that Dr. Blandford's certificate was
not compiled with the requisite care due from a
medical man whilst exercising power to sign away
the liberty of a subject. I now read and move the
following resolution :—

> " That this meeting express to the President and
> Council of the Royal College of Physicians, its
> sense of the utter impossibility of believing that
> Dr. Blandford acted with *bona-fides* in signing
> the Urgency Order for the committal of Edith
> Lanchester to a Lunatic Asylum ; deeming it, in
> the absence of any express admission from Dr.
> Blandford to the contrary, most unlikely that he
> was unacquainted with that phase of the woman's
> movement which exemplifies itself in stern protest
> against the Marriage Law of this country, and
> fixed determination to dispense with the legal
> ceremony ; and that being probably acquainted
> with such ideas he cannot have believed that

Edith Lanchester was merely a subject of morbid idiosyncrasy, or of monomania ; nor can he have believed that the scope of the Lunacy Law included the suppression of heresies, whether of a religious or sociological character.

"This meeting therefore resolves to represent to the President and the Council of the Royal College of Physicians, that Doctor Blandford's certificate was signed without the exercise of reasonable care."

Mr. BADCOCK seconded the resolution. He said the ostensible aim of the resolution was no doubt to take away Dr. Blandford's diploma, but though there might be little chance of success in that respect, the resolution would have sufficient effect to satisfy most people who hated medical tyranny, or sought to gain freedom in sexual matters. They might simply bring about the passing of a rebuke on the doctor's conduct, and this would probably answer their purpose. He added that while Dr. Blandford was at large the public were in danger.

Miss MORANT supported the resolution. She said such conduct as Dr. Blandford's was simply a disgrace to the profession. Whatever else might be gained by condemning him, the condemnation would have the effect of making others more careful. In her opinion there was more harm done by specialist doctors than by ordinary medical men.

Mrs. G. C. E. LAW supported the resolution, expressing the opinion that any condemnation of Dr. Blandford would be of great value, whether or no it was endorsed by the Royal College of Physicians.

Mr. GEORGE BEDBOROUGH also supported the resolution. He entirely agreed that the remonstrance would be a gain, even though help from the Council of a College of Physicians was not given. Having regard to the lamentable wording of the Doctor's certificate, he felt that the evidence pointed rather to incompetence, than to absence of *bona-fides*.

Miss EDITH LANCHESTER next addressed the meeting. She said her confidence had been greatly strengthened on finding that there were so many people ready to rally round her. When she took up with the new woman's movement she had lost friends, but looking back, and looking to the support she now received, she was constrained to feel that the friendship of the lost friends was not of so much value.

Mr. JAMES SULLIVAN supported the remarks of Miss Lanchester, and said that though what had been done by those who had come to the rescue was not done out of personal friendship, he still felt called upon to personally thank everyone concerned for their timely efforts.

Mrs. GRAY denounced the Doctor's action in unmeasured terms, and sincerely hoped that the profession would censure him.

In answer to some questions of Mr. F. Evershed. Mr. J. C. Spence rose and said what was required in the interests of the rights of the lunatic was that which was already granted to the criminal, and that was fair trial in open court. As to urgency orders— wherever danger was apprehended, the nearest policeman could assist without being armed with an order signed by one or two medical men.

The CHAIRMAN, in summing up, said it was perfectly clear that the meeting agreed that the issues at stake were not merely those involved in the reform of the Lunacy Laws, nor on the other hand was it altogether a question of Personal Rights, even with

the capital P and the capital R. Their invasion was.
as any suppression of sociological heresy indeed was
—an invasion of Personal Rights, and the ordinary
Lunacy Laws had been wrongfully applied towards
such suppression. He asked those who supported
the resolution to signify their support by holding up
one hand.

Twenty-one. including the Chairman and the
proposer of the resolution held up a hand. On the
contrary being put, no hand was raised. Three or
four persons abstained from voting.

A copy of this Resolution, and of the report
of the meeting as given above, was sent by me to the
Secretary of the Royal College of Physicians.

A meeting of the Consultative Committee was
held at the Great Eastern Hotel, on Saturday evening
the 30th of December, 1895, when it was unanimously
resolved to send a deputation to the Lunacy Commissioners. It was further resolved to hold a public
meeting, and the hall at St. Martin's Town Hall,
Charing Cross, was engaged for the 19th of December.

Chapter XXXI

THE GREAT LANCHESTER CASE—(*Contd.*).

ASYLUM OR GAOL?

THE following was contributed by me to the *Labour Annual*, 1896:

LANCHESTER AND LIBERTY.

The echo of the glorious blow struck in America by Lillian Harman and E. C. Walker has been heard in England. The chattel slavery of wives is doomed in this " land of the brave and the free." Never again will lunatic asylum doors be thrown open to receive the women who rebel against the tyranny of marriage. That is a foregone conclusion. We have tried to teach our transatlantic cousins a lesson, and we have failed. They, nine years ago. clumsily arraigned Lillian Harman and E. C. Walker before a court of law, and duly lodged them in Oskaloosa jail, thus directing public attention to their crime of unlawful cohabitation. We, cleverer, incarcerated Edith Lanchester in an asylum without trial, save a half-hour's private conversation with Dr. George Fielding Blandford, but we omitted the precaution of putting James Sullivan under "care and treatment" at the same time, and

U

left him free to go and blazon the matter forth in a police court before a magistrate and — a pressman. To this last all praise. I crave space also to praise Mary Gray. I shall never forget her fervid utterance at the second " Lanchester meeting " of the Legitimation League, declaring that she forgot that Edith was her lodger, declaring that she was her " comrade," and that she would stick to a comrade to the bitter end. It is strange (of course I speak merely from my own point of view, and not dogmatically) through what channels the great making-for-righteousness power that humanity possesses works. To my mind Socialism means the accentuation of woman's slavery ; yet here the Power (I dignify it) is working through Social Democratic women whilst some of the leaders of Liberty look on. say little or nothing, or vilify. Edith Lanchester has had greatness thrust upon her at four-and-twenty years of age by an incident, but only her reason and her bravery to act according to her lights made that incident possible. Dr. Blandford would have gone to his grave without doing one tithe of the good the Inscrutable has allotted to his life-task had he not encountered the woman to whom he has given an immortal wreath of fame. But let us remember that Edith Lanchester has not been a mere dummy in the hands of the Power ; a satellite borrowing light entirely from something in the universe outside herself : she has shone. Her filial devotion was the first virtue in evidence ; she was willing to emigrate simply to spare the feelings of her family. When her family thought her migration should be no further than the lunatic asylum, she was anxious to overlook and excuse all who were near to her ; she was weary of the gaze, and criticism, and interference with occupation which sudden celebrity brings in its train—but as a matter of public duty she was prepared to take the necessary trouble to bring Dr. Blandford to book if the Lanchester Consultative Committee advised her that such course would be feasible and wise. What her after work as a soldier of Liberty may be Time will show ; suffice it that she now ranks with her forerunner, Lillian Harman, with the advance guard, to whose lot falls the burden in the battles of Sexual Freedom.

FINIS.

GOODALL AND SUDDICK, Printers, Cookridge Street, Leeds.

LILLIAN HARMAN.
Interim Editor of *Lucifer*,
114, E., 4th St., Topeka, Kansas, U.S.A.

www.ingramcontent.com/pod-product-compliance
Lightning Source LLC
Chambersburg PA
CBHW031033120726

47905CB00007B/2164